The Lake of Fire

Other works by Kate Gale:

POETRY

Blue Air
Where Crows and Men Collide
Selling the Hammock
Fishers of Men

CHILDREN'S FICTION

African Sleeping Beauty

ANTHOLOGIES (EDITOR)

Anyone Is Possible (Short Fiction)
Blue Cathedral (Short Fiction)

The Lake of Fire

A Novel By

KATE GALE

Winter Street Press • *2000*

A first edition of this book
was originally published under the title:
Water Moccasins
by Title Wave Press,
North Hills, California

Author's Note:
This novel is based on a true story.
The location of the commune has been changed.
All names have been changed to protect the guilty.

Cover photograph by Mark E. Cull
Copyright © 2000

Second Edition
ISBN 0-9701057-9-7

Published by
Winter Street Press

Printed in the United States of America

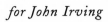

for John Irving

The Lake of Fire

Chapter 1

I grew up in a closed Christian commune that we called, The Farm. This fact is as inescapable to me as breathing. It effects me as surely as my femaleness, my mind, anything else about me. It separates me. How my mother came to join this commune is something I've never fully understood. I can't help trying to piece it all together, but for the beginning of the story I have very few facts. Only what she has told me. I know that in the beginning, before she joined, her name was Sarah, a name I never heard anyone call her.

Sarah climbs the first tree she sees at St. John's. She sits on a branch, swings her legs and takes a swig of beer in celebration. She has convinced her parents to allow her to attend this radical school. She is on her own. The air is cold and bites her bare legs. She smiles and opens her mouth wide. She is ready for anything. She is ready to bite back.

The night of the first dance she comes to her room to find her roommate, Missy, surrounded by empty cans of ginger ale. "I'm sick, Sarah, real sick. You go to the dance. Tell John I can't make it. Tell me what he says. He's so sweet. I wish you could fall in love, Sarah. It's so nice, the way he watches after me. He loves me." She covers her head and turns toward the wall.

Sarah searches the student center for John. "Sarah," he says from behind her.

"Oh, I didn't see you. Missy's sick. She won't make it." He looks her up and down, and she sees that his eyes are glassy. His eyes pause at her breasts, and waist and long legs. "Why don't *you* be my date tonight?"

"Oh, I don't know. I need to get a drink." She squirms into the crowd by the refreshment table and runs into a boy from her math class. "Oh, Sean, I'm so glad to see you." He smiles, and she notices that he's got nice eyes, twinkly green-blue eyes. "Would you do me a favor?"

"What?"

"Pretend you're my boyfriend for a while. My girlfriend's boyfriend is hitting on me."

"Okay, what do you want me to do?"

"Oh, let's hang around together tonight, and let's hold hands when we walk around campus, kiss in public, stuff like that."

"Sure." His smile isn't lecherous like John's, just happy and faintly amused.

A few weeks later she says, "Sean, we don't need to pretend any more. I think John got the point."

"But I like you."

"Oh, you're not my type."

"What *is* your type?"

"The outdoorsy type, beard, guitar playing, that kind of stuff."

"Well," Sean smiles. "I play the guitar, and I sing the blues." She looks him over, his moustache, the still thin boyish chest, his eyes like he's thinking of something he isn't likely to tell.

"You are cute," she says.

"Yes, you're about three months along," the doctor tells her three months later. "How do you feel, Sarah?"

"I can't believe it."

"I can't believe we're doing this," Sean whispers to her in the office of the justice of the peace. "Why are we doing this?"

"So our parents don't kill us," she says.

They visit Sean's parents. "My mom probably won't be there, she says she has no sympathy for me."

"Are your parents really orthodox?"

"My dad hardly spoke to me when I was growing up. He spent his time reading the Scriptures." He opens the door, and Sarah sees an old man leaning over a large book in the pale afternoon sunlight. "Hello, Father. I'd like you to meet my wife." She walks over to the bench where he sits, and he moves over to make room for her. One long, crooked bony finger follows the words along the page. He mutters in Hebrew.

"I've looked forward to meeting you," she says. He does not stop reading. By the time they leave, he has turned the page once.

They fight over morning coffee, over money and over who is going to take care of the yard. "The least you can do is mow the lawn," Sarah says.

"Me? I'm the one who's doing something. I'm going to school and working. You sit around the house reading the Bible all day. The place is a pigsty. You mow the damned lawn." Green crawls up around the house, covers the lower part of the windows. Rats' noses poke out from the overgrown grass at night.

"My parents let us live here if we would take care of the place. If they come down here and see that you're not even mowing the lawn . . ."

"You're the one who should be doing it."

"Okay, neither of us will do it."

When the rats creep into the neighbor's yard, the neighbor comes over with a scythe and cuts it.

"See, you're lazy," she says.

"You're full of shit."

Sarah feels the first contraction just after midnight. She's in the living room reading the Psalms by one small lamp, the Bible resting on her belly. "Get up, get up, it's starting." She shakes Sean.

"It's going to be a boy," he says. "I know it's a boy." She doubles in pain for every contraction while he collects clothes, keys, and locks the house. He carries her to the car. At the hospital, she says, "Put me to sleep, wake me up when it's over," and they do. While Alexa is pulled out with forceps, Sean sits in the waiting room and Sarah lies unconscious. Sean follows a nurse down a long hall and up an elevator to the nursery. She hands him Alexa. He wishes Sarah were awake, so they could touch this tiny bundle together. He feels tears stand in his eyes, and Alexa opens her eyes and stares at him. She feels like a bird that has fallen out of a nest into his arms. He kisses the tiny red face.

When Alexa is one year old, Sarah's parents prepare her birthday party. Sarah is thin; her breasts ache from weaning Alexa abruptly. Her mother had said that she had nursed long enough. The frosting on the cake is pink and fluffy, but when they cut it, the cake itself falls in the center. They laugh and eat ice cream.

Sarah visits the doctor the next day. "I'm three months pregnant," she tells Sean that night.

"We're barely existing now, or hadn't you noticed? I guess you hadn't because all you do is read that damn Bible. That's all you fucking do, read your fucking Bible. I come home to a Goddamn filthy house, and a Goddamn filthy kid, and now you're pregnant. Have you figured out what causes this?"

"You," she says and then wishes she hadn't because he leaves slamming the door.

He doesn't come back for several days. When he walks in, unshaven and in dirty clothes, Sarah suspects that he has come back for the same reason men usually come back; he is out of clean socks. She doesn't ask where he has been. She is already feeling bulky. Alexa seems restless all the time, and Sarah has no money.

By the time Andie is born, Sean comes and goes as he pleases. Sarah has a job her parents found her on campus. She tries to ignore her husband's wanderings because she has little time to worry. She doesn't want to discuss it with her parents. What is the point anyway?

Sarah takes her babies and goes to a church to hear a visiting preacher, George English. She explains to Sean that she is searching for truth. "But truth is reality," he says. "Your life has nothing to do with reality. You don't take care of your children. You don't take care of your house. You'd rather read. What is truth? You can't separate truth and life. See this," he picks up a dirty diaper off the floor. "This is truth."

"There's no point talking with you; there never was," she says. "I wish you'd shave off your moustache, and do what God says."

"He's telling me to take a walk."

At the church, the minister leans forward in the pulpit and stares straight at her as if he had known her all her life. "I am a man of God, anointed by the Holy Spirit, blessed from On High. God has sent me to you this day with glad tidings of great joy. You are free. Free to walk away from the wickedness of this world. Come unto me all ye that labor and are heavy laden, take my yoke upon you and learn of me and I will give you rest." He stretches out his hands over the congregation, and Sarah feels God enter her soul, like lightning, like sweetness, like magic, like peace.

"I was once a sinner, a great sinner, ask my wife who sits there." A gracious lady with careful piles of hair nods and Sarah marvels at her, at George. What a thing it would be, to see this man, hear him every day, drink of him, talk with him. She feels close to God, close to tears, George could not ask her anything that she would not do. His English dialect, and that baritone voice, shimmer on the air, vibrating the part of her soul that has been waiting, empty. "I grew up on the streets of London, wandering ragged and barefoot. When the English Navy conscripted orphans, they took me even though I was way below their standards, scrawny and sickly."

"I started out the lowest boy, the one who was kicked by the others. The biggest boy made us all mop and scrub on our hands and knees. We lined up and swabbed the deck while he walked behind us and hit us with a stick. I did my jobs cheerfully so they called me Sunny."

"I worked hard swabbing the decks, running cheerfully on my bare feet over the deck planks to do whatever I was asked to do. By the time I was sixteen, I was the head boy making the others work.

"I was adopted by an American family, went to school here. Then I went back to live in London and raised a family. I was a smoker. I remember searching every pocket in the house for the last cigarette. 'What are you looking for, dear?' my wife would ask. 'Nothing,' I'd say. Then one day I was walking near the docks in London, bundled in a long coat, and I cried out, 'God, if you are real, reveal yourself to me.' Then God spoke to me. He said, 'Come away and be my son, walk with me.' That's all he's asking of you. He's saying, 'Come away, be my son, be my daughter. Have no more part in this wicked world. Give me your sons and your daughters.'"

The next Sunday, Sean dresses for church. "I'm only going to make you happy."

"What is it with you? You don't have to come."

"This marriage matters to me, do you mind?" Alexa sits on his knee, her long dark curls falling over her shoulders.

What Sean tells Sarah afterward is that he sees a different George than she sees. She sees a man of God speaking God's words. What Sean sees is a man with saltwater soft hands. He sees heavy silver eyebrows, a monomaniacal gleam in his eyes that reminds him of Hitler.

Sarah leans forward, her elbows on her knees, tears streaming down her face. Andie sleeps, and Alexa reaches into Sean's pocket for another piece of candy. "Listen to the word of God," George thunders, "'God waited in the days of Noah, while the ark was preparing, wherein few, that is, eight souls, were saved by water.' (I Peter 3:20, King James) God saved only eight souls. Would you have been one of those eight souls? Christ is coming again to judge the earth, and not many righteous will be saved." George's hands rake the air. "Where does that leave you? The Tribulation is coming. The Beast is coming. The Lord is coming with the trumpet. I will be caught up to meet Him. Will you? He will come in our generation. He will come as a thief in the night."

Sean shrinks away from his wife who is sobbing. Alexa begins to say, "Mommy, Mommy," so he gathers the girls and leaves the church. Sarah never looks up.

When she meets him outside, her face is flushed, her eyes bright, "Oh, Sean," she says hugging him, "I'm saved. Didn't you love him?"

"This George is a fanatic! You're losing your mind. Honey, he's a holy roller, he may wow the ladies, but I'm not going to listen to a madman," Sean says.

My mother's story always became confused at this point. She told me hints, details, I put together my own story from that. I could even picture my father, although I'd never met him, driving out to Vegas to buy a divorce several months later—still trying to understand it all. He had gone with Sarah to one more meeting. She had been baptized, and her name was changed to Hope. On the way home, he kept forgetting, calling her Sarah. George had a religious retreat on a thousand acres he bought in Vermont. Before anyone could come, they had to be invited. Since they had run out of money, Hope had called George. He and his wife had suggested that Hope take the girls and live with a family in Maine who would train them in the ways of the Lord and prepare them for possibly joining the retreat. She had asked whether she should leave her husband. George replied that if she did not she could not enter the kingdom of God.

She did not seem concerned about leaving him or her parents. "You're going to miss your parents," he'd said.

"I'll miss Daddy," she said briefly, and kept packing.

The Blacks live in a large brick house by the river. Hope and the girls have one room. Hope works in a shoe factory and gives all her money to them, while Mrs. Gertrude Black stays at home and cares for the girls.

Sean calls to say he's coming to talk, and Hope thinks for three days about his visit. She imagines him saying, "I want to be with you, no matter what the cost. I'll follow God. I'll renounce my family, anything." She pictures them together, kneeling before George. "Dear children of God," he'd say, laying a hand on each of their heads. She wants to love him again, not because she needs sex, but because thinking about him still makes her heart flutter.

I've tried many times to imagine their last meeting, how it felt for both of them, for him knowing he would never see his children again. Why did he agree to relinquish all rights to see us? I had a lot of guesses. I don't know. She never gave me a hint from which I could construct a story. She told me about that last meeting though, bits of it. I can still see them on a snowy afternoon, putting my fate in writing.

He is coming to see her this evening. She will not touch him. She closes her mind; unclenches and clenches her fists. "If he wants to be with me, let him submit to God," she says to herself.

Sean drives between icy snowbanks to the Blacks' house. He is in a hot anger, not the screaming kind. This anger boils and simmers. Sometimes it seems to bubble around him like stage fog; at other times he feels it rising to his ears, drowning out all other sounds.

"I'll go see her," he'd promised Sarah's parents, "and I'll try to get her back." *His* wife. *His* children. She wants to follow God by following George. She wants the girls and will fight for them. There isn't any point fighting battles he won't win.

He drives through falling snow that makes it hard to see. He wants to figure out for himself what he believes in. God? An invention. Man created God in his own image. God is male and white. Love? Sex is real enough, a physical urge toward an end, but love? A temporary feeling between two people inspired by an empty need, a loneliness. The afternoon darkens around him.

She isn't the same woman he married. That girl was soft, hard edges, but soft in the center, sappy like a tootsie roll; "My sweetheart," he used to say, and the hard corners of her mouth would turn up; the eyes would crinkle. "Oh, all right," she'd say, fawn-like, girl-like.

Now she is changed. "What can I do for you?" she says. She sits on the couch. She sits on both hands.

"I still love you."

"If you shave off that moustache, and promise to follow the Lord Jesus, we can talk, otherwise, there's no point discussing anything."

He sits back, fingering the moustache. "I can't follow George." She sits on the couch like she's stuck there, while he walks around the room. He says, "I can wear what I want, go to bed when I want. You have a need to believe. You have a need to be told what to do."

"I have submitted to the will of God." She's sitting pale and stiff as a school girl.

"Can I see the girls before I go?"

"They're not here, they're out," she says, and he knows there's no softness left; that there's no point looking for it or talking to it. "Why did you come here?" she asks.

"I had to try." He turns at the door, and she still sits head down. He wants to pull the sweetness out of her like a bear fishing in a bees' nest for honey. He reaches out a hand like a paw, but her face says, "Get out." He walks to the car, stung. A dead cold smell hangs on the winter air; it is evening, and fog crowds in, thick and grey and menacing.

Rapunzel

Rapunzel Rapunzel let down your hair
she opens the windows
lets him see inside her head
the prince picks it clean of brains
Rapunzel Rapunzel let down your hair
she opens her garden gate
lets him pick her vegetables
Let down your hair he cries
he storms the walls
She gives birth to twins
Rapunzel let down your hair
but she wouldn't let him in
to see the children grow
Rapunzel let down your hair
I will give you gold
lonely in her tower
she opens the doors
lets him fly through
a vampire bat
smelling hot warm blood
the girls braid their hair
waiting for the call
the sound of their own names
the summons to let down their hair

Chapter 2

When George arrives in Maine, Mrs. Black piles the table high for
breakfast. I am three, tiptoeing down the wood steps one at a time
holding the bannister that I'm not allowed to slide down, "unless
you want a real whipping," Mr. Black said. I smell scrapple and bacon,
toast and eggs. Even my job of setting the table has already been
finished. Gertrude hisses, "Children will be seen and not heard,"
and waves me to my little chair in the corner.

When George enters the room, everyone stands and then bows
their heads for him to pray. The prayer is long. I wonder about the
food. I peek out and see George standing, his hands raised in blessing
over them, "Now unto him that is able to keep you from falling, and
to present you faultless before the presence of his glory with
exceeding joy, to the only wise God our Savior, be glory and strength,
dominion and power, both now and ever, amen."

"Amen," we repeat, and sit down.

Hope serves Alexia and me a little of everything, and puts a hand
over each of our mouths for a second. This means, "Remember, don't
make a sound." The adults talk about things like elections and the
will of God. I want more to eat.

Before he leaves, George stands at the door talking with Hope
while I lean against her leg and Hope pats my head like I am a little
dog. I sit down and wrap both chubby arms around one of Hope's
legs and gaze up at her. "God bless you, daughter. You are one of the
chosen; your husband was not. I saw it in his eyes from the first, but
it is for God, not me, to judge. My wife has left me. But God will
reward us. There will be many who fall away in these times. God is
watching you." George kisses Hope on the forehead and leaves.

One day while Hope works at the shoe factory, Gertrude Black
leads Alexia and me to the river. "It's time for you to learn to swim,"

she says. The fog rests on the river bank early in the morning; Alexia and I walk on either side of Gertrude down to the river bank. Gertrude holds onto our hands tightly and pulls us along. The river rushes coldly and quickly over rocks that look slippery. She orders us to undress. We pile our clothes in a little heap and stand in the cold grey air in our panties, shivering. She sits on the bank, a dark stone among the other dark boulders. "You're old enough, you're three and five, now ready." She throws me in, then Alexia. "Swim, swim, use your arms," she says pulling her sweater around her. Her dark thick hair blows wildly around her square white face. We paddle, splashing with our arms, kicking, gasping to keep our heads above water. The icy current pulls against us as we reach with our feet and hands for a place we can stand. "Come on, you're not even trying." When she grabs our wrists and pulls us out, we say, "Thank you, thank you," and look up at her, our savior. She throws us in again, and again. We stretch out our white arms to her, white arms streaked with red blood from hitting rocks.

In the bedroom, Hope helps us undress. "She's mean to us," Alexia says. "Why don't you help us?" Hope dabs at the blood. "Yeah, help us," I say.

"God is watching out for you."

"I want you, I want Daddy," Alexia whines and puts out her bottom lip.

"Want Daddy," I say.

"God is your Father."

Gertrude opens the door, "Don't coddle them Hope. They're in training. Time for them to come down for dinner. Look sharp, girls." Hope doesn't say anything, and we follow her down the stairs. Ray Black massively occupies the head of the table, and his wife the foot. "Would you like to say grace for what we are about to eat, Hope?"

"Yes," she says, bowing her head, and reaching for my hand under the table. "Lord Jesus, we thank you for another day to be with you."

"Thank you, Lord," the others respond in unison.

"We thank you for keeping us from sin."

"Thank you, Lord."

"We ask you to bless our brethren behind the Iron Curtain." I open my eyes a crack to see what is for dinner. Fresh rolls, mashed potatoes, broccoli; I can't quite see the meat. I stand up a little in my seat, and see Ray Black looking at me. I immediately close my eyes and sit down as we all say, "Amen." We all look expectantly at Ray.

"Andie, did I see you opening your eyes during prayer?"

"No," I say quickly, "I mean yes, maybe."

"I believe we have a little liar in our midst." I feel everyone's eyes on me. I glance up at Hope for help, but her eyes are fixed on Ray Black. "You know what God says; for lying, for not saying "please" or "thank you" and for disobedience, you will sit in the corner and eat a soap bar for thirty minutes. Sit right over there so we can see you."

I sit on the floor in the corner, and Gertrude Black puts a bar of Ivory in my mouth. My mouth can barely close, and my jaw aches. I remember from the time before that the taste does not leave my mouth for a day. The smell of ham mixes with the taste of the soap.

At the end of dinner, Gertrude tells me to go to my room while Alexia goes out to play. I can see Alexia out the window, playing hide-and-go-seek with the other kids. Alexia laughs louder than usual and looks up at our window. She's never had to suck a bar of soap. She runs and touches the base; "Free, free, free," she shouts.

I hear a noise behind me and jump. Hope puts a finger on her lips and hands me two buttered rolls. She makes a hand movement that means, hurry, hurry. The rolls taste like soap, but I smile and mouth, "Thank you," as my mother slips away. That night I dream my first dream.

Ray stands outside the house. He is a huge giant, three stories high, he can look right into my bedroom window to see that the room is messy. He reaches in, takes me out of bed and throws me in the river. While I float away, I dip my arms into the water as if it were sheets. I hug it, and thank it for carrying me.

When I open my eyes, I am curled against my mother's body. I open my eyes but do not move. I do not want my mother to wake and turn away from me. "Only two beds," Gertrude had said.

"Andie and I can share," Hope said, and I held my breath, waiting for a "no" that didn't come.

"All right, it'll save hauling out fresh blankets," she said, whirling to leave. So every day, I remember that at night, I can crawl into the curve of my mother, feel ribs against my back, feel arms around me, feel the breath lightly going in and out. I do not move. I will not wake my mother. I move my mouth to pray, "Thank you God for love, thank you God for heaven."

George calls to invite us to move to the Farm. It is the first time we see our mother cry. "I'm so thankful," she says, "that God has provided a way that you will never have to go to public schools where your minds would be corrupted." She puts an arm around each of us. "Girls, say, 'Thank you, Lord.'"

"Thank you, Lord."

I sit in the back seat of the car while the square brick house disappears and with it, the figure of Gertrude in a white apron in the doorway, her hair covered in a white scarf, her body massive. "Old witch," Alexia mutters.

"Witch," I say.

"Are you two having fun?" Hope says, and we both say,

"Yes, Mommy," in unison.

"You're going to have to learn to call me, 'Hope.' At the Farm, kids have to call their parents by their first names instead of 'Mommy.'"

"Will you take care of us?" Alexia leans forward over Hope.

"Will you?" I ask and pull my blanket around myself and my doll Esther.

As long as I can remember, I have had Esther. I have eleven imaginary children, but my doll Esther is the oldest, the one who always gets to be in charge of the imaginary kids when I am gone. When I have to go to bed early for smiling when I shouldn't, or whistling or singing, I lie in bed with the evening light pouring in the window. I listen to my sister playing with other children, and I hold Esther and talk to the imaginary children and tell myself I don't mind.

"Sit down, both of you," Hope says, "Sit down. I won't be taking care of you. You'll be in boarding school. You'll be in training to be soldiers in the King's Army."

"I want to be with you."

"With you," I repeat.

"Be quiet back there; I can't talk and drive."

Alexia reads her book and I change Esther's clothes under the blanket so she won't be embarrassed. I close my eyes and pray in the name of the Father, Son, and Holy Ghost that God will let Esther go to heaven, let her have her own place under the throne. "I can't be happy in heaven without Esther," I tell God. "I ask you to save a place for her, I ask in the name of the Lord Jesus Christ."

George told us that God only hears and answers prayers if you say at the end of the prayer, "In the name of the Lord Jesus Christ." Otherwise he doesn't hear anything. I always remember to say it, especially for important prayers. "I love you Esther, I love you, I will always be with you." Esther's eyes open and close.

I kiss her and Alexia says, "That's silly, kissing a doll."

I cradle Esther, "I don't care."

Hope stops to fill up the car. She goes into Friendly's and comes back with an ice cream sundae for each of us. The vanilla ice cream sits in a round mound with syrup running around it and pooling around the sides, chocolate syrup for Alexia and butterscotch for me. It starts thickening like taffy. I take a spoonful and offer it to Esther; then I slowly lick it off the spoon myself. I do this with every bite, and by the time I get to the last of the butterscotch syrup, it is very thick and hard.

"Will we have sundaes there?" Alexia asks, eating hers slowly.

Hope concentrates on the road. "I don't think so. Sit down. Gertrude says they eat mostly beans there."

"I hate beans," Alexia whines.

"Sit down, be quiet." The only sounds in the car are the licking sounds. The rain that's been falling ever since we left Maine increases and the car moves on through blinding water. Hope holds up the map George drew for her. I pull Esther with me under the blanket and close my eyes. When I open them, it is dark and the car has stopped.

"Why are we stopped, Mommy?"

"We're here." I see a large farmhouse with a couple of lights on. A door opens and a woman's figure stands in the doorway. Hope turns in the seat, brushes our hair so it hurts and wipes our faces with a napkin.

"Walk behind me, don't talk, don't make me ashamed of you." In the small yellow light, we stumble toward the doorway behind our mother. The woman opens the door wider, "Come in, sister," she says, and kisses Hope. George is inside, and here, in his own world, in his own kingdom, he appears bigger, scarier. We hide behind Hope. He stretches out his arms. "We welcome you. Alexia will be going to Tent City, since she is five. We are in the process of building the school. Until then the kids live in tents in a field."

Alexia looks at Hope, "Mommy, where do we wash up?"

"There is water in buckets. It is cold and refreshing." He looks at me. "She can stay in a room by herself tonight. Tomorrow she will join some other kids. We're forming a kindergarten. Ah, here comes Grace to take Alexia." Hope is still watching George.

"Will I have my things, *Mommy*?" She tugs at Hope's skirt.

"You won't need them," George says. "You will be given a uniform tomorrow. You're going to be a soldier in the King's Army." Alexia's lips quiver; I watch Alexia and Hope.

Hope watches George. "This is Grace, and here's Alexia all ready to go to Tent City." Alexia sticks out her bottom lip the way she does when she *won't* cry. "Mama, will I get my dress?" Hope looks at George and doesn't say anything. "Will I?" Grace takes her hand and starts to lead her away, "Will I?"

"No," Hope says finally, and Alexia cranes her neck around as she walks. "Mama, keep it for me, please, please, keep it for me." Alexia has a light blue dress with a big valentine in front and lace on the sleeves, and she looks at it every day hanging in her closet, and wears it on Sundays.

Another lady comes to take me to my room. I say, "Bye, Mama," and Hope says, "bye," in a grey voice as if it doesn't matter anymore. I haven't eaten anything since the sundaes for lunch. "Do we get dinner, Mama?" I call to Hope who still hasn't moved. "Will we?"

"It's bedtime for little girls," George says jovially.

"Bye, bye," I call thinking she might call back, might say, "It's all right." I can't hear if Hope answers. The lady leads me to a small room upstairs that has a sleeping bag and a blanket on the floor. "Go right to bed," she says. "There's a pot there if you need to go. Good night." She starts to shut the door and notices that I have a tightly clutched Esther under my arm. "The doll will have to go," she says reaching out a large hand for Esther's head.

I scream, "Esther's mine."

The lady bends down and holds me by one arm and snatches the doll. Her fingers cover Esther's face and eyes.

I scream, "No, no."

The woman grabs the doll's feet with her right hand and shakes her right forefinger, "Be quiet this instant." The door closes.

Esther's eyes looking back over the woman's shoulder are the last thing I see. I throw myself on the bed and cry uncontrollably until someone says, "Quiet in there." I try hollering, "Mommy, Mommy, Mommy," and someone knocks on the door, and says, "be quiet or I'm going to give you a spanking." I cry in the dark until I fall asleep.

I wake in the little empty white room. I lie in the sleeping bag for a minute wrapping my arms around myself, remembering where I am and how the horrible lady took Esther.

George opens the door. I stare at him. "When I come in the room, get to your feet and stand at attention." I stand up, my shoulders tight, my mouth a straight line. "You will learn to stand at attention properly," he says. I lower my eyes to the floor. "Here's your cereal," he says handing me a bowl. "Under God's roof, he that does not work, shall not eat. You will work, and God will feed you." I bow my head over my food, but I can't think of anything to say to God. I open my eyes.

"Eat. Someone will be in to collect you for Nursery School," he says and leaves.

I hear a strange sound and footsteps rushing down the steps, and I run out. On the porch, a crowd of adults is gathered, a few little kids like me; a man is blowing a trumpet. But no one is watching him; our eyes are strained down a dusty road toward a group of tents in a hayfield. From an opening in the stone wall, four columns of kids march. As they get closer, I can hear, "Left, left, left, right, left." Children march, heads held high; I see my sister desperately trying to get in step. The leader beside her keeps switching her legs with a stick. Tears run down my cheeks. Alexia's hair has been cut off; all the girls' hair is cut off right below the ears, and the boys are shaved. "Company halt," and four lines come to attention. "Stand at ease."

Alyssum Borders

When I was a child,
Alyssum grew around the border,
Marigolds and snapdragons
in military fashion,
alternating beds of white, purple, rose.

We marched past the flowerbeds
swinging our arms, singing
"Onward Christian Soldiers."
A riding whip cracked; we came to attention,
company halt, by the neatly trimmed hedge.

I sneak out late at night, past the flowerbeds,
under the street lamps. Out there
a car whizzes by going its own way.
Out there a finch listens for a mating call
and floats down.

Where I live now,
we close our eyes and smell jasmine.
Sometimes we lie in the hammock,
telling each other moon stories.

The sparrows watch us in the hammock,
they must have a bird laugh or two.
I remember the child by the flowerbed
at attention, not smiling.

rs of the lawn.

sit with my legs
: better to keep it
n thinking. I am
me place else. I
ut in the fields
says.
, ...ıc other one says. "It's better
... ueen born. If you're dead, you don't know where
, ̇uu be, you might be in hell."

"You're right," the first one says. "I wish I'd never been born." He says this slowly, like he's accepting a bundle unwillingly. I listen to them, several rows over, crawling along the corn row, pulling weeds, and repeat, "I wish I had never been born."

At night, I tell myself stories to put myself to sleep. "Once upon a time," I start, the way my mother used to read to me, the same sing-song voice, "once upon a time, there was a little girl with blond short hair who got lost from her Daddy. She was put in a prison-sort-of-place where no one knew who she was. Then her Daddy found her. Since he was king of the whole world, he took her away from the prison and took her to live somewhere beautiful. In her new home there were lots of orange and white flowers, monkeys, birds and books with pictures. She ate honey on toast and grapes and butterscotch sundaes."

I visit Hope, but Hope doesn't seem glad to see me. Her eyes look troubled when I get out of the van and walk into the dorm where she lives with the other single women. I realize that everything bad I do during the week is reported to Hope, so I feel like I'm getting in trouble twice and nothing is ever forgotten.

Hope doesn't wear long full skirts any more or Scottish wool sweaters. She wears big baggy pants and old sweatshirts with patches. She coughs in the winter. Her face looks thinner and paler, and she doesn't smile. Most of the time, her clothes don't match, and I say, "You said I couldn't wear plaids with prints. You said solid colors with plaids," and Hope pats her head. "Those things don't matter."

"What matters, Mama?"

"Don't call me, 'Mama.' I've told you, call me 'Hope.' What matters is seeking the kingdom of God and his righteousness."

"Read to me in French, please," and Hope reads the Bible in French, pausing lovingly over her favorite Psalms touching my hair, running her hands through it. I lean on her knee; sometimes I sit with my arms around Hope's knees, and I wish we could always stay together, just us, and I could always hear the rhythm of my mother's voice saying, "*Élevez vous, portes éternel, que le Roi de gloire façon entree. Qui est le Roi de Gloire?*" (Lift up your heads, ye everlasting doors, and the King of glory shall come in, who is this King of glory?) (Psalm 24).

"We're going to read Genesis, now; we're going to go all the way through the whole Bible. You must know the Bible. Some day the Russians are coming."

"Who says?"

"George says, and the Lord says. Don't ask questions. You know that will get you into trouble. The Russians are coming."

"Wait a minute, just a little question. If they're Russians, why don't they stay in Russia?"

"Don't ask questions. The Russians are coming to take away our Bibles."

"I'll give 'em mine, I can't read all that good anyway."

"You listen, you need to memorize the word of God. You will need these words to keep you alive in the tribulation."

"Is the tribulation after or before the Russians?"

"Only God knows, now listen, we don't want to get sidetracked. You must learn the Bible. The Russians are coming. The Beast is coming to put '666' on your hand or forehead and the Tribulation is coming. But guess what else, the Lord is coming! And all those who are in Christ shall arise to meet the Lord in the air, so shall we ever be with the Lord."

"Everybody's coming, why can't somebody leave us alone?"

"Andie, this is the kind of thing you say that gets you punished. I can see why you're always in trouble. I've heard you're a troublemaker. Why can't you be more like your sister? She doesn't ask questions. She does what she's told. She doesn't make trouble. Now listen."

Hope reads from the beginning, the Creation, the Flood, the Tower of Babel. "There were giants in the earth in those days;" she reads, "and also after that, when the sons of God came in unto the daughters of men, and they bare children to them, the same became mighty men, which were of old, men of renown." (Genesis 6:4, King James)

"What does it mean, 'sons of God came into?'"

"It means they married."

"Why doesn't it say that? Bible's a funny book. What about giants? Men of renown?"

"It means famous men, and the Bible is not a funny book. Don't ever let me catch you saying that again. Is that clear?"

I sulk, hoping my mother will feel badly for correcting me, and Hope retaliates by ignoring me and reading quietly to herself. "I wanna write books," I say presently.

"What makes you think of that?"

"Well I always tell myself stories, and I want to write stories."

"You must want whatever is God's will for your life."

Hope lives in a little house called the Chalet with eleven other single women. They have a pot belly stove, and they take turns getting up and stoking it; it is winter in Vermont, below zero, the house is walled in by huge drifts of snow. When the girls want tea, they boil down one or two bags for all of them and they huddle around the stove sipping their weak tea. I remember my mom drinking cups of tea before she came to the Farm.

I watch my mother drinking slowly; we are all just sitting around the fireplace, no lights, they are afraid of running up the electric bill. Hope sips the tea, and I slip up beside her and sit down. Hope puts her arm around me. I take off my leather shoes which have big holes in them. They hurt my feet. Hope picks one up and examines it in the firelight. For a moment everyone stares at the shoe, but they're quiet like they're thinking of something else. Then a girl across from Hope starts singing "I got shoes, you got shoes, all God's children got new shoes to wear, since we got to heaven, gonna put on our shoes and gonna walk all over God's heaven, heaven, heaven."

They all join in and they put their arms around each other and sway. I feel for a moment that shoes don't matter, but I'm not sure why. "I got a robe, you got a robe," Hope sings, and the firelight soaks into thirteen pale faces.

In spring, Alexa comes for her yearly visit. Alexa's baby fat is gone, and her eyes look sharply at everything; that soft smoothness to her face and movements is gone. She says, "I'm a Freshman now, and I can march and everything."

"Do you still have pretend children?"

"That stuff is for babies," she says. "Look," she marches and sings, "I'm a little soldier in the Junior Volunteer, but my Lord says I don't have to wait for years and years. I obey on the double, I give the devil trouble, and my feet march the street with the Hallelujah beat." She marches in time with her words. "Do you know why I was allowed to come see Hope?"

"No."

"Well, everybody is going to Fort Number Four tomorrow to pass out tracts. I've seen these tracts. They're little books with pictures that tell people how they are going to hell."

Hope comes in, "Hello, Alexa."

Alexa walks stiffly over to Hope, and they hug like Hope is a reluctant relative, and Alexa a tin soldier.

I watch them, thinking of the way I throw myself in Hope's arms, whispering, "I love you" in her ear, wishing never to let go, how I follow Hope into the bathroom, watching her.

"You take a rest both of you; we're going to have a long day tomorrow. Just lie on the floor, here's a blanket for each of you. Now, don't talk, close your eyes and sleep."

She leaves us alone. "What's school like?" I whisper.

"We're supposed to be sleeping."

"Oh, tell me, what's it like."

"Shsh, we don't want to get in trouble. Shsh." Alexa closes her eyes and turns away, but I can't sleep. Beside me there's a thing that plugs into the wall. I plug and unplug it several times, trying to figure out what the thing does. Alexa opens her eyes and watches. Finally I fall asleep.

When we wake, the room is warm and stuffy. "Who turned on the heater?" Hope says opening the door.

"She did," Alexa says.

"Is this true?"

"I didn't know better, I didn't, I'm sorry."

"You should know better. You cannot go with us tomorrow." I throw my arms around Hope's leg.

"Please, please, Mommy."

"Don't call me, 'Mommy.'"

"Please, please, I'll never, never do it again, I'll never do anything wrong again. I never will. I never."

The next day I am alone at the Farm with one eighty year old woman who I am not allowed to disturb. I am to stay in one room. "You can use this gallon jug to go number one, if you're caught leaving this room for any other reason than to go number two, you will get a spanking and no dinner when I get home," Hope says before shutting the door hard.

"I hate you," I think. I sit in the corner and don't look out the window when the vans pull out. I hear children shouting and running around before they load up. I tell myself stories in the morning and look out the window at the apple tree in the yard. It has tiny green hard apples on it.

Hope read me a story once of a fairy who comes to a man and says, "What would you like?" and he says,

"I would like to turn back time and do my life over, better."

The fairy says, "You have your wish," but when he has his life again, he makes the same mistakes.

"If I had three wishes, I would turn back time so I could go to Fort Number Four." I think about Hope, and somehow, sitting there alone, dazed in the morning sunlight, I see myself as I must look to my mother, running up, hugging her, throwing myself toward the empty space that is my mother. I see Hope touching me, patting me, like I was a dog or a horse. I never see Hope reaching toward me. I remember Hope drawing away sometimes, pulling her arms around herself. I've whispered so many times in Hope's ears, "I love you, better than anybody," and now I remember that like a dream.

"I don't love her any more," I whisper over and over to myself. "She won't touch me. She won't hurt me. I don't care. I don't love her any more."

The old woman brings me a dry peanut butter sandwich for lunch, and I eat it very slowly, and the peanut butter sticks to the roof of my mouth. I sleep in the afternoon, and when I wake, the leaves make strange shadow patterns on the ceiling, and I feel different. I sit up, remembering what has changed. "I don't love her any more."

I hear the vans return, the singing and shouting. Hope comes in, "Come on down for supper." But I don't want to come down. I want to stay by myself and keep thinking. Hope appears distant, strange, like someone I don't know well. I stand up.

"All right," I say in a flat voice. I hear my own voice not moving, like Alexa's voice or Hope's voice. "I'm coming." Hope watches me walking stiffly toward the door, eyes straight ahead, my insides held tightly, my outsides showing nothing.

"Are you okay? Do you need a hug?"

"I don't need anything."

During morning study time, the Nursery School children sit quietly at small desks doing lessons. In the afternoon, we work in the garden or do small chores around the house. One morning, we hear yelling. We peek up cautiously, and our teacher, Joanne doesn't stop us. She is going to open the door, and as she does, the noise enters the room in a scream, "No, Mommy, no," and since no one is stopping us, we run to the window and peer out.

A huge girl is being hauled up the steps by her mother. It's impossible to tell what she looks like, but she seems too big to be in Nursery School, and she is screaming at the top of her lungs.

"Get back in your seats," Joanne yells, and we all scramble. The mother enters the room, dragging the girl by her arms. Inside the room, the girl drops limp in a pile of coat and boots. Her long black hair falls over her.

"She hates stairs," the mother says. Her hair is also black and long. "I don't know," she says to Joanne, and shrugs.

Joanne smiles the special smile she keeps for parents. "She'll be fine; she'll be happy here. All of them cry when they first come." The mother's face looks strained, but she leaves. The girl begins again, an unremitting, earsplitting howl. Joanne doesn't touch her or pay any attention to her. In a few minutes, she tells us we can have our snack and our play time, and we leave our desks to wander over to the toy area. I take my donut and walk over to the girl. I look back at Joanne, but Joanne motions to me that it's okay. The girl is still lying on the floor, a huge lump of dark clothing and hair. She is quiet except for a few sobs. "What's your name?" I ask in a whisper close to the girl's head. The girl doesn't answer, but she moves her head like she's listening. I hold out the donut, and the girl grabs it and stuffs it in her mouth. She sits up, "I'm Ann."

"I'm Andie, I'm almost five."

"I'm eight."

"Why are you in Nursery School?"

"My Mom told my Dad that I is slow."

"Oh."

"Is it nice here?"

"No," I say.

Joanne announces that she'll be going to Bermuda for two weeks to help with the harvest. She says this with eyes shining. George and his secretary Mary go to Bermuda most winters and return in the spring, relaxed and tan. They smile and walk lightly. Now Joanne is going to Bermuda, and she nearly smiles thinking about it.

A teenage girl named Christine comes in to take her place. "Come with me," she tells me the first morning. I pad along behind her to the bathroom. "How old are you?"

"Almost five." Christine bends her dark curly head to enter the small bathroom. She has the children cleaning around the Nursery school room. She pulls down her pants and sits on the toilet. I am puzzled, "Should I leave?"

"No, wait." She takes my soft little girl's hand and puts it in a warm place between her legs. "Rub," she says in a low voice, and I stare out the small square window behind Christine's head. The window is above ground and outside it, a patch of white lilies is growing in the cool damp earth. As I stare at them, a dump truck pulls up and spills a load of gravel, covering the lilies and darkening the room. My hand continues to move slowly, and I continue to stare at the window where the lilies were.

"You can stop now, you can go," Christine says thickly.

Two weeks later, Joanne blows back into the room like spring. Christine bends to say good bye, and her thin lips move in my ear, "Don't ever tell anyone." In the bathroom, black plastic covers the window, and it is always dark.

Boarding School Farewell

do not speak or cry.
I hold on to silence.
A primal howl erupts
from the back of the truck
where we crowd together.
Some children hold hands; some whimper.
The howler kneels, looks through slats
at the disappearing house.
Mommy! he is not tall enough
to see over the back.

Our parents wave at our tears,
turning backs on outstretched hands.
I shut my mouth as tight as my teddy bear.

Chapter 4

I am six when I go to school. The first day at school, we wake to a trumpet blowing. Ann, the biggest girl in the Nursery School, is sent to the school the same day as me. When we walk in the first day, we look at each other out of the corner of our eyes and wish we could hold hands.

The first morning, Ann and I follow the other girls, stacking our sleeping bags, running into the bathroom, stripping off our pajamas and lining up at the row of five sinks. Each girl stands naked and waiting at the sink with her washcloth in her hand. Joyce walks in with her riding crop. She begins to shout out washup calls which I do not understand. "Dip and rinse, up and ring, pass the buoy, foredeck, starboard deck, dip and rinse, up and ring, pass the buoy."

I watch the other girls out of the corner of my eye. I wash myself vigorously. I begin to understand. "Dip and rinse, up and ring," means to dip your washcloth into the wash basin of cold water, swish it around and ring it out. "Pass the buoy," means to pass the soap. "Port bilge, starboard bilge," means under your left arm and under your right arm. "Foredeck" is the face. "Starboard deck" is the neck. I can hardly keep up.

"Wash those bilges," Joyce shouts, cracking the whip. "Dip and rinse, up and ring, port bilge, starboard bilge."

"Why can't she just say to wash under our arms?" I think, "why does she have to call the stupid thing a bilge?"

We pull on our uniforms and line up for workout, twelve minutes of Royal Canadian Air Force exercises, and then a mile run on the school lane. In spring and fall, the dirt is frozen solid, and wind blows through us as we run. In winter, if it is too icy, we run in place on the back porch, counting every time our left foot hits the porch, up to a thousand. Every hundred, we do ten jumping jacks.

After the run, we wait our turn to march out in squads to the Octagon for devotions. The Octagon is the main large building for meetings, weddings, sermons. We march, the boys in their brown ill-fitting uniforms, the girls in long brown skirts and big brown shirts or sweaters. We sit cross-legged on the floor, we girls tuck our skirts under our knees, and George reads to us from the Bible. He starts at the beginning and reads all the way through.

There are parts of the Bible, stories in books like Judges and Genesis and Ezekiel, that George is particularly fascinated with telling us. He reads these over and over. He reads how Ezekiel was ordered by God to eat human feces for weeks and lie on one side and marry a prostitute, and he did all these things for God. He reads about Lot, after his wife was turned into salt because she looked back at the cities of Sodom and Gomorrah. His two daughters living with him in a cave were tired of having no husbands. They got their father drunk two nights and each slept with him and conceived his children.

When Christine comes in to take care of the Freshman girls while Joyce is out sick, she stares at me, but says nothing. I remember the blacked out window, the buried lilies. When the girls go off to summer chores, Christine says, "Andie, we need to talk." As Christine pulls up her skirt this time, I stare at the coat rack. The coats are old and ugly. Christine sits on the laundry box and I stand, touching the shapeless coats with one hand. I put the other hand in Christine's hand and let it be guided down until I encounter hair. I jump back from this; it is prickly.

"No," I say shaking my hand, as if I'd touched blood. "You've got hair."

"Go do your work," Christine says, and our eyes never meet again.

Job, one of the Farm horses, moves restlessly in his stall while I edge around him shovelling manure and sawdust into a wheelbarrow. He lifts his Clydesdale hooves, big as plates and sets them down, and I say, "Easy boy, easy."

"Look at that thing hanging off of him," a voice behind me says. The voice shocks the cold quiet air, and the big horse neighs and rears. I feel fear in my throat, and with a single pull, I lift myself up onto the fence.

"You could've killed me," I scream at the girl looking in the gate.

"Sorry, I didn't know he'd jump like that. I'm Teddy. I'm supposed to help you." The girl grins.

"You're a great help."

"Don't be mad. I'm sorry." She ducks down to peer under the horse. "Look at that thing on him."

"What thing?"

"His penis."

"What do you mean?"

"Don't you know what his penis is, that thing," she points, "that thing hanging down that he pees from."

"Penis," I repeat, tasting the word slowly.

"Well, what can I do? I like horses." Teddy has a thin face, freckles, a small upturned nose, and long brown braids.

"They'll chop those off," I say pointing at her braids while Teddy follows me, helping me finish the horse stalls and going on to the rabbit cages.

"Who cares? How many rabbits are there?"

"Fifteen, we used to have a thousand, then the Lord told George we should get out of the rabbit business. That was when I first came here, and then we had a thousand chickens for a year. Now we have a thousand sheep. How old are you?"

"Seven and a half. Is the Lord into a thousand of everything?"

"I guess."

"I like rabbits. Which are males?"

"The buck is over there, and these are all does."

"Let's put a buck and doe together and see what they do."

"Why? We could get in trouble."

"I want to watch 'em do it, come on, it'll be fun."

"I'm not putting 'em together."

"Why not?"

"You haven't been around here very long. If you break the rules, you get punished. You can get beaten, six-of-the-best, shut up in a room by yourself."

"What's six-of-the-best?"

"Six-of-the-best hits a man's arm can give to your butt with a sawed off mop handle."

"Sounds serious, now listen to me, did anyone ever specifically," she draws out that word slowly and then repeats it, "*specifically* tell you that you couldn't put 'em together?"

"I just know."

"Well shut up and let me do it then."

"If they ever hear you say, 'shut up' you'll get it," but Teddy is already lifting the brown buck by the scruff of its neck and carrying it to a white doe's cage. The doe's feet thump the bottom of the cage, and she presses herself to the far end, but he is on her, his forepaws squeezing her belly. She lets out sharp bunny noises that sound like pain. He presses her down in the corner of the pen, his hindquarters squeezing and moving rhythmically.

"This is great," Teddy says, leaning over the cage, her freckled face pink with pleasure.

"I'm leaving the room," I say. "Put him back when they're done. I'm not getting in trouble."

"Scaredy cat," Teddy calls.

I feed the ram lambs who are going to market. They bleat for their corn, their white faces small trusting ovals.

One half hour of free time a day, and during this free time we do personal jobs. Mondays—shoe polishing, Tuesday—clothes that need hand washing, Wednesday—mending, Thursday—writing letters, Friday—actual free time. The whole day is scheduled, and there are whistles on the hour to remind us to wake up at 5:30, wash and exercise, devotions 6:30, breakfast and chores that are called "joyjobs" 7:30, classes 8:30 until 12:30, lunch, afternoon chores until 6:30, free time 7:30 to 8:00 followed by washups, evening devotions and bed.

It is Friday night free time, and I lie on my side on the bathroom radiator behind the coat rack. If I go for a walk, someone will ask where I am going. Maybe someone will ask to go with me.

I will not be able to refuse without raising questions of why I want to be alone although I always wish to be alone.

"Little lambs all alone wander and are lost," they will say. But I want to be alone. I want to think about a story I am making up in my head. At night, when the others are asleep, I sometimes whisper stories to Teddy.

A little girl lives in the woods with her daddy and mommy and sister. Then a bad witch visits their house and goes around spitting in the corners. This makes a spell, so the daddy and mommy and the little girl's sister all become ghosts. Being ghosts, they are, of course, invisible even to each other. Since they cannot see each other, they wander far away from each other, and the little girl is left alone. She is very lonely, but she takes care of herself and finds a horse and rides it.

At this point, I am not sure what to have happen. In one version, a good witch turns the daddy ghost back into a man. He comes back, finds the little girl, and they live together happily. The mother and sister ghosts are always ghosts because they wandered too far away.

In another version, the little girl doesn't need anyone to take care of her. She rides her horse around the woods, plants a garden, has long hair and is a wild girl. I can't decide which ending I like better.

I hear a new voice on the other side of the coats, a squeaky pleading little voice, "I don't know where to put my things."

"A new girl," I think, with a yellow, cowardly voice.

"Hang your coat with the others. I'll show you where your other clothes go," Grace's voice, a grey voice. The coats part and a white face stares at me, eyes so blue they're almost black and shoulders that seem permanently hunched. I put my finger over my mouth to say, "shsh," but the girl is already screaming,

"There's somebody back here," and Grace says,

"Andie, out of there," in a voice that sounds tired.

I lay my sleeping bag beside the new girl, Stephanie's, at bedtime, and when Grace says, "Okay, no talking, lights out, eyes closed," and shuts the door, I lean over. "How'd you come here?"

Stephanie squeaks, "Shouldn't we be quiet?"

"Shush, whisper, Friday nights they don't check on us. They have off until nine on Saturday morning, and we have to stay in bed until then. So, tell." Stephanie sniffs a few times, and pushes back her brown hair.

"Well," she says, "well, I'll tell you if you promise not to tell a single soul in the whole wide world."

"I promise," I say adding up in my head who I will tell the next day. "I promise."

"Okay, well my Mom died when I was born. My Dad had me and my brother and two sisters to take care of, so he got married to my Mom Julie. Then I had a baby sister and two baby brothers."

"So there were seven of you?"

"Yep, seven, so then we came here, so then after that, George says my Dad and mom Julie are not married under God."

"Why?"

"Because my Mom Julie was divorced before she married my Dad."

"So, they're not really married?"

"They got married in a church, I saw pictures, and I was a baby and my sisters were bridesmaids and wore pink."

"So, then what?"

"My mom Julie left with my younger brother and sister and my baby brother who's just born. I'm not gonna see them again, and I have to live here." Stephanie sobs into her pillow, and I pat her until the sobs quiet and Stephanie falls asleep. I lie on my back staring at the dark ceiling. A father would be fun; at least she has a father. I decide to end my ghost story with the ghost father becoming a real man.

On Sabbath Day, it's the Lord's day of rest, and we don't work except to feed and water the animals. All meals are prepared the day before, special Sabbath foods: Muesli, banana bread, potato salad, vegetable salads, cold sliced meat.

On a Friday night, when Teddy and I finish preparing the food fifteen minutes before dinner, Bertha sends us out to the duck pond with a couple loaves of stale bread for the ducks. "Be back in time to wash your hands for dinner."

We toss bits of bread to the fat white Pekings. Teddy jumps onto my back and kicks my ribs, "Come on, horse. Gallop." I jump to buck her, but Teddy holds on.

"I can't run in these boots," I say. I'm wearing oversized black combat boots that I found in a Salvation Army barrel. On vacations when other children shop for clothes, my mother and I sift through barrels of discards, but there haven't been many shoes lately.

Once in a while, new children would come to school. I always asked to hear what it was like for them arriving at the school. I longed to know what this place was like from an outsider's point of view. Was it unusual, or was it like every other place? When Emma arrived in our squad, I begged her to tell me, but she was shy at first. It was months after Emma arrived that she told me about the whole trip from her point of view. I listened quietly to what she told me. It sounded far away, like it was coming from another world. She told me the story like it was happening to someone else; she said part of her had already died.

Early that morning, a balding businessman in Brooklyn called his family together. "Well, this is the day we've been waiting for," he says.

The older kids, who aren't going off to school, say goodbye to the four younger ones as they load into the station wagon.

When they get underway, the children start off playing games and finally settle into fighting, taking each other's gum, chewing it, then sticking it to the backs of each other's necks. The car rumbles on.

"How often will we see you?"

"Twice a year for two week vacations."

"Who will take care of us?"

"You'll be in squads with counselors."

"Will we eat peanut butter and jelly sandwiches?" Emma asks, eating a hamburger and sucking the last drops of her milk shake. Her long curly hair is sweat-stuck to her neck and forehead.

"And ice cream?" her sister asks.

"I don't think so."

"I don't like this at all," Emma says. "I don't think it's going to be fun."

"I seriously doubt the word 'fun' applies at all here," her older brother says. He is thirteen and has been silent for the entire trip.

The city full of familiar faces and sidewalks has disappeared into greenness stretching out, broken only by white houses and red barns. The kids get quieter, finally huddling together.

As they pull around the bend of the dirt road their father says, "You'll see the school in a minute, kids." Emma sees a dirty duck pond, green as vomit and two girls beside it. The tall one is wearing a long misshapen grey shirt like something her grandmother wouldn't wear. Her hair hangs straight like a bowl over her head. The boots on her feet are what make Emma look twice; at first she can't believe this is really a girl. The boots are huge black clumsy things, and the girl walks awkwardly like they might trip her. On her back, kicking her, is another girl. The tall girl's head is down.

The car stops and the kids get out. Someone comes over to talk to her father, but Emma is still watching the two girls by the pond. They are coming her way now, and she can see both their faces. She shivers, and her father says, "It's cold, let's get inside kids, come on," but she is still looking at the girls' faces.

They are obviously playing, not working; this is their idea of a fun time. But their faces are both blank as if their expressions do not work. She thinks, "They're not nice," and she says, "Hi, what's it like here?" She smiles her best, her warmest, her bravest. The tall one's head jerks up, and she looks right in her eyes like she's surprised.

"What's it like here?" the tall girl repeats. The other girl jumps down, and they both walk by her and go inside without answering, but not before Emma sees liquid filling the tall one's eyes.

By the time I am ten, we have drills at night. I wake trying to remember a half-forgotten dream that was completely clear a moment before; it is already fading. I was swimming in the dream, but while I'm trying to remember it, I'm packing. The whistle blew me out of sleep at midnight for drill call. Each girl jumps up, pulls clothes over pajamas, throws all her clothes onto her sleeping bag, rolls it up and ties it with bailing twine. "Out, out the door," Joyce shouts, "You're slow, we've got to get this under two minutes, come on, out the door. Be back tomorrow evening."

We stumble down the back steps, across the soccer field toward the woods. Emma, Teddy and I walk together as the girls split into different groups. "At least it's not raining," Teddy says.

"Oh, do they make us do this in the rain too?" Emma says, "This is cruel and unusual, you know. I say this is monstrous." "It's not a punishment; it's a drill, this is to harden us up." I push ahead, holding back branches so they won't hit Emma who's behind me.

"Where are we going?" Emma says.

"To this place Teddy and I went last time. We're building a lean-to there. There's an apple tree."

"Are we going to eat just apples?"

"Be glad we have apples. Some of the kids last year ate unripe blueberries; some of them just starved, and two of those guys caught a fish and ate it raw, and then brought back the head to show they did it." Teddy is laughing in the blackness behind us. We're walking along what used to be an old road through the woods, but the undergrowth has taken over most of it leaving only a path.

"Where do you think everyone else is going?"

"Oh, all over. Some of them go down to Beaver's Dam." Teddy's voice sounds like it's coming from far behind.

"Are you coming, Teddy?" I ask.

Teddy says, "Yeah, I was just stopping to look at this tree."

"A tree?" Emma says, and her voice sounds out of breath.

"Doesn't it feel like an adventure?" I say, "Careful Emma, it's getting rocky. Isn't this exciting?"

"No," Emma says still out of breath.

"Oh, give me a home where the buffalo roam," Teddy sings off key.

"Teddy, do you know how much trouble you'd be in, if they ever hear you singing a worldly song?"

"Can't we rest?" Emma says.

"We're almost there," and I push aside a spruce branch, and we step out of the woods into an open clearing on a hillside. A blanket of stars opens above us with the Milky Way splashed across it, one long smudge of white.

By the time we're stretched in our sleeping bags, we're all feeling wide awake, but warm and cozy. "I love sleeping outdoors," I say.

"What I don't get is, what is this supposed to accomplish, making us sleep outside? Tomorrow we'll starve," Emma says.

"See that red star?" Teddy points, in the upper right corner of Orion. "That's Betelgeuse, then the other three going clockwise, are Rigel, Saiph, and Bellatrix."

"Are you sure you have the order right?" I ask.

"How come you guys know the stars?"

"Celestial navigation class, which we took in case we all have to escape this country by boat and sail around in trimarans."

"What's a trimaran?"

"It's a boat with three hulls," Teddy shows with her hands, "a big hull in the middle and two little hulls, one on each side."

"What is it with this school? What is it with these drill calls?"

"See," I explain, starting to feel tired, and trying to think of an explanation. "It's this country. The Lord has shown George that it's going to fall in 1976."

"Why so soon?"

"I thought the Russians were going to take over the country." Teddy sounds tired too.

"No, the country falls first, then the Russians take over, then the Tribulation, the Beast comes, and no one can buy or sell without the Mark of the Beast which is '666' in their hand or forehead."

"So, why do we have to sleep in the woods?" Emma asks.

"Well," I say, "it's just that we'll all be sleeping in the woods all the time then, so we're doing this now and getting used to it."

"Shouldn't we enjoy sleeping inside while we can? Are we going to stay in the woods in the winter?"

"Yeah, I guess."

"Won't we freeze to death?"

"You two can keep talking, but tone it down, I'm going to sleep," Teddy says.

"We'll build fires," I say.

"Good night," Teddy says, "good night everybody."

It's early morning when we wake to sore muscles and crawl out of our sleeping bags. Dew has fallen on everything. "I'm going naked," Teddy says, stripping off her shirt, skirt and underwear.

"You'll freeze." Teddy's body is white, the ribs sticking out, the flat chest like a washboard. "What if someone sees you."

"You're looking at me." Teddy climbs the apple tree behind the huge boulder which hangs over our sleeping place like a wave cresting. She pelts us with green apples.

"We'll get a belly ache," Emma says, but we eat the apples anyway.

The lean-to Teddy and I started the last time out is still standing. We found two trees spaced ten feet apart and placed a log on the lower branches joining the trees. The log is still there.

We carry logs and lean them against the top log and stack branches and moss. "Spruce branches work best," Teddy tells Emma.

"I hate 'em; they're prickly." The sun finally comes out to warm Teddy's white skin. I have stripped to my underwear, but Emma tells us we're both crazy. Our arms and legs are covered with scratches.

We are sick from the apples, but we keep gathering branches. "I'll tell you two something; it's weird that George and Mary live together," Teddy says.

"Weird how?" We all feel tired and hungry.

"Weird because who knows what they do together?" Teddy calls down from the pine tree where she is breaking off branches. She jumps. "I'm getting dressed. Look." She has deep scratches on her legs and one of her legs is bleeding.

"I'm hot." I strip off my underwear and wade into the cold stream. I bend over as I walk so I won't slip on the mossy rocks. I splash my face, and in the middle of the stream, I squat and go under water. I hear Teddy and Emma laughing before I disappear.

"She's getting baptized," Teddy says. They're inside the lean-to when I come up; they're sitting on stumps like two grown women. I wonder if they're laughing at me, at my body, at all the things I don't know. I feel my chest to see if there are bumps there.

Micha Mirror

We aren't allowed mirrors.
Fifteen girls in sleeping bags stare
at a dark ceiling wishing to know one face.

The Russians are coming to brainwash you.
Memorize God's word. The Beast is coming
to put "666" on your hands and foreheads.

We stare at the ceiling in a room below freezing.
"Be ye perfect as your Father in heaven is perfect."
Russians will not brainwash us.

A flashlight in our faces, a whistle in our ears,
we roll toothbrush, sweaters, jeans, in a sleeping bag,
out the door in three minutes, marching toward pine trees.

We drop in a clearing under pale morning light,
scatter for firewood. I crawl in a direction
no one is headed to find my own lair.

I crawl under overhanging rock and see
a piece of micha. I turn it slowly.
My reflection
my reflection
stares back at me,
grey, cold, a mask of every other face.

Chapter 5

Foolishness is bound in the heart of a child; but the rod of correction shall drive it far from him. (Proverbs 22:15, King James)

"It looked extremely rocky for the Mudville nine that day,
the score stood two to four with but an inning left to play,
so when Coony died at second and Burrows did the same,
a pallor wreathed the features of the patrons of the game."

I stop reciting and check to see if my audience listens attentively. Stephanie, Teddy, and Emma sit on the window seat at the back of the dorm. Long paste fiberglass curtains hang behind them.

"A straggling few got up to go, leaving there the rest,
with that hope that springs eternal within the human breast,
for they thought, if only Casey could get a whack at that.
They'd put even money now with Casey up to bat."

"Where did you learn that?" our counselor Joyce's voice behind me makes me jump. I hear myself give a little scream.
"I read it in a book."
"A book that you have been forbidden to read?" Joyce's eyes never blink. She leans forward to look down with narrow eyes, her head cocked like a bird's. Joyce's hands hang out in front of her like useless appendages, and her shoulders hunch forward.
"Go sit in the bathroom." I go, my flannel pajamas swishing the sides of my legs.
I sit on the wooden laundry box. Emma comes in to use the bathroom, but when someone is being punished, the others pretend not to see them. I stare as Emma stands choosing which of the three

toilets to use. She chooses the one closest to the door, then stands choosing which of the five sinks to use. She chooses the one farthest from the door, and nearest to the row of hooks with towels hanging on them. The towels and washcloths are washed once a week. Today is the day, so Emma has to shake off her hands.

Stephanie comes in to brush her teeth. She sneaks a glance at me and shakes her head. The day before, Stephanie was sent to bed with no dinner, and I sneaked her some bread and a donut. Stephanie doesn't say anything. She mouths, "I'm sorry," and leaves.

I watch her go, and think about running away. It is my favorite fantasy, the one I think of every time I am in trouble. Every night when I go to bed, I imagine myself courageous enough to run away. One summer, Stephanie's brother ran away and lived in the woods by an apple tree until one of the school counselors found him. Early in the morning he left in the back seat of a car. Stephanie said he went to be with her stepmother. I saw the field where the boy lived while he ate apples and drank stream water. I couldn't imagine myself living there now that it's winter, sleeping in a snow bank.

I kneel on the laundry box, feel splinters in my knees. I take down two toothbrushes, a red one and a yellow one. In the Old Testament, God had the high priest wear a breastplate with two stones, a black one and a white. These were called Urim and Thumin. When the king wished to inquire of the will of God, he would ask and the priest would take out the white stone of "yes," or the black stone of "no."

I hold the two toothbrushes. "These God, are my Urim and Thumin stones; the red one is 'no,' the yellow one is 'yes.' God, tell me, will I ever be able to leave the Farm?"

I close my eyes and roll the brushes. I stop, pull one out, and open my eyes. The brush is red. "I'm giving you another chance, God. It's three out of five I'm asking for." I roll the brushes again. This time I pull a yellow one. I roll again, red, then yellow. "Okay God, it's even. Now you know I want your will for me, and you know I want to leave the Farm, and I'm asking you God, listen to me. Please stop whatever it is you're doing, and listen to just me for a minute. I don't ask for your full attention very often, but this is important. Please say yes." I roll the brushes slowly this time. I say, "Please, please, please, God" on every roll. Then I drop one, and sit holding the other. When I open my eyes, it is yellow.

It is nearly time for evening devotions, and I wonder whether I will be left in here alone or brought out with the kids. If Joyce is in a good mood, she will consider this punishment enough, if she is in a bad mood, she has already told George, and I will be punished in front of the whole school. I am on the point of asking God with the toothbrushes what is going to happen when I hear, "Andie, it's time for devotions."

The other girls stand at attention in two rows. I get in the back of the line beside Joyce. Six squads of children march, come to attention and sit down quietly. George walks to the front of the room and stands there surveying eighty cold, still faces. The headmaster, Don, stands at attention off to one side. George heads the entire commune, Don is the school principal. George says, "Amen," and the whole assembly says, "Amen."

"The Lord Jesus Christ is risen today." His voice thunders.

"He is risen indeed," we reply in unison.

"It has been brought to my attention," George says, "that one of you has allowed the devil loose in our midst." No one moves. One tiny five year old begins to whimper and her counselor quickly hushes her.

"Andie come forward and tell everyone what you did."

I step carefully between the rows of children. I come to the front of the room staring at my feet, wishing the humiliation could be over, wishing it were tomorrow, hating today. "Do you want me to tell them what I said?"

"No, what did you do?"

"I don't know."

"Rebelliousness is bound up in the heart of the child, but the rod of correction will drive it far from her. You spoke idle words. What does the Bible say about idle words?"

"Whosoever shall speak any idle words, he shall give an account thereof in the day of judgement."

"Bend over." George does not administer beatings himself. He stands and holds the child's hands while Don does the beating. George's after-shave smells hot and spicy, like the breath of God, I think.

He holds my hands tightly above the wrists, so I cannot turn and twist. The stick is a sawed off mop handle.

Don holds it in both hands to deliver six strokes. Each one thuds dully. The children are not allowed to hide their eyes, but they wince and groan at every stroke. I bite my lip, shut my eyes tightly and concentrate all my energy on ignoring the pain. I will not give George the satisfaction of hearing a scream. Through half-shut eyes, I see my sister Alexa sitting in another group, her eyes impassive, her face a mask. I grit my teeth, strike four, a pause, strike five, a longer pause, and six. The sixth is always the hardest, and a squeal like an animal caught in a trap leaps from my throat, a strangled cry I choke and cough to cover. Tears stand in my eyes, but I refuse to wipe them. I stand straight and stare at George. "You may go back to your seat."

I walk stiffly back to my squad and go to the back of the group to stand at attention. I will not be expected to sit for meals or schoolwork for at least a week. My bottom will be a mass of bruises that will turn from black and blue to green and purple.

George raises his hands in blessing, "Now unto him that is able to keep you from falling, and to present you faultless before the presence of his glory with exceeding joy, to the only wise God our Savior, be glory and majesty, dominion and power, both now and ever, amen."

At breakfast time, eighty children file through the kitchen, pick up a bowl and hold it out for cereal. I stole a copy of *Jane Eyre* from the books to be thrown out, and I was amazed to see that burnt cereal is a food staple in orphanages. The smell is enough to make some of the kids want to vomit.

For lunch, there are sandwiches and big pots of vegetable soup. For dinner, Bertha the cook makes baked beans, pork, cornbread and huge salads in the summer. Food goes in phases. One summer when there is less money than usual, we eat dandelion and lamb's quarter gravy over bread. In the winter when food runs low, baked beans are the staple, dry beans cooked in molasses.

We do chores in the afternoon. I march out to a clearing with five younger girls who are part of my team. Our job is to carry logs and stack them for firewood. Some of the logs are eventually carried out of the clearing. I climb "The Hill Difficulty," named after the hill Christian had to climb in *Pilgrim's Progress*, and the other girls follow. The chain saw crew has chopped the trees, limbed them, and cut up the wood into four foot pieces.

Emma carries logs carefully, two at a time. Teddy crawls under piles of brush and finds logs no one else sees. She finds a cat with her kittens, and at the end of the day, she takes them back to the school. "I'm gonna have a boyfriend when I get older," Teddy says.

"What will you do with him?" I ask.

"I donno, stuff," Teddy laughs.

"I'm going to do stuff you can't even imagine with my boyfriends," Emma says. "When I was in New York, we celebrated Christmas."

"What's Christmas?"

"Well, you know, it's when you sing Christmas carols and things."

"We sing carols."

"I know, but you sing them all year round, so it don't count."

"Doesn't count," I say.

"Cut the correcting people's English. No one's listening, you know. Lucky for us."

"You're not allowed to say, 'lucky.'"

"How come?"

"You'll get in trouble, anyway, everyone better get working." I try to set a good example for the team by carrying at least four logs in each load.

Our mittens are always snow-soggy and then frozen, but we take our hands out of them once in a while to warm them under our armpits or blow on them. As long as we keep moving, we can feel our body parts, but if we stop to chat, the chill crawls up the spine and down to the extremities.

"I want a warm fire to stand by," Teddy says, "with a cup of hot chocolate in my hands, and someone standing by me who is a grownup and likes me a little."

"Oh, yeah," Emma says, "that'd be great, but as you know, the lake of fire is north of here." Her voice has that raw brittle sarcasm that comes when you want to repeat something funny, but you barely have the energy for wit.

"Just over the hill," I say, "is a wonderful lake of fire; you could warm up by it any time, and you would feel so comfy. One more sin will take you there."

"Be quiet you guys," Stephanie says, "they're listening; they're always listening."

"The lake of fire is north of here," I repeat, though it's an old phrase we toss around on cold days, "hell is north of here; sometimes I wish we could just go there and be done with it."

"Heaven might be better," Stephanie says, "although the whole harps and white robes thing will get boring."

"It's too cold for harps and snow angels," I say.

We march up the hill for more logs. "Onward then, the lake of fire is waiting to thaw us out," Teddy swings her arms.

"I'm not hearing this," Stephanie says digging her mittens into pockets. "I hear nothing." The sky holds water across its gray face.

A frozen stream runs down the middle of the clearing. The ice makes shapes like it was frozen at intervals, like it tried to stay awake through the winter but failed. "We have to get the logs on the other side of the stream. Wanna go over?" I ask. Emma brushes particles of snow from her mittens. "I'm scared."

"I'll go," Teddy says, as I expected she would. Teddy wants to be a boy. She read *Little Women*, one of the few books besides the Bible that we are allowed to read, and made everyone call her Jo until one of the counselors caught us and said anyone who didn't call her Teddy would get six of the best. Teddy's real name is Letitia, but no one ever calls her that.

Teddy and I step gingerly across the ice. One, two, three steps holding on to a branch, and we are across. Don said we have to start picking up all the logs on both sides of the stream. "I like doing stuff like this, dangerous stuff, it makes me feel like an explorer," Teddy says.

On the way back, we carry four logs each. We cannot see where we walk. I inch across the ice one step at a time watching Teddy ahead of me. Wind whips Teddy's scarf back into my face, and I fall headlong on the ice. I lie still. "You okay?" Teddy asks.

"Yeah, yeah. I can get up. Just get going, I'm okay."

"You sure?" I pull myself up and feel my bruised leg.

"Yeah." The logs roll away, and I crawl after them. The ice is rough and misshapen under my belly. I see cracks where it has melted and refrozen. I look up at Teddy who is on the bank now, struggling, her arms full. I crawl toward the logs which have rolled further downstream. I hear a splintering and cracking and lie still. Teddy screams from the bank, turning, stretching out both hands, but she is out of reach. There is silence for a moment; neither of us speaks.

I lie stretched out, hoping my weight is spread out enough. There isn't a sound. The logs are inches from one hand; the bank looks close and white with Teddy leaning out. I reach for the logs with one mittened hand, and with a terrible crunching sound, a cracking, a breaking, my legs sink into green-white ice water, chunks hitting me at the waist, the numbing water needling through my blood. Teddy screams as my head hits the ice, and I black out.

When I open my eyes, my face is lying on the ice, and the half of my body that rushes in the stream feels unimportant. I feel curiously aloof and am surprised to see Teddy's face close to my own, contorted with pain like an animal. Emma and Stephanie hold Teddy's legs, as she wraps her arms into mine. Numbness and shock make me want to close my eyes. I don't understand the fuss; I just want to be left alone. Behind the girls on the bank I see large white figures which I think must be polar bears. A moment later I realize that they are tall angels, whiter than the snow, their wings folded back behind them.

The girls haul on Teddy's legs, and my lower half inches out of the ice. I look up at the angels who aren't saying anything or moving. "Give us a hand here," I say, but I can't hear my own voice. I say, "Hey, thanks guys," but I find that I can't hear myself. I close my eyes. Taking a nap seems to be the best idea. I think the angels are singing.

When I open my eyes, I feel terrible pain from the waist down. They've pulled off my snow pants and my regular pants and they are furiously slapping my legs. As the pain shoots through them, I sit up and scream, "Cut it out."

I feel confused. The sky is turning from blue white to a dark grey. My legs are blue but turning red. For a second, I look up for the angels, but they seem to have left. It begins to snow lightly on my bare skin. I look down at myself, a smudge against the white snow.

In the dorm, while we change clothes for dinner, Grace comes in to supervise. "What happened to your clothes?"

"I fell in the river," I say as I pull off my things. My feet are blue.

"Is this taking care of your body? Haven't I told you your body is the temple of the Holy Ghost? You are supposed to take care of yourself."

"She would have gotten the Holy Ghost's temple back here faster, but she was afraid she'd get in trouble."

"What?" Grace turns to face Teddy.

"Like I was saying, she was gonna come back earlier, but we didn't want to get in trouble."

"Teddy, get dressed, get a tub of warm water, put it in the dining room. Andie, get dressed, go sit with your feet in it." Teddy gets a plate for me and sits down beside me. "Forgive us our trespasses," Grace prays, and "forgive Andie her foolishness."

The Face of Christ

The headmaster travels by train, asks God
to show him the face of Christ.
Take a picture out the window, God says.

In Christian boarding school
the teachers say every day, look at that picture
if you are clean inside, if you are right with God
you will see the face of Christ.

I look every day. It is shadows on snow.
Go to the corner, sit by yourself
until you see.
The other girls see God; they stand adoring.
I see black and white patches, continents?

They say, this is rebellion.
You're going to start skipping meals.
Forgive me, I pray, for my flesh is weak.
I see it, I see it, the face of Christ.
Thank you Jesus.
I can walk in the breakfast line.
the other girls give me knowing smiles.

Chapter 6

We went through fire and water; but thou brought us out into a wealthy place. (Psalms 66:12, King James)

The older kids raise their heads from taking notes; they wait for George's next words. He stands with his back to the Octagon windows; light streams in glowing through his silver hair.

"God has called us out of this place. I have prayed about where God would like us to go. I have been down to Belize, and the country is good. It is rich and warm; God has blessed that country. It is the only country in Central America where English is spoken. Laws are enforced there. Men are hanged for stealing. God is no longer blessing America because they have turned their backs on Him. God has called us out of this land." His voice rides silky waves and makes me think of what it would be like to live in a warm country; bananas, tropical forests, fish. George's voice treads through the jungles of Belize, tangles our hearts in the coconut forests, and then he stops.

"But we must pray, there are other places God may want us to go. God brought you to this place to be His soldiers to learn to think. You must learn to pray and find out God's will for each and every one of you. God may want us to go to Paraguay in South America. Jojoba beans will be the crop of the future. He may want us to raise jojoba beans there."

We follow George across the plains of Paraguay. With him we live the life of ranchers. We raise sheep and pigs; we kill snakes. We grow up brown, healthy and hard. We gallop horses across the plains to check our jojoba crop. George pauses.

"God may want us to move to the South Sea Islands. Life is easy; it is a matter of catching fish and picking fruit. We would have time for prayer, for devoting ourselves to praying for the leaders of the world, for becoming disciples." This is what I hope the Lord will want. "Pray," he says, "find out what the Lord wants for you."

I have just finished Thor Heyerdahl's *Fatu Hiva* and *Kon Tiki*. I was allowed to get it from the library because it had no wrongdoing in it. Thor lived on Fatu Hiva for a year with his wife just like the natives. He sailed to Raratonga from Peru on a raft of balsa wood.

I know that God wants me on one of the South Sea Islands. I pray quietly, "God, do you want me on the South Sea Islands?" I hear, "Yes, yes, yes."

I have two pencils and paper in case I want to write anything down. I roll the pencils in my fingers while George talks. "This long one," I tell God, "is yes, the short one is no." I roll the pencils in my lap while George's voice goes on, "The water so clear you can see down through it, wave after wave of blue and green."

"Do you want me to go to the South Sea Islands?" I ask God and look down at the longer pencil in my hand. "Are you sure?" I say and roll them again. This time I draw the shorter pencil, "perhaps I should not have questioned you again, but let us say out of five answers, the one you give me three of." I roll again and again. Two times I pulled yes, two times no. My hands sweat on my Urim and Thumin. I roll. "The Lord watches to see if you are worthy to go to this country that He has chosen for us," George says. I close my eyes for a second and look down at the pencil in her hand. It is a long one. "Thank you, Lord Jesus," I write on my paper. "You are altogether wonderful."

George reads from "Revelations." He describes the city of God, the New Jerusalem, where we will go if our names are written in the Lamb's Book of Life. "When you are saved, your name is written in that book, but if you sin, and you do not ask for God's forgiveness, your name will be blotted out." I pray every day that God will forgive every sin I have ever committed or ever will commit. "God, I hope you've got me covered," I say, "because I'm trying real hard."

"The New Jerusalem is a city one mile square. It is the city of the saints who are washed in the blood of Christ. It is to be the Bride of Christ." I wonder if Jesus ever wanted a real woman for a wife instead of a whole city, but I don't want to ask. I wonder if George ever wants a woman for a wife. Mary sits watching his every word. "The city shines seven times brighter than the sun, but we will have new bodies and new eyes, and we will be able to take it."

At the end, we all pray in unison, a half an hour of continuous prayer. Once in a while, one voice will rise above the rest, "Make me part of your Bride, cleanse me in your blood." I never raise my voice. I wonder if those who do are showing off. But when George has blessed us, and we stand up, open our eyes and look around us, the world is new and wet. We are humble as young children. We smile to those around us. "God bless you, my brother, my sister," and for several hours, nothing but God and His kingdom seems important.

I don't know how the other kids feel about Jake because no one talks about him much. Once I hear Emma say, "Bet he hates kids," under her breath, and I whisper back, "If the Weasel hears, you're dead." The Weasel is the squad's tattletale.

Ever since George said the boys and girls squads will be together in one big squad, the Freshman boys' counselor Jake and the Freshman girls counselor Joyce have been taking charge of all twenty kids. We eat all our meals together and have night devotions together. I watch Jake's hands holding the Bible. The hands are huge, with black hairs on them. The rest of Jake is hairy as well. In the summer, when we saw him swimming in shorts, we saw his back and chest covered with bear like hair. His eyebrows almost overshadow his eyes. The hands seem capable of anything. He looks up while he reads to make sure our eyes are on him.

Standing with our backs to the wall, eyes straight ahead, we wait as Jake makes his way down the inspection line. On Fridays, before dinner we line up for inspection: Teeth, fingernails, clothes. Our clothes are folded neatly in open boxes nailed to the wall behind us. If he finds messy clothes, he sweeps them on to the floor with one swipe of his hairy paw, and that person misses dinner and sometimes free time.

I hear him pause at Ann's box. Jake is the only counselor who doesn't treat Ann like she's special just because she's slow. Ann tries so hard to be good, but she can't do things like fold clothes and math. He's swept her box four weeks in a row, but this time he doesn't. I helped her this time, and I almost smile in satisfaction. I hear Ann let out her breath. He pauses and picks up the hem of my dress with his riding crop. "Well, well," he says, "I thought we'd have a perfect inspection here. Even Chunky Bar's clothes are neat, but now we have a torn dress on Chubby Face here. No dinner. Finish hemming the dress by the end of dinner and you can have free time."

I hear Stephanie hold her breath. "Well, Duck Feet," he says, "move aside so I can see your box." She steps forward, shaking.

He pounces on her fear like a wild animal. "Duck Feet, can't you walk straight? Your tail sticks out, and you screw up your face with those glasses perched on your bill." Encouraged by the snickers of the girls he says, "Your belly looks like you've been eating too much corn. Now stand up, stomach in, butt in." We watch her out of the corner of our eyes. We laugh sick apologetic laughs; it could so easily be us.

Stephanie's shoulders shake; her whole body cringes. "Walk across the room for me," he says, "let's see you walk with your feet straight." She takes a small step, and his mouth opens to laugh. His teeth show, and his huge head leans toward her like a shark's head toward a fish when it smells blood. He laughs a braying laugh, and we laugh with him, our laughter grinding over Stephanie. He stops her, squeezes her arm hard, his nails digging into her wrist until a drop of blood appears. "Walk straight I said."

The blood soaks into her sleeve, and she looks down at it, thinking of the stain it will make. She walks across the room, her head down, her butt swaying while he laughs and points. Joyce comes in, "It's almost dinner time." Our eyes flicker toward her remembering the good days when she used to do our inspections before Jake insisted that he should do it.

"I was just teaching Duck Feet here how to walk," he says. "Okay, file in."

At dinner, I sit on the windowbox sewing. I watch the others eat cornbread, peas and meat loaf. I breathe through my mouth so I won't have to smell it.

"On Sunday, we will have organized activities," Jake says.

"For all of us?" Teddy asks.

"Whenever I say that it's just for those of you who want to, only the boys show up. You girls are too soft. Yes, all of you." There is a slight groan from us girls.

"Well, what's the point of playtime if we still have to do something?" Teddy looks around at the other girls for support. Jake's eyebrows meet across his forehead like black arches.

"Would you like to weed the garden while the rest of us play Cowboys and Indians?"

"No," Teddy says, sitting up straight and trying not to let fear into her voice.

Sunday morning, two of the boys pick teams. The boys get picked first; we girls look around as though we don't care. Emma is the first girl chosen, and she walks over to her captain, Luke, with her hips swinging. She has slimmed down since she came to school. Her full lips laugh into the boys' faces, and they all like her.

"She's as full and sweet as a ripe pear," Luke said to me once as we watched Emma walking toward us through a field of strawberries.

"She is?" I asked, not understanding him.

"Yep," he kept looking. "She makes me feel like a dog."

"What kind of dog?"

"Just a dog."

When the teams are picked, we split for opposite sides of the valley. Each team has a bandanna that we will put in a known location. One is going to the Big Rock, the other to the Big Fir Tree. Each team leaves someone to guard the flag, sometimes more than one person, and the rest of the team fans out to sneak into the other camp and get their flag. When anyone sees someone from the opposite team, they shout, "Bang, so-and-so," and the person has to lie down and count to one hundred. The game usually lasts six to eight hours.

I memorize who is on my team because I don't want to be one of the stupid ones who shoots her own team members. Each team has twenty minutes to reach their camp, and then they hear Jake's whistle. I sneak off alone, while my other team members fan down into the valley. I hear the faint sound of someone being shot, then someone else. I go quietly in the opposite direction, climbing the mountain.

I walk through the woods, looking at the trees, the leaves turning red, yellow, orange. I pick up a maple leaf, turn it over, looking at its red points. I wonder how long I would survive alone out here. Could I stay in the woods like John the Baptist and eat locusts and wild honey? I have never seen a locust.

George says that every human being has to work for food, so I wonder if I left the Farm if I could go somewhere and work for food. If I worked for food, could I choose what food I worked for? "I will work for butterscotch ice cream sundaes," I say. My voice sounds loud in the quiet woods.

When I step out of the shadows into the sun lit field where the lean-to is, the light blinds me for a second. I walk quietly, Indian style, toe to heel; I want the animals to think of me as another animal. A snake darts from under the brush, and I step back shuddering; it is a harmless garter snake, thick as a pencil, black and grey and quick moving as a whip. I pick a couple of ripe apples, and eat them slowly. I lie on the ground in front of the lean-to and watch the clouds. One looks like a chariot with a man in the back.

"My father's coming to rescue me." I blow him a kiss the way Emma and her brothers and sisters do. I lie quietly, listening for a while. "Talk to me, God," I whisper, but the only sound is running water and some animal in the underbrush. I watch the snake on a rock sunning itself.

A twig snaps, and I sit up. Stephanie sidles out from behind a tree. "What are you doing here?"

"What are you?"

"I was relaxing until you came," I say, getting up.

"Well, don't stop." Stephanie walks over with her little duck walk and sits down. I move away from her, but Stephanie pretends not to notice.

"This is a neat lean-to you guys built." I look up. The sun has gone behind the chariot cloud, and the cloud is darkening around the edges. I wonder if it will rain.

"I gotta go."

"What's the matter?" Stephanie asks, looking hurt for a moment, and then a little smug.

"I've been relaxing long enough, I gotta get back to the game." I move toward the trail trying to decide where to go next.

"Jake's always picking on me." Stephanie sits down looking at the ground like she wants someone to feel sorry for her. "He really does."

I climb the big rock behind the lean to, and stand on top of it looking down. "I'm so sorry, I'll have to ask him to stop."

"No, really, I don't know what I'm doing wrong." Stephanie's voice comes out in an irritating squeak when she's trying to keep herself from crying. "I don't."

"And I know what to do? Good gravy, girl, I just think you should stop acting scared of him. He feeds on that stuff."

"You're not supposed to say, 'good gravy;' it's an expression, and we're not supposed to use expressions."

"Right."

"Anyway, if it's so easy to change yourself, why don't you stop getting in trouble."

"Forget it. Why don't you just run away like your brother did."

"Do you ever think about running away for real?"

"Would I tell you if I did?"

"I don't rat on people."

"Oh, come off it, we all do when someone's in trouble." I sit cross-legged on the rock looking down at Stephanie who's slumped against a tree. "We just sit in that circle, and he goes around and asks each person, 'Well, Stephanie, tell me, what has Andie said recently that is against the will of God,' and then you'll come up with something. 'She's thinking of running away. She told me."

"Well, are you?"

"You don't listen to anything."

"*I* wouldn't ever think of running away. You'd go to hell for sure. Anyway, if you were out in the world, anything could happen. George says if we can't make it to heaven here, where we have the Word of God delivered to us every day and we have saints who love us, how could we ever make it on the outside?"

I jump down between the two parts of the huge rock. "They say this rock was split by lightning. Imagine seeing that, lightning striking down out of the sky, hitting the rock; it shudders and splits in two."

"Like the veil of the Temple."

"Yeah, well, I gotta go." I look back at Stephanie who is still leaning against the tree, her head and shoulders hunched over her knees. Her shoulders shake, and she cries silently.

I walk away thinking, feeling a bit mean, a bit superior. I can't help Stephanie, that's for sure, but pretending to try would have counted for something. I wish I could help myself though, and I can't. Every night, every naptime, every time I go to sleep, I tell myself stories, and I dream of writing the stories down someday. I could be a book writer, a story teller. The stories are about running away, or being rescued by my father. Sometimes I come back to the Farm years later, grown up, beautiful with long blond hair. I am riding a white horse. I rescue everybody. Sometimes the horse rears up, just as I reach the Farm. My mother rushes out, sees the black silhouette of the horse and me against a red sky. My mother cries in her apron in gratitude. But I keep wondering if everybody wants to be rescued. I can't tell. No one knows what I think. I do not know what they think.

Red Salamander

"Thou shalt not suffer a witch to live."
I raise a cautious hand,
"What's a witch?"
"What do you think?" he looks over his glasses
to see who interrupts the flow of God.
"A witch is a story, like the witch
that wants to eat you in Hansel and Gretel?"

"A witch is a woman who practices the occult,
or reads horoscopes, or talks to animals," he says,
and continues to read who else
God will not suffer to live.

I walk on dead leaves through woods
touching oak and maple trees.
"Occult, horoscope," I say,
mouthing unfamiliar words like candy.

I almost step on a red salamander
walking on wet earth toward clear water.
"How are you today, Mr. Salamander?"
I pick him up on leaves.
I've heard he likes his skin kept cool.
I don't want to warm him with my fingers.
"Mr. Salamander," I look in his beady eyes,
his tail flickers, his whole body twists like rubber.
I put him down, lean into a tree
to watch him slither away.
I look around, did anyone hear?

Chapter 7

I am growing up; I am twelve. I still tell myself stories, but I have trained my face to say nothing. I have learned not to cry.

In the middle of December comes the first huge blizzard, snow falling all night. Joyce leaves the light on outside of our dorm, and we watch the flakes pelting down madly, chasing each other into shadows. In the morning everything is white, huge drifts cover half of the Octagon windows; the sun shining on all that whiteness hurts our eyes.

"A snow day, a snow day, could we ask for one?" we scream when Joyce comes to wake us, and we are already at the back windows staring out.

"Wait until breakfast, and you can ask with the boys," she says and hustles us off for washups. During breakfast, we march in to see Don who is eating with the seniors. One of the boys hands him a note, "On top of this mountain all covered with snow, there will be no school today if it's okay with Don O."

He reads it, and slams his fist on the table. "Done," he says, "no school," and we cheer. "Finish your joyjobs, and you can go sledding. Your counselors will tell you what to do in the afternoon."

At lunch time, we are wild after being out in the cold, the rush of toboggans on new snow, down the hill where we grow squash in the summer across the playing field, down through the orchard and into the horse pasture. "This afternoon," Jake says, "We will have a Treasure Hunt. You will follow signs to find a treasure."

We line up while he writes the first clue on the blackboard. "Your electric bill is way too high; go to the Tower and find out why."

We're off, stuffing our hands into mittens, scarves streaming out behind us. The radio tower two miles away dominates the landscape for miles.

Walking along the snow covered road, silently, the sun glistening off the snow, I think about the tower. I have always wanted to climb it. At night, sleeping on the porch, we can see the lights at the top of it twinkling. At the top, is a cloverleaf of red objects that look like huge chairs. I think about what it would be like to climb to the top of the tower and sit in one of the chairs, so close to God I could almost touch him. Perhaps he would explain everything.

When Teddy and I arrive at the Tower, the boys who have run ahead are still there. The sign on the fence reads, "To find this you'll need eagle eyes, think of fir, surprise, surprise."

Two of the boys start off in one direction, while Teddy and I run the opposite way. "The fir tree by Beaver Brook where we picnic, right?" Teddy says.

"Yeah, I wonder where they're going."

All afternoon we scramble through snow drifts, finally slowing to a plod, careful not to knock branches and cascade snow down our backs. One sign says, "Water used to flow down there; it now is frozen ice, the only things alive down there are shivering little mice."

Teddy and I have just climbed down from the top of an apple tree where the last note had been, and we sit still trying to figure it out. It is cold, even under our snowsuits. "Well, it's obviously a stream somewhere."

"Why, down there?" Teddy chews a twig.

"Jake just used that to make it rhyme. He's just making everything rhyme." I am tired, and my feet hurt in my too-small boots.

"Down there, down from a bridge."

"The Bridge," I jump up, "where we all found that nest of mice last spring when we were out walking."

We get colder on the way to the bridge; we're not talking. We stand at the top of it and look down for other footsteps. There is not a mark anywhere, just one perfect expanse of white stretching down toward the frozen stream.

"Weird," Teddy says, and we look at each other. There is no wind, hasn't been all day. We look down, but nothing breaks the surface. Only our eyes show now; we've covered our faces with scarves. "I don't get it, not even Jake's footprints, what other bridge could it be?"

"The Farm bridge?" Teddy groans.

"That's about forty-five minutes from here, and it's getting dark."

Luke and Nathan come up, and we all look down. "No footprints, Jake hasn't been here."

"Maybe it's the Farm Bridge," Nathan says through his scarf.

"That's what we were wondering," Teddy says.

"I'm going down," Luke says, "We're here, we gotta check."

"There's no note here," Nathan says, but we all follow Luke down the untouched slope. The last of the sun's warmth glows on the snow red and orange, as we slip down the hill to the stream. Nobody talks much; we fan out and paw through the snow.

"Nothing, nothing," Nathan says finally, and we climb carefully up that side of the slope and down to the other side of the stream. Under a drift of perfect untouched snow, Luke uncovers a note stuck onto a branch.

He reads aloud, "Indians are flying, cowboys on the loose, running through pine cones, hiding in the spruce." He buries the note; we whoop and yell. The spruce grove where we play Cowboys and Indians is only five minutes away.

In the twilight we run, bounding over snowbanks, pulling each other along, and then in the spruce grove, hanging from trees are silvery packages glimmering from behind the branches. Each one has one of our names on it, a tinfoil package full of candy.

Back at the school, we find Jake and Joyce chatting in the dorm. "How did you do it? How did you get it under there? It was like you were never there."

"Get changed for dinner," he says, smiling. The other kids can hardly believe that the snow was untouched when we got there. Under the glaring fluorescent lights in our dorms, undressing from our outside clothes, dressing for dinner, it doesn't seem possible that we stood on that bridge, the dying light glimmering on all that perfect snow.

"It was magic," Jake says, and won't tell us anything else.

At dinner time he says he has an announcement to make. We put down our forks full of baked beans and our hands full of brown bread, and Jake says, "Joyce and I are getting married." There is a moment of silence. No one has ever announced a marriage, and we don't know what to say.

Luke says, "I thought something was cooking between you two," and Jake laughs, a big full-bodied laugh. We all join in, tentatively at first, and then laughing hard, not sure what is funny, but feeling good about laughing. Jake stands up. He goes to Joyce's end of the table, pulls her up, and hugs her from behind. "She's going to be my little wife," and he laughs again. Everyone laughs and starts to clap, while Jake leans over and kisses her cheek. Joyce doesn't smile, but Jake's teeth are showing.

After a spring wedding, Joyce seems more subdued. "Sure, sure," she says when we ask if we can do something. Every night that it isn't raining, we sleep on the back porch and identify stars and planets. We sing for a while in our sleeping bags before Joyce says quiet for the evening, and then we listen to hear the angels sing.

George has been telling us about angels. "Each one of you has your own guardian angel, a ten foot tall person who stands at the foot of your bed every night to watch you. The angel follows you during the day. We are the new Israelites. We have a Pillar of Cloud by day and a Pillar of Fire by night, and those pillars are angels watching us. If you want to see an angel, open your eyes; they're all around you. Some day you might be walking into a barn, and there will be an angel sitting on a hay bale. You might be driving a car, and there will be an angel in the passenger seat. If you listen at night, you can hear angels sing."

We listen at night after we've stopped singing. We know hundreds of gospel songs, all the verses. But when we stop singing, we lie still and listen for the angels.

Ann says, "Listen, they're singing the 'Hallelujah Chorus,'" and we all lie still listening for the four part harmony. For a long time no one says anything, and then Ann says, "Think, high, silvery, white." We breathe as quietly as we can; nobody coughs or sneezes.

I think maybe Ann can hear because she is the most pure of spirit, and then, I too hear the angels singing. My hands begin to move, conducting a heavenly choir. One by one, we sit up, listening, moving in rhythm.

Every night, we listen for the angels singing. Sometimes we cannot understand the language, sometimes we don't recognize the music. Once, I wake in the middle of the night and see a tall white figure at the end of my bed. I don't speak to it; I don't move. I just watch it until I fall asleep again.

One night we are singing "Glorious Things of thee Are Spoken." George says we aren't singing it with feeling; we aren't singing like this is a city where we will be spending eternity.

He describes the New Jerusalem, the City of God. "This is the city where you will live forever and ever. You will have a white robe, a golden harp, and you will play on the harp, forever singing praises to God. Each of the twelve gates of the city is one single huge pearl. The streets are paved in gold. The city shines seven times brighter than the sun."

That night I dream that I am waking up. I am looking out the huge picture windows in the back of our dorm. The City of God, the New Jerusalem, is slowly coming down out of the sky. The light dazzles me, and I cover my face with my hands. But I can still see the city, through the palms of my hands. I can see it shining like the sun like all the light in the universe. I am afraid for a moment that I will die, and then I wake up.

When the snow starts to fall during dinner, Jake turns off the light in the room, and turns on the outside light. We all run to the window and watch the flakes racing madly, floating down and back up on the wind. Outside on the porch, we let the flakes fall on our tongues.

Jake says we can slide down the hill after dinner but only if we do not wear any clothes except our underwear. "Really, really we can?" and he says,

"Yes, in your underwear. Boys and girls will take turns." That's what we do the rest of the winter, every night when the snow is good for sliding. We run out the back door, grab an inner tube, and jump off the porch in our underwear onto an inner tube and slide down the hill. We run up the hill as fast as we can, and run inside. Teddy and I show off by doing it twice before coming inside, but nobody cares. We have fifteen minutes, and then it is the boys' turn. We scream as we jump up and down to warm ourselves. Joyce watches us without saying much; she is usually not feeling well.

Jake stands behind her, "My little kangaroo," he says, "She's going to have a baby." He grins and puts his arms around her belly. Joyce looks embarrassed. "The baby is due April 17th."

I pray every day that the baby will be born on April 25th, my birthday. This will be the first new baby I have seen, and I know he will be special. I stop reading when I am supposed to be working. I don't talk back; I do everything right. "I believe Andie has turned over a new leaf," I hear Joyce tell George.

"Well, praise the Lord, it's about time." By the beginning of April, I pray when I wake up, when I go to sleep, after every time I eat, after every time I drink, every time I use the restroom, every time I wash. I run to do what I am told, and I talk as little as possible so that no idle words will escape my lips. I catalog words that could be considered idle. Is asking for the salt and pepper idle? I decide yes.

The night of April 24th, I try to stay awake all night praying that the baby will be born the next day. The next morning it snows; I go to school; it is lunchtime; it is dinner time. At evening devotions, Joyce sits with her huge belly in front of her. She shows no signs of labor.

That night I do not pray. I say nothing to God. Matthew is born three days later, three days after my birthday, eleven days late. He doesn't have a red mark or a wrinkle; he is nearly ten pounds. When I lean into his cradle to touch him, he opens his eyes to look at me, grabs my finger. I am twelve years old; I do not believe in God, but I want a baby.

We come in, panting from our mile run; we wash our faces, comb our hair and sit in a circle for devotions. We have morning devotions in squads so George can spend his mornings praying. "He probably just wants to sleep in," Teddy whispered to me when the announcement was made.

"Blasphemer," I whispered back.

The boys march into our room, and Jake sits on a chair; we look up at him. We stare into his black eyes. "If you are guilty or unclean, you will not be able to look me right in the eyes," he says. We stare at him; we do not shift our bodies. I think of my body as a stone that cannot move.

"God says that if you confess your sins He is faithful and just to forgive your sins. We are going to confess our sins aloud, so God can forgive us." I can taste the air tightening around me. Someone will get caught; someone will confess something that will get them in trouble, someone will wind up on the chopping block.

"Starting with you, Teddy."

"I ah, well, I . . ."

"Speak up, we can't hear you. Speak up so God can hear you."

"I ate some grain."

"You did what? Let's name our sins for what they are."

"I stole some grain and ate it." Jake takes out a book and writes in it.

"You know what the penalty is for stealing."

"Yes."

"What is it?"

"For all lying, stealing and cheating, there shall be six-of-the-best."

"That's right, go get the stick. Andie, what do you have to confess?"

I paw through my mind for something that won't involve six-of-the-best, something small, harmless, "I said an idle word."

"What did you say, exactly?"

"You mean, repeat, now, what I said?"

"What you said, exactly."

"One bright morning in the middle of the night," I start tentatively. "Two dead boys came out to fight. Back to back they faced each other, drew their swords and shot each other." A couple of the girls smile, and I continue with greater emphasis. "A deaf policeman heard the noise, came to rescue two dead boys. If you do not believe this lie is true, ask the blind man, he saw it too."

"Where did you hear that?" His voice has a cold empty quality. "Where?"

"In a book."

"Where did you get the book?" I search through my mind for another lie. The truth is that whenever there is a new arrival at the Farm, someone is given the duty of taking all their personal possessions out to a truck where it is hauled away to be sold. Their vehicles then become Farm property. I volunteer for this job; then I sneak books and hide them in a secret place in the woods. But nothing will make me confess this.

"Some book that got thrown out later," I say.

"You can't stay out of trouble, can you?" I say nothing. "Can you?"

"I guess, I don't know. I want to stay out of trouble."

"But you don't want to bad enough, do you?" He asks questions to which there are no answers, and then he asks them again. "Do you?"

"I don't know."

"You don't know. Well, I tell you what's going to help you find out. You are going to spend today and tomorrow by yourself repenting. You will not have any food. I want you to fast and pray. You are not to talk to anyone. You can take walks in the woods, but when you are here at school, you can sit on the windowbox." My face does not move. I have trained it to stay still like a map lying on a table. I do not move while Teddy is given six-of-the-best or while the other children march off to breakfast. When they are gone, and I am alone in the room, I smile. Two whole days to be alone! I run out the back door, down the steps, across the fields and into the woods. I run to my book stash pull out *David Copperfield* and find a pile of leaves to lie down in and read.

By the next day I am hungry and feeling strange. When I am around, the other children take special care to talk more loudly and to act as though they are having a great deal of fun eating or setting out their sleeping bags for the night. I am spending my second day alone in the woods, and it is the Sabbath Day.

I kneel under an old apple tree. It is blooming and the smell is suffocating, sweet, heavy and white. The petals drift down around my skin. The blackflies and mosquitoes hang around my head. I feel my skin crawling with their sticky wet blood-filled bodies. I swat hopelessly at them, listening to their song, the high wail of an insect who will die if he does not have blood soon.

I walk carefully on an old wet log, picking lilies of the valley. Three or four perfect white bells hang from every stem; I pick one stem at a time. When I have a handful, I crawl out from under the tree toward the stream that keeps the lily bed wet and marshy. I follow the stream down to where it flows beside a sandy bank. I spot Ann sitting on the bank, quietly watching the water.

I don't want to startle her. I crack a branch, and Ann looks up smiling. "Hello." The expression on her face is peace. Her buck teeth stick out, covering the lower half of her jaw; her straight black hair hangs down like the framing for a picture, and the picture is of contentment.

"Sit down," she says. "I've been picking lilies too." Ann has a wet cloth wrapped around her lilies and another for her lilacs. I wish for something to say.

"I just, I just," I say, sitting down. Ann wraps an arm around me and begins to sing quietly. "I have found a friend in Jesus, He's everything to me." She rocks back and forth slightly. "He's the lily of the valley to my soul." Sunlight spills down between the newly budding leaves.

From the Bible to Poetry

I walked between the Bible's
thin pages, stepped out
like the truth from a liar's mouth.
I scrambled to a rock where I hear
my own voice, muddled by echoes.

I turn myself around.
I turn from that white wall,
from black marching orders
on thin paper. I get out of line
and run

to a bookstore, where poetry
flies toward real life,
and swallows it, spitting out
a new world on pages
where lines are not even symmetric.

Chapter 8

At one o'clock in the morning an alarm clock buzzes between two sleeping bags. A hand emerges from one of them to shut it off.

"Wake up, Andie," Teddy groans. We slide out of our sleeping bags onto cold hardwood floors and stagger into the bathroom. We pull on coats, mittens, boots, scarves over our pajamas.

Outside we trudge along, two figures swathed like mummies, breathing ghostly breath through scarves, snowbanks plowed up on either side of us.

"Even at night," Teddy says, "God watches us." She flings her hand as if she were George directing singing. "God has his eye on you. Behold the heavens." She says this with a southern accent.

"Where'dya hear that?"

"On TV once, long time ago."

"You watched TV? It's a sin, you know."

"It's not like I knew; anyway it was somebody preaching on TV. 'God can see you everywhere.' That's what the TV preacher from Alabama says."

"You better not be making fun, God'll hear you. He'll tell George. Your number'll be up."

"Oh, God speaks to me too. He says, 'Teddy, I am a woman. I have breasts. I . . .'"

"You're gonna get in so much trouble, if they ever hear you saying that stuff."

"I just say it to you."

The barn smells of hay, warm bodies, wool. A thousand sheep are separated into two long pens. I switch on dim lights. Teddy and I each climb into a pen and walk slowly, checking the mothers who have lambed that night. We each have a sack of ear tabs, a hole punch, iodine. We swab the umbilical cord with iodine, punch the lamb's ear and mark it with a smaller tag that has the same number as its mother. If we find a lamb that the mother has rejected, we put it in with the orphans.

"C'mere a minute." I call, kneeling down by a small Dorset ewe. Teddy climbs over, kneels in the hay beside me. "Easy, easy," she says. The ewe backs into a corner, bleating, the whites of her eyes showing. Two tiny hooves stick out of her back end. She bleats loudly.

"Hold her head. I'll help her," I slip a sterile rubber glove onto my hand. The ewe groans and pushes. The lamb's nose appears pressed down on the legs, covered with mucous.

"Come on, mama," Teddy says. "She's a yearling. She's small. You think you're not ready for this, baby. C'mon,"

The ewe pushes and sinks down in the hay. The flattened skull of the lamb appears for a moment and slides back. We pull the ewe to her feet, and she grunts and pushes. Her head moves from side to side. Her bleats come out in short breaths like a baby crying. The lamb's head pushes out and hangs there for a second while the ewe breathes heavily and takes a step. Teddy holds the ewe's head. Her hands dig into the lanolin-greased wool around the ewe's neck.

"Ease it out, ease it out, I got her," she says. I cup the lamb's body in my two hands, and slowly ease it out, the shoulders lump out, and then the rest of the body slips down like Jello. I wipe the mucous off with a cotton rag, but the lamb is dead. "It must 'a been in the birth canal forever. Let's just wait for the afterbirth, make sure she's okay." The ewe pushes, groans and falls over in the hay.

"Come on, you're okay," Teddy says. We pull her to her feet. "Come, on, come on, mama," Teddy croons. The ewe pushes again and two more hooves press the bloodied opening.

"Look, look, she got twins," Teddy says, "come on, mama." But the ewe refuses to push; she walks over to the manger and takes a bite of hay.

"Back you come," Teddy pulls her into a corner. The second set of hooves has disappeared. "Come on, you're not losing this one." The ewe pushes, and the hooves appear, another push and the nostrils are visible, slowly, the whole nose appears, closed eyes, ears flattened against the skull.

The ewe pulls to get away from Teddy, "Easy, easy," the head slips out in one huge convulsion, "Come on, come on, one more push." The sheep's head writhes from side to side like a snake. She bleats loudly.

In one huge push, the shoulders come part way out, and my hands are around them, easing the slippery body onto the hay. This lamb is smaller. It lies on the hay, wet and slimy for a moment while I clean its nostrils. It climbs to wobbly feet and begins to walk on tiny hooves toward its mother. She gives another push and the afterbirth falls on the hay. She walks away to the long manger and begins to eat. Other ewes make room for her. They stand in a long row eating, their fat backsides a long line of white wool.

"Come on, mama, look at your baby." Teddy turns her around and puts her nose to the lamb's wet wool, but she pulls away.

"Oh, leave her alone, she doesn't want it. That's the thing with these yearlings. It's a ewe, what d'ya wanna name her?"

"I donno. Let's go feed her."

The little lamb lies in a box lined with cloths while I mix her first bottle. Teddy washes and fills the feeder for the other orphans. It's a stainless steel five gallon tank with protruding black rubber nipples. She mixes Land o' Lakes milk and fills it while the orphans crowd around bleating and pushing.

"Periwinkle. She got a little black star on her forehead. She don't need her Mama." Teddy strokes the lamb's nose.

"She doesn't need her Mama."

"You and your English, look at this little Periwinkle, would you, she's tugging at that bottle. She gonna be fine." We take Periwinkle into the room where the orphans are kept warm with a gas heater.

The next morning I feed and water the sheep, but I check Periwinkle first. The little lamb is up, pushing the other lambs aside to get milk. She "baas" loudly. "You're gonna make it, I can tell," I say lifting the lamb out for her bottle. By the third day, Periwinkle follows me while I do my chores. By the time she's two weeks old, she has found the corn bin and steals nibbles. Her slim white nose twitches when she is hungry and she taps her front hooves as she eats. I gives her special corn and molasses and nurse her from a bottle. Periwinkle comes when her name is called, she jumps onto a chair for corn or her bottle, and she will lick molasses off my cheeks.

Twice a year during vacations, all the kids whose parents do not live at the Farm go home to places like Pennsylvania and New York. I don't remember Maine well, but I think Pennsylvania and New

York would be exciting. Their parents drive up to get them, sweeping around the bend in clean cars. Fathers sit gallantly at the wheels, while mothers wave frantically out the windows. These kids return with new clothes, teeth fresh from the dentist and new writing paper with flowers.

A van comes for the kids whose parents live at the commune, but are married. These kids come back with thrift store clothes and new toothpaste. The kids whose parents are divorced usually stay at school to care for the animals. We stand in the driveway watching the van disappear, full of waving kids going off into their parents' waiting arms. We turn and look at each other and smile.

The only counselors are Grace and Nancy, and they are on vacation too, so we five kids do the work and leave the counselors alone. We hardly see them, and we have two weeks of vacation, to laugh, to run, to go sledding after chores are done.

My older sister Alexa stands apart. I only see her at meetings and we hardly ever talk, I don't know her well except to know that teachers who have had her in their class are always surprised when I come along. "Why, I taught your sister last year, and she wasn't nearly this much trouble!" they say. When I think of her, what I think is that if she were chicken soup, she'd be just the broth part, the part that's supposed to be good for you, the boring part. I don't think I'd be chicken soup at all, I'd be the smart chicken that ran away and never got put in the pot.

"Well, fun, fun, fun," I jump up and down a couple times.

"We better go feed the animals," Alexa says.

"Better go, why don't you go?" I say.

"I'm going to do what we're supposed to be doing." She starts to walk off and turns to look back at us. We look at the sky, then at our own feet. We walk around like pieces rearranging ourselves on a chessboard. The wind blows, and we turn up our collars and start walking slowly toward the barn as if it pulled us.

Stephanie starts singing, "I'm a little soldier in Junior Volunteer," and we join in and march in step. "I obey on the double, I give the devil trouble, and my feet march the street, with the Hallelujah beat," and we join in a little halfheartedly. We can hardly hear our own singing; the wind carries it away.

I run to catch up to Alexa, "You hardly talk to me any more."

Alexa pulls her light blue scarf over her face and says through the scarf, "I don't see you; we're not in the same squad."

"Well, we're doing the sheep, it's vacation, so talk to me."

"What is there to say?" Alexa stumps along, her body thick under layers of winter clothes. "I haven't seen Hope for a long time."

"You'll be out of school soon."

"When I'm fourteen."

"What do you want to do?"

"Whatever God wants; it isn't up to me."

"Well, what if it were, I'm just saying, if you could choose, what would you want to do? Work in the bakery, in the office, what?"

"I don't think about it, okay, that's what gets you into trouble. You're always thinking." Her voice rises in exasperation.

"Yeah, I guess George'll give you your marching orders. I want to teach or maybe take care of horses."

"You want the will of God," Alexa says with a finality that means, "this is the last word, you better not argue with me." We walk between the mangers to the grain chute and each fill two buckets of grain, pour on a little molasses and then walk down the mangers pouring in the grain mixture.

"Why don't you even try to stay out of trouble; every time I hear about you, you're getting six-of-the-best for something. It's like you don't even want to be good."

"Yeah, Hope wishes I'd be more like you."

"I just want to walk the straight and narrow, I don't know what you're trying to do."

"Do you ever think about our dad?"

"Sometimes, but he didn't love the Lord Jesus."

"I pray all the time that he and Hope will get back together."

"Well, you can just forget that prayer, because it's not going to happen. It's not going to happen at all. Why don't you pray that God change you, and then do something like trying to be different."

"Well, that's no fair. I want God to make Hope and Dad get back together, so I can pray for it. He can do anything. Anyway, if I just pray for him to change me and then I try to be different, I'll never know if he changed me or I changed myself."

"That's what I mean, that's what gets you in trouble, talk like that. Sometime I'm gonna hear you say something like that, and I'm gonna report it to George and that's gonna be it for you. You run the waterers, okay, look out, I'm gonna throw down hay bales."

I am dreaming. I lie in my sleeping bag on the wooden floor and roll restlessly. I dream that I am awake and hot. A hole has opened in the floor beside my bed. It is a red gaping hole, like the jaws of a huge wolf. I look down into it and see flames licking up, screams coming from a lake of fire. Demons fly up on black wings snatching people and whizzing back down into the red vapors. I smell sulphur. The floor under me gives away, and I grab for the edge. I hang there for a moment. My sleeping bag falls away from my body. My nightgown is hot on my legs. The wood I am holding on to gives way, and I fall. I can see a red glow around me. I jerk awake, and stare at the ceiling. The red glow is there just as it was in my dream. The room is full of shadows and an eerie light. I sit up in the cold air feeling the dream rush past me.

I reach over and tap the floor beside me. The hardwood floor is firm. I walk to the window and see a luminous patch of red against the night sky above the barn.

The next few hours are very confusing, and when I try to think about it the next day, it comes back to me in scenes like parts of a very long, bad dream. I get up, turn on the lights. Someone calls the fire department, but in March, when it is ten below and roads are icy, it takes them almost an hour to arrive. The back of the barn is blazing and too hot to go near. There is a steady boom and crack of timbers.

"You, Andie, Stephanie, get the sheep out, now!" Grace shouts.

Alexa and one of the boys carry long cages of chickens down the road. The chickens' clucking mixes with the snapping and crackling of burning wood.

Stephanie and I open the two huge gates that enclose the front of the barn. We run in among the sheep and try to move them toward the opening, but they cower back toward the back of the barn. We can see the fire moving in the back of the barn where the pigpens are. In back of the sheep pens, we see the horses rearing against the orange flames. The screaming of pigs mixes with the high whinny of horses, the bawling of the calves. The sheep crowd back like masses of cotton clinging to each other. We look in at the white masses, the eyes, and behind them the rushing crackling fire at the back of the barn.

I move behind the sheep, talking to them, coaxing. Stephanie runs to the calves and horses. She opens the calf pens, and the calves run, bounding on their long awkward legs toward the black opening at the front of the barn. The sheep move forward in bunches, slowly as if they had their whole lifetimes to make this maneuver.

"Don't let them move back." Stephanie runs from the calf pens to the horses. The fire crackles louder behind us, and we feel the heat building.

"Come on, get out of there, it's in the hayloft," I scream. "Come on." I can see Stephanie running under the hayloft, opening the horse pens.

"Get the sheep moving," she yells, but her voice is almost lost in the growing rushing sound, the fire eating the hay loft. The sheep need no more urging. As the horses gallop by, their whinnies high like children screaming, the sheep stampede for the open doorways. The huge gates like open mouths spill out onto the black hilltop.

We run behind the mob, picking up lambs abandoned by their mothers. Other kids rush up and help herd the sheep to the old barn. Outside on the hillside, the sheep move in mass, the stars are brilliant. Behind us in the towering blackness of the barn, something is moving. The fire rages like a monster who will not be finished until it has a belly full.

I run back toward the barn I see pigs running about. Three firetrucks parked beside the barn seem to be out of water. A fireman is kneeling beside the duck pond, chainsawing a hole in the ice. One of the pigs walks up behind him and nudges him into the water. I run past him toward the door. "The rabbits and ducks are out," Nancy shouts to Grace.

"Where are the orphans?" I ask.

"We couldn't get all of them." Grace and Nancy stand in a snowbank. From where they stand, the barn is hot as an open furnace. The metal roofing curls like bacon. Smoke pours skyward from the windows.

"Periwinkle!" I run toward the barn. I hear Grace's voice behind me.

"Get out of there!"

Inside it is black and the air is thick and burns my throat. These rooms have concrete walls, and the rafters above them are not yet in flames. But I hear the sound of fire rushing, eating, hungry, and the cry of animals. I stumble in the direction of the orphan lamb pens. I hear timbers falling. I pick up a warm woolly body and another. I hope I have Periwinkle, but I can't see a thing. I can't breathe. I try to find the door, but it has vanished in a cloud of smoke. The smell suffocates me. On my knees, I begin to crawl toward the area where I last saw the door. When I get there, it is a wall. My throat feels unbelievably hot. I can't remember why I am here. I begin to remember the dream. I am being dropped into hell; the flames are all around me. I am falling past flickering walls of flame; it all makes sense after what I've done. I think of asking for mercy but I can't remember who to ask.

I open my eyes to see Grace looking at me, and the fireman who carried me out saying, "Is she okay?"

"Yeah, she's fine," Grace says. "You okay?"

In my arms are three lambs; one is Periwinkle. All three are dead. Tears burn my cheeks.

"Go down to school, help them put the goats and rabbits in the cellar," Grace says. My feet drag. I carry Periwinkle's dead body carefully. She feels limp, the tight curled wool is damp. I turn to see the barn as I walk away. Most of the pigs must be trapped in there. The fire is beginning to smell strongly of pork.

Moon Child

I climb the hill behind the barn.
Moonlight glistens on a manure pit
eight feet deep where cow shit is bulldozed every week.

I talk to the moon, Get me out of here,
I say, aren't you listening?
Don't you see I'm living close to a manure pit
where I might fall in forever?

Moon walks are time alone
in boarding school.
"Where were you? What were you doing?"

Praying, I'll say.
They'll never know it's the moon I talk to.

Chapter 9

Heavy, wet air clogged with the smell of Clorox and dirty socks greets us every time we open the laundry room. But we like it; doing laundry is so much better than other jobs we could have been assigned, like doing dishes, scrubbing floors or cleaning bathrooms. Twice a year we assemble in the Octagon, and Don reads out our new joyjobs. We sit in squads waiting. He reads my name from his list, and I hope desperately I will be off the log crew and on an animal crew. "Andie and Teddy, laundry and horses." We look across at each other and barely nod. We do not smile, but we both know inside we're sucking in a smile. We're screaming with joy. We say, "Yes sir," together, loud, so Don knows we understand.

After breakfast, during joyjob time, Teddy collects the laundry boxes in each school building. The big school building is an octagon with six wings. The Thirty-by-Forty has four floors which Teddy runs up and down carrying the clothes tied in dirty sheets. She runs with the clothes on her back, a tiny girl weighted down like Christian in *Pilgrim's Progress*.

I load the big white machines and line up the load for the rest of the day. "You're more organized," Teddy had said. "I'll run."

We hardly speak as Teddy runs in and out and I sort the clothes: Darks, whites, reds, towels, sheets, kitchen. George and his secretary, Mary, have us wash their clothes separately by hand.

During the five minutes between classes, we dash out, throw a load from each washer to a dryer and from the dryers to the sorting table. We then throw fresh loads in the washers, add soap and bleach, and rush back to class. There are no excuses for being late to class. Latecomers sit outside their class for fifty-five minutes and make up class in two Friday night free-times.

After lunch, the sorting table is a huge mound of clean clothes. Lunch is over at one; at three, Teddy and I are usually finished.

Teddy folds each piece, checks for a name tag, puts it in the correct box, Freshman Boys, Freshman Girls, Hardy Boys, Hardy Girls, Senior Boys or Girls, and the little kids, the Butterflies. I iron more than one hundred pieces. I time them, one every two minutes, and leave myself a half hour for George and Mary's ironing.

When the laundry is finished, we clean out the stalls. We give fresh water to the horses and throw down the hay from the loft; then we can ride. We start with the Welsh mountain ponies, Taffy and Lightning, because they're smaller, maybe easier. When Stephanie took care of the horses last year, Taffy bucked her off, "But that won't happen to us," we tell each other.

In the summer we go camping, so we don't ride much. Usually by fall, the horses are ready for a good gallop, and so are we.

I tighten the chin strap. "So, you want to ride Lightning?" Lightning is black with a white streak across her withers. Taffy is brown with a black mane and tail.

Teddy leads Lightning over to a fence, climbs up the fence and says, "Stand, stand, stand still Lightning." The little mare skips around nervously, and Teddy jumps on. Lightning immediately begins rearing.

"Rearing's nothing," I say, "I'm going to get bucking."

"Come on." Taffy stands by the fence; nothing moving except his tail. His ears lie flat on his skull. The whites of his eyes show, but he stands still while I jump onto his bare back. Then his bulk convulses; he twists like a pretzel. I dig my heels in and lie down on his neck like a monkey clinging to a branch. My lunch pauses at the edge of my throat, and I promise myself that if I can stay on, I will never ride again. I bend low over his withers, urging him to a gallop. He can't gallop and buck, I think, but as we thunder around the curve, Taffy throws his hind legs in the air twice in front of the school in full view of the windows of the Faculty Room.

I feel my legs loosening. I think for a moment, "Flying." I flip three times Teddy tells me later, and I land on my side. Taffy comes to a stop by the hay strewn on the pathway to the laundry room and begins eating. I get up gingerly and confront Don. "Are you okay?" he asks.

"Fine, never better." I stand on wobbly feet. I want him to go back inside and stop looking at me.

"You sure you're okay?"

"I'm fine." I straighten up, come to attention.

"Collect the horse, and get back on him." I walk slowly over to Taffy. I'd been wishing I could take him back to the barn and get another horse. I've never gotten on without a fence. I take his reins, and he keeps eating. He looks awfully tall. "Please, get me out of here, Taffy."

"I haven't got all day," I hear Don say. I jump, and Taffy takes off down the lane. I hear Lightning's hoofs behind me.

"Gosh, I was hoping you could do it," Teddy says.

"I was scared, could you tell?"

"You weren't shaking. I don't think he knew, but I knew." The ponies slow to a trot.

"I think we're supposed to go up and down with their trot," I say. "I wish I were a horse."

"Wouldn't you rather ride one?" Teddy says, coming up beside me. The whole silent day in and out of the humid laundry room has rushed us to this point of riding the ponies, feeling the wind sift past us, going wherever wind likes to go.

"Ann and Stephanie never got to go riding when they did laundry and horses. They finished just in time to feed and groom."

"Ann's careful."

"Yeah," Teddy says. "D'ya want to go by Mr. Whipple's?"

"Sure."

Mr. Whipple lives just over the hill from the school. He lets us graze our sheep in his fields. His fences are overgrown with weeds; his ears and nose have hair growing out of them. The shingles are falling off his house; the paint is peeling. His hair and beard are long, grey and uncombed. When we ask how old the house is, he shrugs, "Old." When we ask how old he is, he says, "Older." He grows huge beds of johnny jump-ups, little miniature pansies with purple and yellow faces. We ask him for a couple of bunches to take home and plant. He digs them up himself, careful of their roots and puts them in a cardboard box. "My babies," he says in a slurred voice, handling the flowers as delicately as one hands a newborn. One whole side of his house is a mound of beer cans. "My medicine," he says pointing at the can he is drinking from.

In the winter, we take food and firewood to him every week. When the electricity goes off, we flounder through snow drifts to check on his water supply.

Teddy and I ride through the orchard, through his fields to his house. We knock on the door, but he doesn't answer. It's a cool wet day, but no smoke comes from his chimney. His traps lie in the sun, ugly metal mouths to catch the animals he will eat all winter. We ride toward Beaver Brook and find him lying naked by the stream.

"Ladies," he says, sitting up, wrapping his waist with an old towel.

We look at each other, our eyes asking, "Did you see?" our eyes answering, "Yes, the thing between his legs." The thing lay between his legs like another leg, surrounded by grey hair. He scratches his head and sits up, looking cleaner, freshly stream bathed, younger.

"Sleeping," he says.

"Sorry to disturb you," Teddy says as both ponies start drinking. He waves a hand as if disturbing him is unimportant.

"Do you believe in God?" Teddy asks. George has been preaching on "Let your light so shine before men." George says we should witness to others, but the only outsider we ever talk to is Mr. Whipple.

"God?" he asks, his speech a little clearer than usual.

"Yeah, you know, God who created the world and sent His Son."

"Creation," he says with a wave of his hand that covers trees with sunlight spilling between them, the water singing its water song over rocks, the horses, us.

"Do you believe?"

"I believe."

"In God, and Jesus and everything? We didn't even know you were a believer." His small chest covered with hair moves. He coughs. "Do you worship God?" Teddy asks.

"I worship." He waves his hand, coughs again, lies back on the pine needles. "I worship Creation."

We wave to him, wave off the words we do not understand, and ride up the mountain trail. Leaves crackle under the ponies' hooves. Most of the leaves have already fallen, a few cling to their trees, brown and limp from bare branches. The ground has begun to harden during the nights that drop below freezing, and the ponies hooves tap on it. "D'ya know people come from all over to see New England leaves turning color?"

"I know," I say. "I saw a sign, 'Come to New England foliage.' Big deal."

"That's cause we see it all the time. D'ya think you'll be here your whole life?"

"Taffy's getting spooked by something."

"Probably a bird, I mean, d'ya think you'll get married, have kids, and everything?"

"I'd like to travel. Look, it's over there; there's flies around it." I guide Taffy's head in the direction of the thing, mostly covered with leaves and buzzing with flies. Taffy snorts and kicks one of his hind feet. "Easy, easy, boy."

We both dismount by something large and dead. "It's a deer, poor thing."

"Probably some hunter's story of the deer that got away." Teddy uncovers its face which looks peaceful, almost smiling in the afternoon sun. "It ran a long way after it was shot, probably."

"D'ya think it left a fawn?"

"Who knows?"

The doe's head rests on a hummock like a child on a pillow. It smells of decay. If it weren't so cold, it would reek. Its white belly is bloated, its eyes closed. The hugeness of the death silences us. Somehow a small animal, a cat or a rabbit dying, would be less frightening.

"Poor thing," I repeat.

"Oh, let's get out of here. Everything dies."

"Don't say stuff like that."

"Why not? It's true."

"Just don't."

"I'm sorry." Teddy comes over, touches my arm lightly, and begins covering the deer with dead leaves. I think for a second about this gift Teddy possesses of shutting her mouth when it needs to be shut. We pile leaves on the deer's belly and its long legs. We cover the head carefully.

"Shouldn't we say words over it like they do at funerals?"

"What words?"

"I don't know," Teddy says. "I've only been to one funeral, and I wasn't listening."

"Who was dead?"

"My Grandma, but I didn't know her too good, and I was looking at the sky."

"You didn't know her too well."

"Whatever, but they did say words."

"Well, you say something."

"Okay, and you say, 'Amen.'"

"Okay."

"May this deer go to heaven."

"Amen."

"And be blessed forever."

"Amen."

"And rest in peace."

"Amen."

"And may her fawn survive winter. Amen."

"Amen. The sun's setting; we better go home."

George calls a meeting to discuss the coming school year. "The Lord has provided for you to all learn French," he says. "Let's hear a cheer," and we cheer, the steady rhythmic clapping of children trained to applaud on command. "Hip hip hooray," we shout, clapping in rhythm. "Hip hip hooray." All eyes directly on George, all backs straight. "Hip hip hooray."

"Will the new French teacher come to the front of the room?" We look back, and I see Hope getting slowly to her feet in an embarrassed way, then moving forward, head down.

Hope steps between us children, blushing, embarrassed, her hands twisting, one strand of her hair in her mouth. She ducks her head to avoid being looked at. I feel an unexpected rush of sympathy and find myself with a pain in my stomach, watching my mother.

"Sit down," George says, pointing to a chair beside him. She sits, pulling her legs up onto the chair, hugging her knees with her long arms. "Sit up straight." She sits straighter, but doesn't let go of her knees. Her short, cropped black hair falls forward around her face. "Look up, chin up." Hope picks up her face slowly. Her face says, "Get me out of here."

"Say something in French for the kids." Hope doesn't speak. Her face becomes red and then white. She squirms in her chair. The silence lengthens, and I begin to feel sick watching her. Everyone looks at George, waiting for him to stop this display of helplessness, but he seems perfectly comfortable. His fingers touch each other, and he looks at his soft white hands lovingly.

The silence becomes longer until it is a palatable thing, Hope's discomfort hangs in the air like bitterness. Hope's mouth opens, and a sound comes out, then she chokes as if she were going to cry. "Stand up, turn around," he says, "and try again." She stands up, turns, sits down; a sound escapes her, and then silence. I look at George, hating him for showing off my mother like some puppet, turning and twisting her so we can see her fear of him. I hate him for sitting there so comfortably. I want to hug my mother. I feel bound to this woman in the chair who is related to me even though we rarely touch.

I hear my own voice break the silence. I raise my hand. "Can I say some French that she taught me?"

George looks at me and back at Hope. "Sure, stand up and speak up."

"*L'Éternel est mon Berger*," I start, "*Je ne manquerai de rien.*" (The Lord is my Shepherd, I shall not want.) "*Il me fait reposer dans de vert paturage.*" (He leadeth me in green pastures.) My voice becomes louder as I warm to my recital.

When I finish the Psalm to applause, George says, "You can sit down," and waves Hope to her seat. Hope walks past me and I watch her face as she passes, hoping to see a rush of love and thanks. Hope does not look at me.

The hospital smell hits me when the automatic doors open. Grace says, "Come on," and my feet follow through white shining corridors to an elevator crowded with people, their eyes staring straight ahead. I wonder why they don't look at each other and whether they are guilty. When the door opens, Grace says, "No, we're going to the ninth." The elevator lurches again, and I watch the other people who are looking straight ahead.

I was called out of class this morning. "There's been an accident," Mary said. "Hope was not in the will of God, and she has been injured."

Grace and I step out of the elevator, a strange little room that made my stomach queasy. I follow Grace down the glistening hallway past open doors from which I hear murmurs and moans.

Grace says, "Here she is, I'll be back for you," and disappears. I walk in, glancing at the white still figure on the bed. I move a little closer. My mother's body is covered with white sheets; her face is swathed in white bandages. "Like Jesus in swaddling clothes or Lazarus coming out of the tomb," I think and move away from my mother to the window and look down. I have never been on the ninth floor of anything, and the world seems very different from such a height. Cars and people look tiny and unimportant like bugs you could squash. "That's how we must look to God," I think. I think about what it would be like to jump, and I try to open the window, but it is solid and welded in place.

I turn to the still figure on the bed. "Are you asleep?" I whisper. No one answers, and Hope's body on the bed looks perfectly still. I watch for the slight rhythmic movement of breathing under the sheets, but there is nothing.

"God? Is she alive?" I whisper, but he doesn't answer, and she doesn't answer, and the room is silent. The skin around Hope's mouth is white; her lips are a bloodless pale; her whole body seems to melt into the sheets.

"What if she is dead, what would I say, 'Nurse, nurse, I've been left here with my dead mother?'" I try to decode my feelings. Am I sad? Will I cry if my mother is dead? Will I be relieved of the effort of trying to decide if I do love? Should love?—ever did love?—am loved?—ever was loved?

What happened to my mother with her fragile wrists to bring her to this white antiseptic space? Hope teaches French in the mornings, and in the afternoon she marches with the chainsaw crew out to the mountain and cuts wood. One team fells the trees, and the team Hope is on, chops off the limbs and chops the trees into firewood. This is the latest business venture; clear-cutting the mountain side. George tells them that at town meetings. The townspeople complain that the mountain that used to rise behind the town, cushioned with green in summer, dressed in glory in fall, is now just one big ugly scar as the chainsaw crews strip down the trees to send firewood to Boston and New York. "They complain because they do not know the will of God. Being unbelievers, they are out of the will of God. God gave us this mountain," George says.

Alexa has been on the crew that falls trees since she was pulled out of school at fourteen. Boys who are thirteen and fourteen drive Pettibones and skidders, massive machines for winching the trees out of the woods and lifting the limbed trunks onto trucks where they can be hauled out and cut into firewood.

I am leaning over my algebra book attempting an equation for the second time, and I jump when George's secretary, Mary, taps my shoulder. Mary beckons for me to follow her and we slip out. I know the other students are wondering what I have done this time. I paw through my mind; there are so many things; it could be anything. Outside the classroom, Mary says, "Andie, Hope's had an accident." I don't say anything, don't do anything, but I think, "I hate you." I think of my mother, slim, light, with streaks of grey in her hair, a slight stoop from a back injury the winter before, out there in the icy cold with a fifty pound chainsaw. I remember Hope telling me, "I'm on the chainsaw crew," with the same pride that she said, "You're a little soldier in the King's Army."

"You will be going to the hospital this afternoon. They operated yesterday, but she can have visitors today."

"When? when?" I can't finish.

"It happened yesterday. You will be leaving right away. Tell Hope that Alexa is working, but she says, 'hello.' Get in the Valiant, Grace will be out to drive you."

I walk outside, climb in the car and stare out the window. "I wonder what they would have done if she had died." I remember Grandma Jane dying in a fire when I was in Nursery. I heard them talking about it afterward saying things like "faulty wiring." I didn't know what wires had to do with Grandma Jane being burned to death.

Visiting Grandma Jane was the best part of the our week. At her house, we would have cookies and milk, and she would play the organ. We were going to see her the Friday afternoon that the house burned down. Joanne suddenly screamed and went to the window, and one by one we joined her, and she didn't stop us. The white house across the field was a framework against an orange sky. We watched the firetrucks arrive and spray the flame.

I am in the hospital with my mother and the smell is chemicals and chocolate. The sky outside the hospital is a clear cold blue. Clouds float white and so still it looks like a postcard. I wonder if I should call a nurse. She isn't moving. But then I would have to speak to a stranger, someone who isn't part of the Family of God, and I don't know how to do that. I look back at Hope, still motionless under the sheets. I move to the window and look down again. "Hello," a whispering gravelly voice floated behind me, a voice I hardly recognize. I jump and turn. Hope's eyes peer through bandages at me.

"Hello, Hope."

"Hard to talk," Hope's lips move slowly. "hurts face." I wave her hand, "It's okay, I talk too much. I'll talk enough for us both. Alexa says hello, but she had to work. Mary said your chainsaw bucked and your head was cut open, but you're gonna be fine." Hope tries to smile; her lips move a little. "Thank you, Lord," she whispers.

"Yeah, thank you, Lord. Look at all this stuff people brought you." Hope's eyes follow my arm pointing at the array of homegrown flowers and homemade fudge. I move over to the fudge. "Do you mind?" Hope waves her hand to include all the food. "I can help myself?" I say biting into a piece. "This is all for me?" Hope starts to smile again, but the smile never makes it to her eyes which have big bruises under them. "So how close was this cut to your brain?" I ask, then I wish I hadn't. But I don't know what to say. Hope raises thumb and forefinger, barely apart.

"That close, so, your brain was showing?" Hope nods. "And you're okay now?" I peer at her as if expecting brain damage to become apparent in my mother's face.

"Thank you, Lord," my mother mouths again. I take another bite of fudge which is very good, full of walnuts, and think, "For what?"

I've been learning about brains, and I think of my mother's quivering indented grey matter exposed, staring up at the treetops in the clearing.

Hope looks like she's frowning, like she's upset. "What?" I walk closer to the bed. "What? You want something? You want the doctor? the nurse?" My mother's lips move. "What?"

Hope points to the table. "Juice?" She shakes her head. "Pen and paper, here you go." My mother scrawls in her half sitting position. "Say thank you, Lord. You seem angry."

"I'm not angry at you. I'm just angry you got hurt." My mother's eyes are dark surrounded by the bruises and bandages. She points to, "Say, thank you, Lord."

"Thank you, Lord. Okay, I'm sorry, it's just I don't get why you were chainsawing in the first place."

"Will get you kicked out," Hope writes.

I open and close my hands in exasperation. "Everything is going to get me kicked out. So, I'm going to get kicked out eventually. Being alive's going to get me kicked out." Hope's eyes fill with tears.

I drop to my knees by the bed. "Look, I'm sorry. We shouldn't even be talking about this. We shouldn't. You're going to be okay, and I'm going to repent. I'm going to be a new person." Hope's lips turn up a little.

"You want me to pray right now?" For a moment I think, "What if a nurse comes in," but Hope nods, almost smiles. I close my eyes, "Father in heaven, please make Hope well, please heal her quickly. Let her have no pain. Please forgive all my sins. Please wash me clean in the blood of Jesus." I pause. Silently I pray, "If you will heal her quickly, I will never again think of leaving the Farm. I will obey you the rest of my life. I will keep in step." Out loud I say, "In the name of God the Father, and of Jesus Christ, the only wise God, our Savior, amen." I open my eyes. Hope's lips are smiling.

Beethoven Reminds Me

Old sadness creeps over me.
Beethoven slides under my skin.
I am a child,
too small inside to say
cut it out.

Is this poetry?
I take care of dirty laundry.
When people say, let me see it,
peep into the tub where I'm scrubbing
blood-stained panties,
I hesitate, is this poetry?

Beethoven brings me back to the stream.
I write a child standing white, naked,
no sound but crash of water on rocks,
a bundle of stripped fern stems slapping legs.

Chapter 10

"Ann's sick all the time," Emma says. "Get up, Ann, no one else is allowed to be sick. Get up." Ann crawls slowly out of her sleeping bag holding her side. She doesn't say anything, just looks around at the activity swirling around her, at us girls stacking sleeping bags, pillows and blankets.

"What's wrong, Ann?" Joyce calls.

"I don't know," she closes her eyes for a second; she keeps holding her side.

"Get back to bed; get out her sleeping bag," Joyce says in a tired voice. Ann is often sick. Sometimes her father comes to take her to the hospital. She comes back reporting ailments with long names that sound impressive to us; bronchitis, walking pneumonia. When we get sick, our ailments have short names like pink eye or flu.

Someone comes back from vacation with the flu one winter and within two weeks almost every child has it. We lie on the Octagon floor each with our own paper bag to get sick in. The counselors walk around taking temperatures as we drift in and out of consciousness and wish we were well enough to enjoy not being in school, not doing joyjobs, not working in the afternoon.

Most of us get sick once a year, and when we are sick we have to confess our sins. George says sin and sickness are linked. People get sick because they have unconfessed sins; except Ann. She's often sick, but no one accuses her of having unconfessed sins. She never does or says anything wrong, so no one ever mentions her sins.

I have seen Ann's mother twice, the time she dropped Ann off, and one time when she and Ann's father came to pick her up to go home for vacation. That time she hadn't been feeling well, and she had leaned against Ann's father. She had buck teeth like Ann, long dark hair that fell in a mist across her face which was as white as a mask. Her fingers looked white, cold and long, and she moved her hands in graceful waves. The hands looked different to me, not like hands that work, but like hands that wave. Ann's father supported her slender figure in his arm. Her hair drifted across his arm, and he smiled proudly like a man who has won something.

"Mums is usually sick," Ann explains, "or working; she works in a nursing home. She's usually sick." She says this proudly as if it is a mark of distinction where she comes from. "My dad is a jailer."

"You mean a security guard at a prison?" Emma says.

"A jailer," Ann repeats. She smiles when she talks about her parents.

"What's wrong with your mother?"

"She's diabetic, that's why she gets sick." Ann's parents live in a trailer park, and Ann says that when there's a thunderstorm they turn off the electricity and sit in the dark because they are afraid of the trailer being struck by lightning. Ann says she has spent many afternoons and evenings in the trailer sitting in the dark listening to her father sing or recite Bible verses while they wait for the rain to stop.

Joyce says, "Wash up, girls, I'll go see about Ann."

"I don't see why she gets away with being sick all the time," Emma says. "I mean just because her mom is a friend of George and Mary's."

"She's special, Ann's like an angel or something," Teddy says grinning.

When we get back from joyjobs, Ann is gone, and we hear later that she had appendicitis. She only comes back to school one more time, and that is to say goodbye. "The Lord made it clear that I'm supposed to stay home and take care of my parents," she says. "I'm gonna get a job at the nursing home where Mums used to work."

"Doesn't she any more?"

"She's sick."

"I'm gonna miss you."

"I'll miss you, Andie, but I'll remember your birthday, April 25th, and I'll say Happy Birthday to you. Maybe I can call you or write you a letter. I love you."

Ann remembers everyone's birthday although she could never pass seventh grade math. She stuffs her clothes in a green utility sack. "I gotta go now," she kisses me and walks out to her father's car. I sit on the windowbox looking out the back windows.

I wake up at 5:00, before the morning whistle, and I lie in bed, my eyes squeezed tightly and promise, "God, I'm going to turn over a new leaf, be a new girl, I will not talk unless necessary. No idle word will escape my lips. Please help me for I know I cannot do this alone. In the name of the Lord Jesus Christ and of the Father, Son and Holy Ghost, amen."

What I spend most of my time thinking about these days is trying to change myself and, if that doesn't work, running away. I can see that there is something wrong with me. People like my sister Alexa and Ann never get into trouble. They don't have to try to be good; they just are. I, on the other hand, am essentially a bad person. On our infrequent visits, my mother confirms this. "I don't know what went wrong with you," she says, shaking her head. Tears often stand in her eyes when she looks at me. I think I love my mother, so I would like to be good, to prove something to her, but I have decided that if it doesn't work, I will run away. I think of my favorite story, the one about the Ugly Duckling who turned out to be a swan. Though I suspect that I am not a swan underneath as I would like to be. I am suspicious of myself at every turn. I see myself failing. I believe I am rotten to the core.

One afternoon, I am working with a group of girls in the pasture below the orchard. We are chopping out thistles that get stuck in the sheep's wool when Don calls us. We stand in a semi-circle facing him.

"I understand," he says, throwing his head back, "that you are afraid of John Striker." He moves his head for emphasis when he talks. "None of you want to get in the sheep pen is what I hear."

We nod tentatively. The ewes scattered behind him nibble grass followed by their half grown lambs. The flock's ram leader, John Striker, stands alone watching us. "You aren't afraid of the cows." We laugh a little.

The day before, some strangers had come to inspect the school. In the barn they had asked two of us to show how a cow is milked. Emma and Luke brought in old Mary. Mary had some strange defect in her let down reflex, and as soon as a pail was placed under her, the milk began pouring out of her udder. Emma led Mary into the milking stall, and as she slid the pail into place, Luke began pumping the tail. Milk streamed into the pail, as Luke pumped up and down. The strangers smiled. One said, "I had no idea a cow could be milked like that." Just the thought of it made us want to laugh now. "Strangers are so stupid!" we had said over and over to each other.

"I won't have you neglecting your chores. These are the Lord's animals. We are in control of them. Now, I don't want to hear anything more about any of you being afraid of John Striker." Behind Don, John Striker begins backing up. He raises and lowers his huge black Suffolk head and begins pawing the earth. "If you are not afraid, he will sense that and leave you alone." The ram snorts.

"Ah, Don," Emma says, putting up her hand to get his attention.

"Don't interrupt when I'm speaking to you. God wants you to be bold." One of the other girls clears her throat. The ram paws the ground, backs up a few more paces, paws again. He lifts his head and lowers it. "You are soldiers in the King's Army. Stand your ground." The ram charges, head lowered. Don sees our faces change into fear and looks behind him. "Run," he yells and we dash for the fence looking back as the ram's head crashes into his backside hurling him forward. He picks himself up and runs, tripping once as the ram hits him again. As the ram backs up for another plunge, he vaults over the fence, and sits on the ground for a moment unmoving. We crowd around him, and he looks up, staring at each face for a trace of irreverence.

I smile, and then start laughing. In a moment, we are all laughing. Don's expression is blank as he stands up.

"You," he says to me, "you are mocking me. What happened to the children who mocked Elijah?" His anger cuts through our laughter, a dark streak across a bright day.

We can quote the Bible like breathing, "And he turned back," I say, "and looked on them, and cursed them in the name of the Lord. And there came forth two she bears out of the wood, and tare forty and two children of them." (2 Kings, 3:24, King James) I shiver, as I always do when I think about that story.

"God will not be mocked." He stands up, brushing the dirt from his trousers, and the film of dust blows on to me, envelops me in the knowledge of my own wickedness.

"Go sit on the laundry box in your bathroom."

I sit on the laundry box, smiling when no one is there at the thought of the huge ram burying his huge head into Don's butt. Any punishment is worth it.

Joyce comes in, hours later, after dinner and joyjobs. "Report to the office," she says. I march behind her, across the Octagon.

I remember last winter being sick when we all had the flu. I'd been very sick, with a temperature of 104 degrees, and I'd been put in the room with the other very sick ones. Someone watched over us all the time and kept us supplied with grape juice. I remember looking out the window and seeing long delicate strands of morning light between the trees' branches, the whiteness of light on snow, and then closing my eyes and opening them to early afternoon winter darkness. I said, "I'm going to get sick," and Joyce said,

"Get up, run to the bathroom," and I had run down the hallway, across the Octagon. "Run, run." I vomited purple, a long horrid stream of grape juice.

I fell, my ears ringing and felt my head hit the floor and the side of the toilet, the cold porcelain against my skull. "Get up, mop up this mess," Joyce said. "Get up," and I looked at the mop being shoved into my hands like it was something I had never seen before. A mop bucket sat in the corner, and I walked over to it, swished the mop in the water slowly, watching the strands of the mop head swish dull and grey in the flat water. I watched myself as though I were no longer attached to my body. I worked over the mess. The smell hung heavily around my head, and I leaned to vomit again and vomited on my feet. Joyce screamed, "now you have more to clean up." My feet felt heavy as though they were tied to something, and I slid onto the floor, my hands sliding along the splintery mop handle. "Get up," Joyce yelled again, but I heard only a ringing in my ears. I could not feel my head at all. When I tried to think, my thoughts ran past me, chasing each other.

Walking across the Octagon, I remember mopping the grape stain until my body gave out. The Faculty Room is lined with books.

Don says, "The Lord has made clear that you have to leave. We're sending you to your mother. Go pack." He speaks slowly and precisely. The clock behind him strikes two.

I say, "Yes sir."

"Dismissed," he says, and I turn sharply, and march out.

I wait, sitting on the floor in Hope's dorm, leaning against my bag of clothes, and when the door opens, I open my eyes and see that Hope has been crying. Her eyes are full of disappointment and bitterness. Her hair has grayed early, and her whole thin body looks defeated. The last time I visited my mother, we showered together. I looked at my mother's body and wondered if someday it would be my body, the breasts and belly sagging downward, the white planes of her pelvic bones thrusting outward, the dark hair on her legs.

"Are you sorry?" my mother says, tears in her voice.

"Yeah, what are you going to do with me?" Her voice sounded small and pale.

"How could you do this to me?"

"I don't know." Hope sits on the floor, her head between her knees, her arms wrapping her like her life closing in around her. The afternoon sun disappears, and the room darkens.

"They're coming back soon," I say. We both know Hope shouldn't just sit around talking with me when I've been kicked out. "I'll go out for a walk and pray. I'll be back before dark."

Hope says, "Okay," in a low voice, like we're two conspirators. "Pray, repent, maybe God will forgive you and you'll be allowed back."

I have three days of walking alone, writing in my notebook letters to God. I write, "I have seven devils inside me. George says I am full of devils. My heart is a habitation for demons. God please cast them out from me. I pray this in the name of the Lord Jesus and of the Father, Son and Holy Ghost, amen."

George has been reading to us about orphan children in China. The missionaries who cared for them, taught them about God. The orphans could see demons and angels. While they prayed, they saw heaven and would walk around in heaven playing harps and singing. The missionaries never got to go to heaven, but they would see the kids moving about singing in a language they didn't understand.

What fascinates me most are the demons; the children said they were different shapes and sizes, some small with snouts like pigs, some huge seven foot creatures with many legs and eyes. I wonder about the demons that I asked God to cast out of me, what they looked like, where they are now, and whether they want to get back inside me. In the Bible, a man had a demon inside him. When it was cast out, it wandered around. Not finding a place to go, it found seven other demons worse than itself and went back to the man, and they all went into his heart to live.

The children saw demons climbing on the roofs of a house and sometimes going inside. They saw the demons crawling over a man like monkeys, screaming in his ears.

I still get confused by hearts and souls, but when I asked George about it, he said I was blaspheming, and I was put in a room for three days. Whenever someone is in trouble, they are told to ask God for a new heart, a clean heart, and to ask the Lord Jesus to come live in their heart. But then after having one's heart replaced any number of times, when you die, it is your soul that goes to heaven or hell. It seems like the heart should go. No one ever explained this to my satisfaction.

I write, sitting on a flat rock in a glade, a pool of sun in the middle of trees. I climbed there early in the afternoon after doing Hope's chores; cleaning the cupboards, doing dishes. I sit still, only my pen moving. I glance up and hear twigs cracking. I sit perfectly still in my grey skirt and brown sweater, a lump of earth on rock.

A fawn moves out of the woods into the sunlight, its tail high, its nose twitching. It dances forward, its body rocking like it has not fully discovered the stride of its growing legs. Its spots have almost disappeared. It dances closer to me, only ten feet away, and then it stops, and I see the whites of its eyes gleam. I can see its mother's dark form for a second in the trees, and then they are both gone.

I think about hunting season coming soon, and write, "I can't run away."

"Not yet," I think, "not yet," but I don't write that. Someone could read this book. "Now is the time for repentance," I write.

I tear out a couple pages to write a letter to George and the school children. I need to get everything right. George has said that you can tell the truly saved because when they talk about their life with Christ, they talk about the cross, the blood of Christ, and the Resurrection. They refer to him as the Lord Jesus Christ, their Savior and Redeemer. I try to remember everything. I say that I have been given a new heart, and the Lord Jesus has come to dwell in my heart. I assume this is true because I asked in the name of Jesus, and he says he answers prayer. I finish the letter and climb down the hill, already missing the sunlit glade between trees.

When I return from my walk two days later, Hope is waiting on the porch. "A letter for you," she says, eyes shining. I hold out my hand suddenly feeling a cloud of sadness dampening my day. I reach out my hand into Hope's happiness and touches the letter. I know what is in the letter, and I wish the days of walking alone would go on.

"Read it out loud." Hope's dark head leans over my pale blond one.

"Dear Andie,

The Lord has seen fit that you be invited back to school. Love, the School Family."

"Oh, Andie." Hope hugs me. One of the other women walks in and sees us hugging. "She's going back to school," Hope's voice has tears in it. "The Lord has had them invite her back." The other women who Hope lives with haven't looked at me or spoken to me during the four days I've been sleeping beside my mother's bed. They've treated me like a ghost, a dead person. But now the other woman hugs me, and says, "Praise the Lord." The women come in from work, "Praise God, Hallelujah." They hug and touch me, and I turn in the circle of women, surrounded by their outpourings of praise.

That night I am back in my sleeping bag at school. Long after the others are asleep, I stare at the ceiling. I shut my eyes and see the fawn learning to run behind its mother. I tell myself, "I love you," before I go to sleep.

Teddy and I walk up to the barn to say good bye to the sheep. "I'm going to discover boys," Teddy says.

"Then what?" I don't feel like saying much.

"I'm going to do stuff with them," she says.

"I still don't get why you have to leave."

"My dad and mom say they want to see us more than four weeks a year. They need help on their farm, and my dad says, 'What's the point of having eight kids if they can't help with the animals?'"

"Are you glad?"

"I'll miss you. But I'm going to give you something before I leave."
My mind skips through Teddy's possessions, things she's hidden with
her sewing kit, writing paper, shoe polish in her windowbox: A dead
bird that earned her a beating, crickets pinned to cardboard, dead
butterflies, live snakes. "What is it?" Teddy reaches over and slides
the thing into my hand. "It's not a frog is it?"

"Open your hand." The thing's coolness lies in my palm, and for
a moment, I'm not sure what it is, an egg, a marble, a shell? I look at
the thing, turn it over; it's a rock, smooth and shiny, shaped like an
egg, brown with twists of green and orange running through it.

"Where'd you get it?" I hold it up to the sun. I want to suck on it,
to feel how smooth it is, but I won't do this in front of Teddy.

"From my Mumsie, you like it?" In Teddy's family grandparents
are Popsie and Mumsie. "She told me how they make these things,
see, they put all these rocks, just regular rocks together in a machine,
and they roll them over and over with water that's cold, and they
keep rolling in there all brushing up against each other, and then in
a long time, they come out like this, all smooth like marbles or jewels.
They aren't rocks anymore."

"But underneath, they're still a rock," I say, "I mean the surface is
polished, but they're still a rock, they still know they're a rock." We
both are speaking almost in whispers. "You keep it, okay?" Teddy
runs her hand through her hair. "I'm gonna grow my hair long, I'm
gonna have a mane like a horse."

"You're one lucky girl," I whisper.

"I'm leavin' so I'm sayin' it, I'm lucky, lucky, lucky." Teddy says
loudly, and we both laugh.

One year later, during class, Grace calls me into the office. "Teddy
is visiting, and she wants to see you. Do you want to see her?"

I try to hold back my excitement. "Yes, if it's permitted," I say.

We are allowed to go outside and walk down the lane. One of
the dogs comes with us jumping and frisking. "I'm gonna kill that
dog," Teddy says.

"You shouldn't say that, Teddy."

"Oh, tell me about it, it's a figure of speech," says Teddy. "You
still follow all the same rules, but then I guess you would, you're
living in the same old place."

"Where else would I live?"

"I don't know, don'tcha have any folks outside this place?"

"I wouldn't want to live any place else," I say. "This is my life. I wouldn't know how." I try not to stare at Teddy who has blue-green streaks above her eyes, painted fingernails, red lipstick, and tight jeans.

"Are you just sayin' that, or do you really mean it? I can't believe you really like it here."

"I've never thought of living any place else."

"Look, you don't have to lie to me, I'm not living here any more; I'm not going to rat on you, give me a break. I've been here. I've been with you. I know you." She lowers her voice to a whisper, "The truth, Andie, the truth, you think about leaving every day. Not a morning passes, not a night that you go to bed when you haven't dreamed of running away."

I almost smile. "If I dream about it, does it do any good? Not that I've noticed."

"I'm telling you, there's stuff to do in the world, you haven't even thought of. Stuff you're gonna like."

I smile. "What kind of stuff?"

"You gotta get out of here," Teddy says. "I miss you." September red, yellow and orange leaves drift down around us.

"I still have the stone," I say.

"You still got it?" Teddy looks at me curiously as if she were a different species. "You know, George was always saying that we're gonna end up on some desert island? Well, islands are tropical, there aren't desert islands."

"How'd you get to come and see me?"

"My dad and mom owed some money, so my dad was coming over, and they let me come along. I'd forgotten, this place is too weird. You still just do what you're supposed to." She mimics my walk, marching down the road, arms swinging.

"Do you remember building lean-tos in the woods?"

"I try to forget," Teddy picks up a red maple leaf and shreds it.

Disappearing Tails

We collect frogs' eggs in gallon jars,
watch them yellow and green in the sun,
hatch wriggly black tadpoles.
One boy eats them on a dare,
swallows four tadpoles, heads and tails.
We listen for frogs croaking in his belly.
He encourages girls to lie on his stomach listening,
asks us to walk in the woods.
He wants to show us something.
I hang back, watch my tadpoles hatching.
The other girls have seen enough.
Their pollywogs are losing tails.
They follow him to a woods place
near the meeting of two streams
where he says grownups never go.
The girls come back red-faced and laughing.
I watch my tadpoles emerge from eggs.

Chapter 11

Emma and I swing in a playground in Regina, Saskatchewan as the sun sets. It feels good to be out of the cramped bus. A little girl, a stranger, comes over to talk with us.

"Why do you dress like that?" she asks, eyeing our skirts, matching kneesocks, blouses and sneakers.

"We're from Vermont," Emma says.

"Vermont? Where's that?"

"North of New York," Emma says.

"South of Canada," I add.

"Is it nice there? Why are all you kids here?" the little girl asks, staring at us as if we were from some different planet.

"We're going to British Columbia for the summer. Do you always live here in Regina, Saskatchewan?" Emma asks. I can tell she likes saying the word, "Saskatchewan," likes the flavor of it on her tongue. She rolls the syllables over one another.

"I've never left Regina." The girl climbs on the swing and pushes her foot on the ground. "Push me, please." I push her higher and higher in the blue twilight. The swing lifts her and her dress blows up around her legs. She laughs, her laugh drifting down through the cool air.

"Why is she laughing?" I ask.

"She's happy," Emma says. "People out in the world laugh and smile. They're allowed to."

George called us together at the beginning of the summer. He walked into the Octagon followed by his blonde secretary, Mary. They were back from several weeks in Bermuda, and they glowed, tanned and relaxed. They wore white, she in a white blouse and skirt, he in white shorts and shirt.

"As you know, we have just returned from visiting the brothers and sisters in Bermuda." George had three flocks over which God had made him Shepherd: The Bermuda Family, the Farm Family and the BC Family. He travelled between them, and sometimes people were moved from one flock to another as their skills became necessary.

"Well, the Lord has seen fit that we should now go to BC. The Lord has also made clear that you are going too. We are going to fly, and you will come by bus in two weeks." His words fell out into the silence. We were sitting stiff and upright, legs crossed, hands folded.

"You can cheer now." The clapping began, rhythmic, and we shouted, "Hip hip hooray, hip hip hooray." George stood at the front, Mary behind him, and the clapping washed over him. We almost smiled in our excitement. Some of us have never left New England.

The next two weeks are frantic preparations: Packing the bus for a week's travel, sewing clothes. The kitchen in the back of the bus is packed with bread, sandwich makings, canned fruit, snack mix.

"Emma, you shouldn't talk with strangers."

"She talked with me first. I couldn't be rude." We walk across the park. The bus has broken down and has been in the garage for four hours. The counselors finally got tired of telling us to sit still or march. They relax on blankets beside the bus, while we wander around the playground.

"Know why my parents don't live at the Farm?" Emma asks.

"No."

"Well, my dad was married before and they got divorced, and he married my mom. So I have a half sister, plus my seven whole brothers and sisters."

"Well, why can't your parents live here?"

"Because George says if you're divorced and you remarry you're not really married."

"Oh, yeah, I remember, that's why Stephanie's parents can't live together."

"Well, George told that to Daddy, but he already has eight kids with Mommy, so he says he is married. He says George comes up with some weird stuff."

"You're going to go to hell for saying that."

"Oh, blow it out your ear."

"You're not supposed to use expressions. Where do you get those expressions?"

"Brooklyn."

"I'd like to go to Brooklyn."

"I thought you said I'm going to hell."

"Well, yeah, maybe."

I write to my mother every day of the trip describing the prairie dogs in Saskatchewan, the Rocky Mountains in Alberta, Lake Louise, a little glacier lake nestled in the mountains where artists paint the mountains, lake and sky. I practice to be a painter, coloring elaborate pictures of birds with my pencil crayons. My letter on the day of my arrival ends, "We have arrived."

Hope writes back, "Got your letter and couldn't believe you ended like that. We want to know all about the place. Where are you living? What is it like out there? What are you doing?"

The bus stops long after dark in front of a farmhouse outside of Nanaimo, British Columbia on Vancouver Island. George bought the BC Farm when the young men at the Farm needed a place to dodge the draft. The man who owned it joined George and sold him his farm, called Swallowfields, for one dollar. We heard about Swallowfields and have waited to see it: The stream running through it, the fields where horses run, the cherry orchards, the sawmill.

We follow George through trees to a huge campfire surrounded by dome-shaped plastic houses. "These are your hogans where you will live for the summer." Signs above the hogans mark which squad will stay in them. We crowd around the fire, and Emma's little sister sits down on her rolled sleeping bag, and then falls over, "Are we there yet?"

I wake up early and go out to reconnoiter. I like that word because I feel it lends some importance to what I am doing. There are cold water spigots at the end of each plastic dome-shaped hogan, and I wash at one. There is a laundry tent with tubs and washboards lined up where we will do our laundry all summer, and beside it there are long clotheslines. The cook tent consists of rows of picnic tables, two big refrigerators, and a big diesel stove. A couple of the older girls are making breakfast, and they recruit me to butter toast.

Emma and I scrub our clothes together in the wash tent after lunch. We grind our socks on the washboard and sing songs in French. "Tout çe que vous faites, faites le de bon coeur, comme pour le Seigneur, et non pour les hommes," which means, "All that you do, do it heartily as unto the Lord, and not unto men."

"After work, I'm going to build the house if you want to come," Emma says. She is the acknowledged leader since she knows more about the world, having spent her first ten years in New York.

"Can you tell me some stories?"

Emma and I build a secret lean-to and name it Fifth Avenue which Emma tells me is the street where books are published. The boys play softball in the Bull Pen Field. Emma tells me stories while we build Fifth Avenue.

"So tell me a story, please." I have saved my banana from breakfast for Emma. I don't like bananas, and Emma insists that I sneak them under my shirt. We are sitting under the lean-to which faces a gravelly bank running down to the Bullpen stream. The sunlight comes through the tree branches to help the purple and white violets grow.

"In New York, there are millions of bad people, simply millions. They're everywhere like ugly on an ape." I know Emma heard that expression from her father. He lives in New York, but he'd met George and had been convinced that the boarding school was an ideal place to have his kids raised. He is round, jolly and bald.

He is sixty years old, and his wife is pregnant. "If I wasn't busy having all these kids," he'd say, "I could make some money." Emma tells me that this is a joke because he owns three companies and works all the time.

"A company," she explains, "Is a bunch of people working for you, and they're making stuff while you're driving a Cadillac and wearing white shirts. After the stuff is sold, you give a little bit of the money to the people that worked and keep the rest for yourself."

"What's a Cadillac?"

"It's a big car that older people who are parents or grandparents drive. It's so big you could let your whole family drive in it, but you don't want to, because it's fine and the seats are all nice, so you just drive it to work yourself, and you make the wife drive the kids in the station wagon. On weekends if you take the wife somewhere fine, you let her ride in the Caddy."

Emma's dad gives big hugs to his kids when he leaves, and they yell, "Love you, Daddy" as his car pulls out of the school drive. None of us kids whose parents live at the commune are allowed to call our parents "daddy" and "mommy," but Emma says everybody out in the real world does that.

"So, tell me about the black guy jumping the fence."

"Ok, so one morning, I'm sitting outside my house watching the planes go over to the airport."

"What airport?"

"The airport, silly, the one that's in New York near our house, and I can see all the planes coming in. I'm watching, and then this black guy jumps over the fence into our yard with a big bag of stuff he's robbed from our neighbor's house. The neighbor's dog is chasing him but can't get over the fence, so he's barking, and the man runs across and jumps over the fence. I watch him jump three more fences, then he runs down the street. Then I hear a siren and a police car drives up, and these policeman try to grab the guy but he runs off and jumps another fence."

"He can just jump a fence, just like that?"

"Oh yeah, he's a big guy."

"Ok, so tell me something else."

"Well, there's a lot of rape going on in New York. You read about it in the papers all the time."

"What's rape?"

"What do you think?"

"I don't know, there's the grass called rape we pick for the sheep."

"You're such an idiot, sometimes. Rape is when a man forces a woman to have sex."

"Let's talk about something else."

We walk along the stream picking early blackberries. "I wanna see New York sometime," I say.

I think about asking Emma about rape, but I don't think I want to know the answer.

This is a summer for camping, and George and the counselors plan a long hike for us, fifty miles along the West Coast Trail. I am captain of a team consisting of Liza, Stephanie, and Emma. We make tents for ourselves out of plastic. Each tent is a plastic sleeve which is to be strung through a rope which will be attached to two trees. No one explains what we will do if two suitable trees are not found with a space between them for a tent, or what we will do if it actually rains, and the rain pours in the open ends of the tent. The food we pack is granola, canned beans, tuna, crackers, honey, spam and rice. Our packs weigh an average of fifty pounds which includes sleeping bags, tents, food, hatchets, ropes and clothes. The day we are to leave, Liza comes up to our counselor and says that she was lying about something. She is told to go to her hogan. We never understand why these summer huts are called "hogans," but George has told us solemnly that they are hogans, so they are. She is not allowed to go, so all the stuff from her backpack is stuffed into Stephanie's, Emma's and my packs making them still heavier. Don and Steven are coming along, but they are the only adults. They are supposed to stay together, and let the team leaders do the leading.

At the beginning of the trail, an old Indian rows us across a river, one team at a time. We pull our ponchos down over our faces; it is raining hard. Our teams start off the hike fifteen minutes apart, so we can hike separately. Don and Steven wait until last. "What do they think we'll do, run away?" I say to Stephanie as our team gets started.

"Yeah, into that," Stephanie waves an arm at the rain forest. Long shaggy moss hangs off of trees. Water drips into the grey, soggy woods.

"Looks like something out of a storybook."

"Some story, if you were inside looking out."

We slog along; the mud comes up to our ankles, and makes a squishing sound as we walk. "Where's Emma?" I say suddenly when I fail to hear two pairs of shoes behind me. Emma has fallen in the mud at the top of the hill we have just come down. We climb up. Emma's face is gray, her eyes closed. "Emma, Emma, get up," I shake her.

"She fainted," Stephanie is excited. "She completely fainted. She's carrying too much stuff." Emma opens her eyes, and says,

"What's going on?"

"You fainted." Stephanie says impressively. We help her up, take off her backpack and take everything out of it that we can fit in our own packs. I put some canned food in my jeans and tie Emma's sleeping bag on top of mine. My backpack is precariously off balance.

"What are we gonna do with her tent. She can't carry all this stuff, we got too much stuff, we got enough food for one more person, and we got an extra tent," Stephanie says.

I kick the tent over the cliff, "So much for the extra tent," I laugh.

"I'm really sorry."

"Don't worry about it," I say. We walk a little more slowly. Emma nibbles on crackers and honey. We have been hiking for an hour and a half when we come to a gorge. A stream rushes at the bottom on its way to the ocean. The stream bed is a mass of rocks and old logs. There is one long log across it with a wire cable to hold on to. It is wet, slippery and has no bark. A little sign says, "Fifty-foot bridge."

"They call this a bridge?" Emma asks. We hesitate, there is obviously only one way across it.

"I'll go first," I say. "Wait till I'm all the way across before you come. We'll do it one at a time, so we don't shake each other." I stand there arranging my pack for a while and take a drink from the canteen. I don't want to look like I'm stalling. Stephanie and Emma aren't saying anything. Water drips off their ponchos, and they both have set, tired expressions.

I start inching across one step at a time. I put one foot in front of the other slowly. The wet wood of the log feels slimy. I hear my heart, and I keep saying, "I'm fine, God help me, I'm fine." When I get to the middle, I look down at the stream water which rushes and bubbles along. I can see it, and I can just hear it over the steady drip, drip of rain. I think for a moment about whether I would go to heaven if I fell down and died.

"Dear God, please forgive me for all the sins I have ever committed. Keep me safe, in the name of the Father, Son and Holy Ghost, amen." I feel pretty good after the prayer, and I turn to wave at the others. The arm movement swings the backpack out over the ravine, and jerks my feet off the log. The pack catches on the wire, and I hang there.

For a long minute while my feet feel air beneath them, I watch my life, all the sins I have committed passing in one long chain. "Save my life, God," I say, "and I'll never think of running away, I'll never read another book except the Bible, never speak another idle word."

I listen for the rain and hear the angels singing. The sound of water mixes with the smell of my fear hanging from my wet hair. I can hear every sound distinctly, my heartbeat, the water, the nothingness.

"I'm coming," Emma says. I see Emma out of the corner of my eye, creeping along the log careful not to touch the wire. Her hair gets in her eyes, but she doesn't notice. She creeps on her hands and knees. Her pretty face is scrunched up. Stephanie is standing still, her body tight. Emma creeps closer. When she gets to me, she sits up straddling the log.

"What're you gonna do?" I whisper.

"I got it all under control. I'm gonna grip the log with my legs like I'm riding a horse. I got a rope and the other end's tied to a tree. I'm gonna swing your legs over here."

She can reach my legs by leaning out a bit. She grabs my feet and the back of the pack, and swings me forward onto the log. I land, straddling the log face forward. My forehead hits the log and blood stings my eyes. For a moment, I grip the log with both arms and both legs and let out a little scream. Then I am quiet and lie still. "Are you okay?"

"Yeah, except my head's banged up, and I feel like throwing up." We lie there for a while, and then start crawling forward. Stephanie comes last, crawling across the log with two backpacks. The others pretend not to notice that I am crying a little. They just shoulder their packs and look back across the log. Stephanie starts laughing, and suddenly we are all laughing.

"I was petrified out of my wits," Emma says.

"I thought I was gonna die for sure, I was a gonner, you saved my life."

I kiss Emma. We're still wiping our faces when Don and Steven appear at the other end of the log.

"We gotta get going," I say. The laughter stops. We turn back to the trail single file.

Our feet move slowly in and out of the mud until the water, the sky, the mud, all are trudging through the afternoon toward dusk and the camp by the donkey engine. We want to stop, but the rain forest, thick as a briar patch dares us to try to get off that trail and sit down for a moment.

A huge rusting hunk of metal sits in the middle of the path overlooking us like some water god, vines for hair, one huge stick across its belly ready to be used for justice. I open the map I carry in a plastic bag, but we are sure that this thing is our first marker, our goal for four o'clock in the afternoon. It is now six o'clock, and we have just arrived at the donkey engine.

The West Coast Trail runs along the rockiest part of the West Coast. It is fifty miles of rugged trail that used to be called the lifesaving trail because of the hundreds of shipwrecks that occurred there. Between the two trails, one running along the beach, the other through the woods, are connecting trails because most of the beach trail is underwater when the tide is up. We would have preferred to use the beach trail, but hikers of the West Coast Trail usually go back and forth between the two trails carefully consulting a tide chart. Being caught on the beach trail when the tide comes in could be fatal. There are places where the trail runs beside rocky cliffs that stretch straight up one hundred feet or more.

I say we might as well spend the night and hope to make better time the next day. The first team has already gone on. Emma is not speaking. She collapses on a log while Stephanie and I string up the tent between two trees. We try to pick an area where the openings of the tent face away from the rain, but the plastic sleeves clearly are not involved with anything so mundane as keeping out rain.

Stephanie collects wet wood and lights a feeble fire with newspaper. The rain muffles it, and finally, Stephanie kicks it and walks off. "Let's just eat our food cold." I take out the canned beans and hotdogs I have stuck under my sweater. I eat beans from the can, and bite into cold hotdogs. "Think of fried chicken," Stephanie says.

"Or pizza," I say.

"Even meat loaf," Emma chews her cold hot dog.

The other teams set up their soggy homes between trees. Hardly anyone talks. The only sound is the water dripping and drowning out all attempts to make a fire.

When I wake up, I must have been wet for a long time; my skin feels like raisins or prunes. The water is all the way through the sleeping bag, but I feel warm and wet, and not at all like moving. "Are you gonna give swimming lessons, Captain?" Emma says, her voice sounding damp out of the darkness. "I wonder what time it is." We listen to the rain water which seems to be getting louder and closer. "Isn't that getting louder?" Stephanie's voice has just a hint of a shake.

"Maybe the donkey engine is sneaking up on us," and then someone shouts, "There's a bear in the camp!" And I think about the bears we'd seen at the dump, big black bears eating garbage, gentle looking bears, and I say, "It's a grizzly, I know it's a grizzly," and think about how grizzlies probably like waterlogged girls, and Emma says, "He'll peel us right out of our sleeping bags like bananas," and hides her head.

Then we hear Don shouting out, "Andie, Andie, get me a flashlight!"

"Ours doesn't work."

"Well, then get me a candle."

"They're in our backpack, strung in the tree, and I'm in my underwear."

"I'm in my white underbottoms, get it," he yells. I dash across on bare feet thinking of all the other kids who could do this. By now there are other girls running in their underwear; the boys say in the morning that they would have been eaten in their beds before they ventured out wet and naked.

I get the rope end of the backpack where it is strung in the tree to keep it safe from bears and lower it. I fumble through it with the clumsiest hands, find a candle and light it, cupping it, and hand it to Don who's there in his underwear. My cotton panties are wet and stick to my butt.

The candlelight gleams on Stephanie and Emma's eyes peering out of the tent laughing at my white legs and Don's hairy ones. We look through the shadows for the huge bulk of a bear, probably a grizzly, and the rain forest glimmers and drips grey green shadowy across the tin plates by the dead fire, "And that's all there is," Don says, "water on tin plates," and hands the candle to me. But Emma, Stephanie and I still scan the camp for that stupid bear who might have left his bear wife to go on a hike in water and mud.

I climb into my sleeping bag, now cold and wet. The water is all around us now. Stephanie scoops up a handful and tastes it. "Tastes salty brackish. What time is it?"

"Two o'clock," Emma says, "so, we have two and a half hours."

"Tell us a story, Andie."

I start, "There once was a tin grizzly bear . . ."

Instead of Kissing

We rake leaves and burn them.
scrape fungi from old logs,
the size of a hand,
write on them,
my name, your name.
We name the tree, the "Shininin Tree."
Skin scrapes off our legs
as we climb, dive
into brackish cold pools,
come up in beavers' houses.
Night settles
around us
sitting on rocks,
slipping in quietly
as trout, one last time, looking
up through stream water,
through night air,
we see the moon shining
down to touch
creatures in shadows.
We hold hands
under water,
rise to the surface,
part, climb out
alone,
hurry into clothes
and through woods
in separate silence.

Chapter 12

Under a black sky that slowly lightens, we pull wet jeans onto damp bodies and tie the straps of our waterlogged backpacks. We pack handkerchiefs under the shoulder straps where we have blisters from the day before. "At least we don't have to see how bad we look." Emma's wet hair sticks to the side of her face like whiskers.

There is no point trying to cook anything. We eat rancid hard boiled eggs and cheese as we walk. Through the wet grey light, we see other kids stirring, but there is nothing to say this morning. I start off followed by Emma, and then Stephanie. I trudge along silently through the mud, and then the sun bursts over the trees, shining through the rain, sparkling on our faces which appear ghostly in the morning light. "Mashed potatoes and fried spam for dinner," I say.

When we stop for a break and look at the map, we see we're coming up on a trail that leads down to the beach. The map shows where ships wrecked along the shore, dozens of ships. "I want to go and see one of those wrecks when the tide's down." I say.

"Who wants to see a stupid old wooden skeleton? That's all it is." Emma sounds grownup.

"Oh, I do," Stephanie says. "I think ship wrecks are creepy, all those people just floating along the waves of their life and they see this shore and try to come in and they crash, and try to get out on this trail where lots of them died."

"Yeah, Emma, these woods are probably full of ghosts," I lean over and stretch out fingers like claws in Emma's face.

By the time we get to the trail leading down to the beach, it is almost midday, and it turns out to be more of a cliff than a trail. Stephanie goes first, edging her way from tree to tree, and I stay to help Emma who has her eyes closed. "I'll stay at the top of this cliff forever. I'm gonna end my days here in peace. I am not coming down."

"Don't be ridiculous. Look at Steph, she's climbing down like a monkey."

"I'm not a monkey."

"Try."

"No."

"Well, I'm not staying here all day. I'm climbing down. You coming?"

A man's voice behind us says, "What's the problem?" and we both jump, afraid it might be Don or Steven, but it's a man with long hair and a beard with a backpack full of cans.

"You're carrying beer?" Emma asks.

"I sure am. I'm the beer carrier of our group. Need a hand?" Emma gets up, and puts out her hand to him, and together they crawl tree to tree down the slope. I crawl along behind them, but near the bottom I lose my balance and tumble the rest of the way down, scraping my knee. Blood soaks through my pants, but I hardly notice because a moment later, I break out of the jungle and into the blazing bright open stretch of beach. A ship wreck like the massive skeleton of some dinosaur shoves up out of the sand, and gulls circle. The rain forest behind me is a forgotten prison, and I walk out blinded by the light and walk into the man with the long hair. "Did you hurt yourself?" We look at the knee, and he says, "Come on."

In his camp, long-haired men and women walk around cooking and drinking beer. One of the women rolls up the jeans leg, washes my leg and bandages it. "You kids by yourselves?"

"No our counselors are behind us."

"You in camp for the summer?"

We've been told never to answer questions of strangers.

"Yes, we're in camp. Thank you very much." I leave, frightened.

Stephanie and I climb through the ship wreck, examining the ribs of the ship stuck deeply in the sand. Emma sits on the sand, calling up, "Are you two almost done poking around that smelly old ship?"

"It isn't smelly," I yell. It's washed clean by the wind and sand. It's bleached and beautiful.

"Beautiful is getting to our campground for the night and eating."

"You only think of your stomach."

Stephanie feels the wood with her hands. Our backpacks and

Emma look small below us as we scramble up to the bottom of the ship and sit on the keel. "Can't you just feel the souls of these people?" I rub the wood and look up at the sky.

"These people just going on with their lives think they see a light on this shore, and they sail their ship closer, and then crash on the rocks, and then wander in these woods. That's it, they never sail again."

We shiver, looking at each other, our faces close, our knees squeezing the sides of the boat as if it were a horse. "We could get lost in those woods too," Stephanie whispers.

"Why are you whispering? We know the way out. We know the way." We laugh climbing down. The wind is picking up.

"I thought you two were going to stay up there forever," Emma says.

By four o'clock, we see the waterfall that marks that night's campsite pouring down through the trees over rocks and that night we sleep on flat rocks above the tide line. Near us pools of anemones lie in their clear habitats waiting to suck in fingers.

The last three days on the West Coast Trail are the easiest. The rain stops, and we spend more of our time on the beach trail. We come to a huge lighthouse on a promontory, and near the end of the trail a long, thin waterfall-like crystal pours down through the sunlight reflecting its colors. Don and Steven take pictures of all the teams by the waterfall to send back to our parents. In the pictures we look older, thinner, unsmiling.

At the end of the trail, a ferry named the Lady Rose takes us to where the bus will pick us up. We stand waiting for the ferry, amazed at ourselves for making it, feeling like warriors or explorers. But beneath it all, is a rumble of fear. Everything we have done on the trail will be reported to George. Each team has kept a log book recording their progress. One team got ahead and camped by themselves for the entire trip. No one talks to them. It is expected that George will punish them. Even the bear story might make George angry. One can never be sure.

Each of us gets one dollar to spend in the ferry cafeteria. Gum is forty cents, a piece of cake is fifty, a bowl of soup is a dollar. Stephanie buys gum and soda. Emma and I pool our money to buy cake, gum and lifesavers. We eat by the railing letting the wind blow our hair.

"Do you think you'll ever leave the Farm?" Emma says.

I don't know why she's asking me this, maybe to get me in trouble, you can never tell. "I doubt it, Hope's never leaving. Would you?"

"I bet I will," Emma chews her gum. "I just bet I will."

It turns out that George is in an unexpectedly good mood when we return. He says that the team who got ahead did the right thing by plunging on, and they are accepted back as though nothing went wrong. We tell stories of our trip around a roaring fire. George sits beside Mary and they both smile.

The next trip is a hundred mile canoe trip through Upper and Lower Campbell Lakes and Buttle Lake. I am on the team with Luke and Nathan. As the weakest paddler, I am often put in the middle to prepare the dinner for the night. I slice wood into kindling, shell peas, shuck corn and wash out clothes by hand while Luke and Nathan paddle.

On the second day, Nathan says, "Look," and points to a bear cub eating huckleberries by the side of the lake. We paddle over to get a closer look. "Let's see how close we can get," Luke says. He's excited. "Just tie up the canoe lightly, so we can untie it in a minute in case the mother bear comes. Come on, Andie." He's the captain.

"We better be careful," I say, but the boys are excited. Luke steers the canoe quietly, and the bear cub lifts its head, but he doesn't run away. His mouth is full of huckleberries, and leaves are sticking out the sides. The boys slip out of the canoe and climb the slope while I tie a slip knot. The cub slowly ambles away looking back at us. He walks on four feet and turns around to rock on his back feet to watch us. He appears confident, "The way a baby looks when his mother is in the room," I think, and then shout, "Look out, you guys, stop." A huge muzzle comes out of a patch of dense trees further up the slope, about twenty feet from the boys. The cub is halfway up the hill ambling toward his mother, stopping to look around. The black hulk of Mama Bear emerges from the bushes, and she snarls. Luke and Nathan run tripping on branches. She takes a step toward them, but her cub is closer than they are. By the time they get back to the canoe, she is nosing the baby bear and slapping him with one paw. I cannot get my slip knot undone for three minutes. "This would have been terrific if that bear were eating us," Luke says.

We camp under pine trees and eat dried mashed potatoes, corn and peas. On two trees near the camp there are long scratch marks. Before camping we had learned about the wild animals on Vancouver Island, and we know that bears will scratch the same tree every year, long deep scratch marks, and return to see how much taller they are. The scratch marks are about twelve feet up the trunk. We decide to keep watch so bears don't nose through our food.

Nathan and I take the ten to eleven shift. "Tell me about what you want to be when you grow up," I say. We keep wood on the fire, and move about to stay out of the smoke.

"A missionary, probably, bringing people to Jesus," he says, "what about you?"

"Maybe a missionary's wife," I say, "maybe something else, maybe I'd like to go someplace."

"Like where?" He pokes the fire with a stick.

"Oh, you know one of those places George is saying we might all move to, like Belize or Paraguay or something, maybe here."

"Yeah, I know, sometimes I wanna go someplace, but we gotta know what God wants for us." His brows furrow like he's thinking about this seriously. I think of him as a real believer, unlike me.

"Does God, like, really talk to you?" I ask cautiously.

"Oh yeah, I gotta listen for a long time sometimes though."

"Yeah, sometimes it's just that I hear this little voice inside my head, and I don't know really, if it's me talking or God or the devil," I say.

"Well, that's what George is talking about getting to know the Lord's voice, like he says, 'My sheep know my voice.'"

"Well, see that's actually what bothers me, I wanna be one of his sheep; I really think I am."

Nathan doesn't say anything for a while; he just stares into the fire. I think about how nice it is talk with him about this. We girls are always telling on each other. If I told Stephanie or Emma or Liza this, they'd run to tell one of the counselors and they'd repeat it wrong, and then I'd get into trouble. Emma exaggerates everything and loves tattling.

"Well, you might be one of his lambs, and just learning to know his voice," Nathan says.

"Yeah," I feel a sudden relief. "Yeah, I'm learning. Sometimes, I know it's God's voice, other times, I'm not sure. I bet George knows all the time."

"Yeah, well, George has been walking with God a long time." We sit quietly poking the fire for a while. When it is time to wake the next team, we crawl into our sleeping bags and stare at the fire. I pray, "Help me God to know your voice, to be a good soldier in your Army, to have a clean heart, to speak no idle words, in the name of Jesus Christ, amen."

The next day is grey and overcast; it starts to rain about ten. By four in the afternoon, we are wet and tired from rowing against the storm which is blowing water in our faces in sheets. We have twenty-one miles to go every day, and we want to make our camping place before stopping for the night.

By two, we were ready to give up. But since then, we have not found any campgrounds. The sides of the hills rise steeply away from the man-made lake. The wind blows harder, and our rowing is not taking us anywhere. We see an abandoned saloon, and decide to camp. Luke is steering and Nathan is rowing in the bow. The canoe ahead of us is faced straight into the wind tossing on wave after wave, and without warning, it suddenly capsizes into the grey mass of foaming water. The three kids on board are all wearing the obligatory life vests, but Emma and Joy are not strong swimmers.

I yell, "I'm going for their packs." Luke and Nathan turn around to steady the canoe, and I dive. The water isn't as cold as I expected. The storm has churned and boiled it. I dive where I saw the pack go down thinking, "I hope they've bagged their food well. I don't want to starve the rest of the trip because we're feeding three extra people on our meager rations." I'm excited by the water sliding over my body, by the danger I suppose myself to be in, by the need to do something. I grab two packs and hope they have the other. I come to the surface holding them and see Stephanie, Joy and Emma holding onto the side of the fiberglass canoe with one backpack on top, its belt hanging in the water. Luke and Nathan are nearby, paddling. "Are you all okay?" Nathan bawls over the water.

"Yeah. Joy, you and Emma let go of the canoe and hold onto your packs, we're going to flip it." Stephanie and I have practiced this dozens of times in clear lakes when our feet could touch the bottom, but in this weather, I'm not sure. Stephanie hands the top rung of her pack to Luke.

"Ready, get set, go," she says, and we both dive and come up under the canoe in a few inches of air under there. We remember when we did this for fun, dumping canoes and diving under to talk in inches of airspace where none of the counselors could hear us.

"All right, ready? Flip to the right?" Stephanie's teeth chatter.

"Ready," I say, and we grab the gunwales of both sides of the canoe and lift it high above our heads and flip it. It lands right side up and shoots away from us down the lake.

"Get it, get it," Luke screams. I am the faster swimmer, but the canoe is far away from me bobbing on the waves.

"You get to shore, Stephanie, I'll get it."

"You idiot," Luke screams, "get to shore." He and Nathan paddle after the canoe in a familiar rhythm, stroke, pull, stroke, pull.

On the side of the hill is an old house with a sign, "The Rest Easy Saloon." We manage to start a fire in the old wood stove on the porch and warm our socks and shoes. The blankets and sleeping bags hanging to dry make the whole place humid. Stephanie makes biscuits from the carefully ziplocked flour baking powder mixture, hot chocolate, corn and peas.

"We could have been killed," Emma says.

"I know, it was great," I grin.

"Yeah, it would have been real terrific if we hadn't been there. You would've been stranded."

"Maybe some stranger would have come along to help us," Emma says, her eyes gleaming. "That would've been something."

The next day we come to a huge dam where we will need to portage. We like the sound of the word "portage," and keep saying it over to each other, "Are you ready to portage? Will we portage everything at once?" The counselors had marked "portage" on our maps by the dam. In the end, we manage to do it in one load, but we need many rest stops. It is backbreaking work carrying our backpacks and walking slowly with three people holding the canoes up five hundred steps and down the other side. "Just think we only have to do this one more time," Luke jokes, but no one laughs. Every fifty steps we stop to catch our breath, and finally, we just go for it.

It is sunny on the trip back. Buttle Lake, which had seemed so frightening during the storm, is a mirror reflecting reforested slopes owned by the logging company Macmillan Bloedel. The big MB is everywhere on signs. Down, way down through the water, Luke, Nathan and I stare at tree stumps, tires, an old car. "This whole lake used to be woods. Animals lived here, people ran through it."

"All those little lives washed away," Nathan says, "You want to sing?" He always wants to sing; he has a beautiful tenor voice. "With Christ in the vessel, we can smile at the storm, smile at the storm, smile at the storm, as we go sailing home."

No one is very happy when it is time to go back to the Farm. Living in British Columbia felt like the closest thing most of us have experienced to words like "freedom" and "vacation." We spent long periods of time unsupervised, with no one asking questions. We were allowed to get up early, go salmon fishing in the Georgia Straits, spend afternoons wandering through woods. Going back to the regimented life of the school, all whistles and horns blowing for us to do things, feels like death. Not even seeing our parents again can cheer us up much. The drive seems too short across the provinces, just as it had seemed too long on the trip out.

When the bus pulls up the hill and around the curve of the School Lane, I see the crowd of adults waiting; I know my mother is there. We round the curve at sunset just as I always dreamed I would pull up to school, only I would be riding a horse, and the sun setting behind the school would be casting long shadows behind me. The setting sun streaks the sky glorious pinks and reds. The parents are waving and shouting.

I feel love rise like a lump in my throat, love and happiness to be home. I havn't been in trouble all summer, I think as we tumble forward out of the bus to our parents' arms. I see Hope pushing forward smiling and wet-eyed. I reach for my mother, and we both realize as our hands connect, that I've grown taller. I look straight across at my mother. We stand away from each other laughing. I'm thirteen; I stare at my mother's body and my own and see myself with the height but without the breasts and hips. My mother wipes her eyes and I watch her, wishing for something, I'm not sure what.

Red Sun, Black Morning

My sister and I fish in the Georgia Straits,
the salt water between Vancouver and the mainland.
We hold rods between young narrow knees,
keep our eyes on the water. Her line pulls.
It isn't salmon. It is black, heavy,
pulling her line, pulling the boat
toward the mainland. She reels while I paddle
toward the island. Above the waves, appears
the open broad mouth like a joker's smile.
I caught him, I'm eating him. He's mine.
I say, It's a dogfish, but she clubs
the shark across the nose as the sun rises behind her,
glowing red. She eats the dogfish on the sand.
The meat tastes like zucchini or rubber.

Chapter 13

I glance at Stephanie's chest in the mirror. I stop, look again, pretend I'm not looking. The mirrors have recently been put up so we can comb our hair better. But we aren't allowed to stare in the mirror. "Glance at yourselves, do not stare. Do not admire. Vanity and pride are sins."

I take another look at Stephanie's chest where bumps are growing. Stephanie glances sideways at me, and her face turns red. Joyce walks behind us snapping the riding crop. She pauses for a second, looking at the bumps on Stephanie and frowns. "Those will have to be covered up," she says, and I look over at the bumps, the ones that make Joyce frown, the ones that need to be covered up, the wrong things on Stephanie's chest, and I hope that I will never get them. "What's wrong with her?" I ask.

"You get those when you grow up," Joyce says.

"You have to?"

"Yes." I think about this.

Within weeks, the bumps are larger, Stephanie says they hurt; they itch. They swell under her blouses. Joyce says, "Come with me." Stephanie tells me afterward that Joyce took her to the basement of the Thirty-by-Forty where recirculated clothes hang in the Thirty by Forty shop. In the bottom of a barrel marked "Underwear" she found bras.

"They look like old women, and they smell like old women," Stephanie told me. "She pulls them out of the barrel, and they hang flat and yellowing in her hand, and she holds them out to me, and tells me to try 'em on, and I pull it around myself. She says, no, and makes me fasten the hook with my arms behind my back; she twists my arms. It feels terrible hanging off of me, and people can see it through my blouse."

"I want one."

"Why? They're a pain. I only have one, and I have to wash it by hand every night."

"I want to be a grown up."

Stephanie outgrows that bra, bursting through it one morning right before exercises, and Joyce purses her lips and goes to the Thirty-by-Forty Shop and comes back with one that is a C cup which hangs limply around Stephanie's white torso, until four months later, she bursts through that one too, and stands still for a moment with the straps of this useless thing and her large white breasts pressing up and out into the open air.

I hope my breasts will not grow like huge globes. I pray for little ones that will lie unnoticed on my chest. Hope's breasts hang like deflated balloons. I wonder if my breasts will grow in like that.

I visit Hope every few months. "I'm worried that my breasts might get big like Stephanie's," I tell Hope.

"You shouldn't waste your time on such foolishness." Hope has a lot of grey hair, and lines in her face. She strokes back my hair.

"Tell me about whether you've ever been in love. Did you love my dad?"

"Have you been in love?" she asks me.

"Not really, I kind of liked one of the older guys for a couple weeks, but nothing really; I really want to be a boy, take walks by myself, write a book maybe."

"Yeah, I wanted that." Hope sits on a picnic table touching my hair. "Andie, why can't you be more like your sister?"

"You like her better than me." I stir my yogurt and applesauce with one finger, and lick the finger. "She works in the office, you like that." Hope's lips press into a thin line. "She plays the piano, recorder, accordion just like you taught her. Is it just that I'm not musical?" Hope doesn't say anything. She's looking off at nothing, and her shoulders sag.

I take my bread, walk over to the pond and throw it to the ducks who paddle over, their little tails going up and down as they bob for crusts. "If I were a duck, I'd hate having my wings clipped and being fed bread," I say. I put up my arms. "I'd want to fly."

"You'd be cold in winter, and die." Hope throws a piece of bread, and the duck's orange webbed feet appear for a moment as he bobs for the soggy bread. "I was in love once, with Jacob, when I first came to the Farm."

"Jacob Johnson?"

"Yeah."

"Well, so then, what happened? How did it feel?"

"I felt tingly all over whenever he was around. I wanted to marry him." Hope's eyes take on an unfamiliar shine.

"Wow, then what?"

"George said if you've been divorced, you can't get remarried. It's against God's law."

"So what did you do with the tingly feeling?"

"I put it away. I didn't think about it any more. I stopped loving him. You'll fall in love one of these days, and if you're not allowed to marry him, you may cry too."

"What happened with your husband?"

"Your father, well, he had another girlfriend while he was married to me. He kept her as a sort of insurance policy in case it didn't work out between us."

"What's an insurance policy?"

"Oh, just take my word for it, your father had to have somebody on the side. Then he sends me flowers."

"What kind of flowers?"

"He sends me flowers when he has another girlfriend." Hope's getting angry thinking about this.

"So you throw them away?"

"You bet I do. Then he divorces me and leaves you kids."

"Did you love him? Was he good looking? Did he ever like me at all?"

My mother stands up to signal the end of the conversation. She reaches for a branch and snaps it off; then she breaks it several times. She clenches and unclenches her fists. "I don't want to ever talk about your father again. Do you want to go for a walk?" I don't, but I say yes. What I want to do is stay by the pond and keep reaching fingers back into my past and coming out with nuggets. I don't want to look into the future. It looks like more of what I am experiencing now.

I doubt that I will tell anyone about Hope falling in love with Jacob Johnson. For one thing, Jacob is not well-liked, a loner. He is not bad-looking, but he is awkward, shy and keeps to himself. But more than that, it is always wise to hesitate to pass on news that could get you in trouble.

When I start to get the itchy feeling on my chest, I don't tell anyone. If I can wait until vacation, Hope will take me to the thrift store in town, and I won't have to get the mildewy smelling bras that lie in barrels in the Thirty-by-Forty Shop.

In the summer, most of us wear just shorts most of the time to save on clothes. We don't wear shoes, socks or shirts, and that way we don't wear them out. I make excuses to keep my shirt on that summer, and Joyce lets me get away with it. Her baby takes a lot of her time.

"I think I need a bra," I tell Hope. I haven't been going around without a shirt all semester, because of it. I take off my shirt, and Hope glances at my chest embarrassed.

On the way home from the thrift store, Hope looks straight at the road and gives advice. "Be modest, be careful, cover them up. Wear loose sweaters so they do not show. Don't wear anything low."

The headmistress's son, Luke, asks me to go for a walk on the Sabbath. He walks with a loose swinging gait as if he is very comfortable in his skin. His eyes are blue and alive. He looks at girls out of the corners of those eyes. He gets away with more than the rest of us. His good looks have a confidence that make him shine.

We walk down the lane. For a while we don't talk. I feel the sun on my face. It is late spring, warm enough to be comfortable in only a sweater, too early for blackflies and mosquitoes which will come later and make life miserable for walkers. "Do you know what makes a baby?" Luke asks.

"Sort of, I sort of know." I feel embarrassed for not knowing, but I don't want to brush the question aside. If I act like I know, he may not tell me whether he knows. He tastes my curiosity on the air sharp and obvious as the smell of soap.

"Like what do you know?" I am fourteen, a little older than Luke. I do not want to appear ignorant.

"Well, I know it takes two married people, a man and a woman."

"You don't know anything," he says loftily. "But, I'll tell you, if you promise with your hand on your heart never to tell a single soul."

"I promise with my hand on my heart, never to tell anybody." I place my hand on my heart, and look Luke right in the eyes.

"Okay," he says. We are at the end of the lane, and we sit down by a big white rock. Luke and I sit on the grass, and Luke picks lambs quarter to chew on.

"You know how animals do it?"

"Yeah." I've seen stallions leaping on mares who neigh shrilly. I've seen boars grunting as they squeezed sows, dogs pinning the bitches to the ground, cats caterwauling like crazy while they mated.

"Well, human beings do it the same way." I gasp, and Luke lies back enjoying my reaction. I visualize my mother on hands and knees screaming, my shadowy father behind her.

"Do the women get on their hands and knees, or do they. . . ?"

"Their backs, they lie on their backs," he says cheerfully.

"Oh. Does it hurt?"

"It hurts the women." He pauses and says in a lower voice, "I've heard they bleed. But the men like it."

"Why do the women let them?"

"Well, they gotta, if they want to have kids."

"Everybody does this?"

"Everybody who's married, who's got kids. They do it, they do it all the time. The men really like it."

"How disgusting. I can't stand it. Don't tell me any more. You think Hope did it?"

"Sure she did, that's how she got you."

"That's disgusting. I wish you hadn't told me. It's repulsive."

"We better start walking back, you know."

We don't talk much on the way back. I look away from Luke into the woods. I think about all the people I know who have kids, the women lying on their backs with things stuck in them making them bleed and cry. They do it, the women lie on their backs, and the men like it.

Late one night Joyce finds me sitting on the wooden laundry box reading. "What are you reading?"

"Ah, ah, *Jane Eyre*."

"You know what you are doing is wrong."

"No, no, I didn't know."

"What do you mean?"

"I mean," I feel tortured, I know I'm getting in deeper by the second. "I mean, no one ever really said I couldn't read at night."

"Go to bed, the Lord will deal with you in the morning."

In the morning, George stands me up in front of the school and says that for an example I am to be sent away to repent until God reveals to me that I am forgiven.

The school has two buildings. The Thirty-by-forty has three floors and a basement, classrooms on the first floor, bedrooms for counselors on the second, dorms on the third. The big School building is an octagon with wings, each wing a dorm/classroom, except for one which was a kitchen. One of the staff bedrooms is kept vacant as a room for people to go and be quiet until they are right with the Lord. Sometimes one of the staff members is put there. Once the principal was there for two weeks. When he rejoined his wife, he seemed meek and frightened.

Don shoves me into the room. "Only come out to use the bathroom. If you are seen in the hallway for any other reason, it will be six-of-the-best." In the half-darkness, I fumble around and find a sleeping bag rolled up in a corner. I roll it out, and look around at bare walls. The closet is empty except for a book on a high shelf and a pair of binoculars. I climb up and pull the book down. It is a big thick green book called *Dear and Glorious Physician* by Taylor Caldwell. I hold it carefully like precious treasure. How it came to be left there I have no idea, but I feel a thrill run through me as I think about the days I have to read uninterrupted.

I read in the half light. Every time I hear footsteps, I shove the book under the sleeping bag and pretend to be asleep. Finally, I fall asleep.

In the morning, Grace comes to give me a bowl of cereal. "You will only have one meal a day until you repent. So no one will come see you the rest of the day. Watch and pray, the Lord may come at any time." I think about the book and nod, head down. Grace leaves, and I get the binoculars. I look out from behind the curtain at the little trailer where George and his secretary Mary live.

Mary stands in the kitchen stirring something. She is wearing a white shirt; it looks like a man's shirt. I study the womanly figure, long white legs and blond hair. George walks into the tiny kitchen area, and walks up behind Mary. His arms go around her waist. He is pressed up against her back. "What a funny hug," I think, and then for a moment I remember what Luke told me. I hear a noise and dive for the closet. I put down the binoculars and lie on the sleeping bag. Someone walks by. I wait until I hear nothing and get the binoculars. The curtains of the trailer are drawn, and I cannot see anything. I go back to the book.

The young Greek is being seduced by the beautiful Empress who likes beautiful young men. What does she want them for? I am unclear, but the whole thing seems wildly exciting. The morning turns into afternoon, the shadows grow long, and my stomach begins to ache. I try looking with the wrong end of the binoculars; the trailer seems tiny and far away. I see George going into the trailer. He looks tiny, a little bug of a man. It is hard to remember how terrifying he is in person with his heavy silver eyebrows. I wish looking at people with binoculars would shrink them.

Orange Windows

There used to be a little window.
Out of it I saw the sea
clapping for its own music.
Leaves of a maple tree
fluttered down, orange.
I pressed them beneath
wax paper.
I lay sick.

Now the sun filters
through smog
and never
reaches me.
My house is
K-mart curtains.
I start my novel
the eighteenth time
to please him.
I drink orange-spice tea.
My sunset swirls
in a teacup.
There is no sea.

Chapter 14

"I'm not going to live my whole life just being a little person living at the Farm doing my chores," Emma says, crawling along beside me. We're in the garden preparing the soil for seeding, crawling between rows. We reach into the soil and break it down to soft soil for seeds. The Vermont soil grows rocks. Every spring new rocks sit on the surface.

George allows long hair now, provided it is tied off the face; it requires no cutting. I've pulled my long straight brown hair back in a pony tail. I wear glasses, and I can see, when I look in a mirror, that I have a pale egg-shaped unsmiling face. My face has learned to show no emotion. Even my eyes are still. If anything goes on in my mind, I never let it rise to the surface.

I have human beings divided into troubled waters and still waters. My sister Alexa is still waters; she will flow steadily; you can count on her. The troubled waters are people like myself, Stephanie, Teddy, Emma. We froth up on the bank when the river turns unexpectedly, cutting our own course, channeling our own river bed.

"I can't believe you're always talking about leaving," I say.

"Someday you'll get in big trouble."

"Oh shut up."

"If they ever hear you saying, shut up." Luke walks by and smiles down at Emma. She smiles back, a smile full of promises. "What do you smile like that at him for?"

"He likes me."

"He likes you? We're not supposed to have boy-like-girl, girl-like-boy relationships."

"Ah, are we gonna get in trouble?" Emma drawls, drawing out the word, "trouble." "I don't like him anyway."

"But you know he likes you?"

"I like Mike."

"Mike?"

"Mike likes me. Who do you like?"

"I don't."

"He and I are working together on sheep, and we hold hands."

"You hold hands?"

"And look at each other." Emma stands up and stretches out her arms and as she turns, her cotton skirt whirls up around her legs. "They like me," she laughs.

"The Lord has begun to speak to me about health." George stands at the podium and the school kids and counselors sit around on the floor. On Sabbath, during meetings which last three to four hours, we are allowed to sit in any position, not just cross-legged as we have to during devotions. We can even change positions, as long as we do so quietly.

"The Lord has told me several changes we must make in our diets." Bessie the cook sits beside him. "Bessie and I have discussed this, and we're going to implement the new health program next week. First of all, there will be no more milk products. Yoghurt will be made from soy milk, muesli will be made with orange juice, no cheese, no pudding. Milk builds up in the intestines. It clogs them up, makes them stagnant.

"Secondly, all of you who have glasses are going to wash your eyes out with an herb called eyebright seven times a day. I will have the counselors distribute this herb. You mix it with water and then wash your eyes out with a sterile eyecup. There is no reason the Lord cannot heal your eyes. There is no reason so many of God's children should be wearing glasses. You will wash you eyes with eyebright, and you will pray. If you are right with God, he will heal your eyes, and you will no longer have to wear glasses.

"Thirdly, all of you from twelve on up are going on a one week cleansing fast to cleanse out your lower intestines. Mary and I have already been on this fast. We feel much better as a result. You drink colonic cleanser mixed with juice every two hours, and then every night you take enemas with coffee." Everyone sits watching him, wondering what's next.

"Lastly, it is unnatural to sit on a toilet. In nature we squat. So from now on, you will get up on the toilet, and squat. Any questions?"

There is a long silence. George's daughter, the school headmistress, smiles and raises a hand.

"We just want to say, thank you Lord for showing us how to be healthier." George smiles approvingly at his daughter Lucy. In another squad, Lucy's son raises his hand. Lucy's five children almost never get in trouble, and behind their backs we call them "the princess and the princes."

One of the princes says, "Just one question, are we talking about getting right up on our feet on the toilet seat, and then, aim and fire?" Everyone pauses. We hold our breaths so we will not laugh, and George says, "Yes," and the prince says, "Yes sir."

I will always remember the next few months: Repeated fasts, drinking that horrible colonic cleanser that jelled in juice, drinking it every two hours all day. At night, the smell of coffee grounds in the bathrooms, as we lined up to take enemas. Coming off the fasts gradually, and then going on a juice fast for twenty-one days. Feeling weak in school, faint at work. Sitting at the table while others ate and watching the baked beans and brown bread rise up off the table and drift toward me only to get away when it got to close. Kids lining up to wash their eyes out with the eyebright that burned their pupils. All the kids with glasses having red eyes all day. When the health kick dies down, there still are no milk products, and we still have to squat on the johns.

Emma and I walk up Chamberlain Road on a Sabbath Day in spring. "This is the only good season, and it's only for two weeks." I push back strands of my hair.

"I know," Emma says, "then blackflies, then mosquitoes, wet and hot all summer, fall isn't too bad, disgustingly cold all winter. I hate it."

"It's nice now," I say.

"I hope you don't mind something."

"What?"

"Well, I asked if we could go for this walk, just us. Mike's sneaking off by himself today, and he's going to meet us so he and I can talk."

"Want me to go off by myself?"

"If you don't mind."

"Whatever," I try to sound hurt. I don't care, but I want Emma to feel badly.

"I'll make it up to you."

"How?"

"Well, I'll sneak you a book when I come back from vacation next time."

"I want *Lorna Doone*, I read a condensed version of it from one of the books in the library."

"Write it down for me, *Lorna Doone*?"

"Where's he meeting us?"

"In the glade by the big rock."

"How long do you want me to disappear?"

"Two hours, I'll loan you my watch."

On the way down Chamberlain Road, Emma's face looks flushed, her eyes dewy. Her blouse is wet and sticks to her as if she's been walking a long ways. "What did you do?" Emma hums and doesn't answer for a while. She sighs twice. She says, "We talked."

"I walked and then I lay back and watched the clouds."

"That's good."

"Do you still like him?"

"I love him."

"You love him?"

"You know what we did? He kissed me."

"Kissed you?"

"On the lips. We're lying on the pine needles, and I roll over on the rock, and he says, 'Oh, you're hurting your head,' and leans over and puts his hand under my head, and kisses me on the lips."

"On the lips?"

"We kept kissing and kissing. He held me in his arms and his heart just kept beating and beating against my heart. I said, 'I can feel your heart,' and he said, 'I love you.' Andie, I love him so much." I stop and pick a pussywillow.

"You aren't saying anything."

"I'm not because I know this is bad. You'll be crucified for this."

"Crucified?"

"Kicked out."

Next Sabbath meeting George says, "There will be no boy-girl relationships unless God ordains them. Did any of you know Mike and Emma were having a relationship?" No one answers. "Can you each stand before the Throne of Grace and say you did not know this abomination was taking place in our very midst?" Everyone nods. "Well, the Lord has found the unrighteous thing, and it has been cast out."

I have only one classmate, and we study together in a small room unsupervised. We are given our assignments at the beginning of the day, and we do them until we finish. Nathan is definitely still waters, never gets in trouble. He has long eyelashes like a girl, sandy hair, and a gaze of infinite sympathy that he fixes on me whenever I am struggling with my school work. He has a thin body that will probably fill out later, green eyes and large hands. He is the sort of person who is as comfortable to be with as a cat. I do not think about liking him or disliking him. I feel safe with him.

I cannot find an answer to a geometry question, and I look up at him, as if just looking will pull it out of him. His head is down, and he is diligently working. I look out the window as the pale yellow afternoon sun filters into the colorless room. Nathan does not look up. He glances at his watch, sees that there are five minutes until break time and returns to his studying.

Most of us are pulled out of school by age fourteen or fifteen, but Nathan and I have been allowed to continue so we can be teachers. George called us into his office. He sat behind his desk with Mary beside him. "You will be allowed to go together your senior year, and after you finish high school, you will be teachers. Study well, and may the Lord be with you."

At break time we stand up and walk stiffly around the room where we spend seven hours a day. We start school at seven and study until ten. Then we exercise an hour, cycling or running and come back to study until 12:30. By 3:30, we are finished and ready to care for the goats.

"We have an English test next."

"I know," he says.

"Ready for it?"

"I hope so," he says. Nathan never gets lower than a ninety-five on an exam, and it's hard to say what he excels in because all his grades are high. We don't look up during the test. We don't have time. We move our essay writing hands rapidly, and when the hour is over, Nathan says, "Time's up," and we both stop immediately and shake out our hands. "Are you finished?"

"I think so," I say.

"Praise the Lord," he says and hugs me. The hugs are all we ever do. Hugs have always been permitted at the Farm.

After a meeting George will say, "And now greet the brother or sister next to you with a holy hug of affection," and we all hug our neighbor, a hug on command; only I notice that when the girls hug it is a short embrace, but when a boy hugs me, he holds me against him as if he wants to keep me. I like the boys' hugs.

I think about wanting to be a writer. I sleep with stories in my head, tell myself stories of women who break out of prisons. The first three lines of most of my stories are, "I am a girl, I am in prison, this is repetitive." I dream of being Joan of Arc, Florence Nightingale, Amelia Earheart. I want to be a writer, have wanted to ever since I read my first story by a woman, *Jane Eyre*. If she could write that story, I can write one, and I have so many stories to tell. I lie in bed at night imagining a room. On one side are bookshelves, on the other, open windows with sunlight pouring in. The bookshelves are full of books I can read whenever I want. Several of the books have my name on them. I open my hands and close them; I beg God for something to happen.

Crawling Under the Sky

Before my mother made me, she knew
it was a mistake, the shine
of my father's eyes, a mistake, couldn't he
take his glittering long self
somewhere else? Yes, he said,
I do, I will, and walked away.
My mother held me in her hands,
a round fat thing, a play-doh ball.
She said, I do not want this.
Want what? my father said.
Oh, you again, go away.
I do not want you,
and she held me close.
That holding convinced me,
little did I know it was
a with-holding, that she wanted
me, and I snuggled into
my whole world. She dropped me
and my back broke. Now look
what you've done. Look.
But I was crawling away.
I crawled out the door,
and I've noticed as I heal,
stand, and start walking,
that other crawlers smile at me.
I see the sky.
There's a lot of room under the sky.

Chapter 15

When George calls a special meeting after breakfast, I think someone else is being kicked out, and I hope it isn't me. When we're all seated, George walks to the front of the room followed by Mary. He has grayed completely. He walks naturally, a king in his kingdom. Mary walks a step behind him, carrying the perpetual clipboard on which she takes notes of what he says. She rarely speaks, but she records George's words. His daughter Lucy, once Mary's schoolmate, follows and they all stand in front of the room facing the children.

Mary's thick blond hair curls around her narrow face. Her smooth skin and thin bones tell the rest of her child-woman's story. As George looks out over the crowd, smiling, her pale blueprint of a face moves into his expression.

"I have an announcement to make," he says. "The Lord has spoken to me and made it clear that Mary and I are to get married." Silence. "The Lord has also made it clear that others who have been divorced will be allowed to marry." Silence. "You may cheer now." Deafening, steady clapping, no other sound. Not a face changes expression. Lucy embraces her father and Mary. George raises his hand, and the clapping stops. "Let us sing, 'I am the Lord's,'" and as he raises his arm, we sing, "I am the Lord's, oh joy beyond expression, oh sweet response to voice of love divine. Faith's joyous yes, to the assuring whisper. Fear not, I have redeemed thee, thou art mine."

I smell cakes baking before I open the door marked "Cake Room." Chocolate cakes and white cakes cool on the counter in front of the window. Hope frosts the largest cake, and I watch silently. "Hi," Hope says, not turning around. "A wedding cake, the Lord's really blessing the bakery and the cake decorating."

"You're good at it. They said I could stop in to see you."

"It's all the Lord, I couldn't do anything without him."

"Yeah, well, I think you're talented," I say, moving over to a completed cake covered with lilies of the valley and sweet peas. "You know, George said Nathan and I could go together."

"Yeah?"

"Well, I was just saying, I mean. We don't do anything. We study, you know. We talk, I guess some. He says, we could really go together. I don't know."

"Well, what are you saying?"

"Nothing, there's nothing I want to do with him or anything."

"Jacob and I are going together."

"I thought you didn't like him anymore."

"Well, since the Lord has made clear that divorced people can be married, we're going together. The Lord made clear that we could."

"Do you love him? Everyone's always saying they *love* somebody."

"Who's everyone?"

"Oh, Emma did before she got kicked out."

"I love him."

"Well, I have to go. Can I taste some of this frosting?"

"Yeah, there's a piece of chocolate cake I saved for you, too. How do you feel about Nathan?"

"Nothing, honestly Hope, I don't feel anything, and I'm not doing anything. I just want to stay out of trouble for once. I gotta go." I lick some more frosting.

"Don't eat so much, you'll be fat. Are you going to stop and see Alexa?"

"I'll wave at her, she never talks to me."

"The Lord be with you," Hope says, stacking the last layer on the wedding cake and centering it.

"The Lord bless you," I say, returning the blessing as I close the door.

"It's a different thing for you to like Luke," I say as Stephanie and I break up chicken into chicken pie. "It's a lot different."

"George said you and Nathan could go together, why not me and Luke?"

"Need I explain everything to you?"

"You're getting weird. And I don't just like Luke, I love him."

"Oh, right, there's that again. Let me tell you something, the reason they don't let you be with someone you love, is because you might start doing things with that person, I don't like Nathan, so we don't do things."

"What do you mean? What kind of things?"

"You know."

"Well, I touched Luke's leg the other day when George was reading to us *The Last Battle*." *The Last Battle* is one of the Chronicles of Narnia by C.S. Lewis. George reads the Narnia stories to us once a week. Listening to the Narnia stories is one of my favorite things to do.

I want to scream at Stephanie because what she's doing is so incredibly stupid; I can't believe she isn't trying to get kicked out. "That's just what I mean, touching is going to get you in trouble. Anyway, Luke is a prince. He's George's grandson."

"No one ever says anything about that. They just say that we're all the family of God."

"They don't need to; we're all nobodies. We better hurry with this chicken."

"What about all that, we have neither father nor mother nor sister nor brother, we are all the children of God," Stephanie says.

"You are too dense for words. The Bible's full of contradictions," I say sourly. "'Honor thy father and thy mother.' Is this before or after God takes them away from you?"

"I can't even believe some of the stuff you come up with."

"Rebellion is as the sin of witchcraft," I say eating a bite of chicken.

"Do you still study history? I liked history." Stephanie picks the chicken off the bones, and I dice it.

"Remember, 'Secular history is a vast panorama?'" I say, and Stephanie joins in the litany, we repeated before every history class. "Secular history is a vast panorama detailing man's disobedience and rebellion against God. Viewed with the Scriptures, God's omnipotence, mercy and justice are clearly revealed."

"In our history book, it says there's a national anthem. I read it; it's about bombs and the flag and stuff. Can't you stop liking Luke?"

"He likes me."

"Oh sure he does." Stephanie's face is clear white. Her face has the pinched look of someone constantly afraid of getting in trouble. Her hands and feet are small, her shoulders rounded over large breasts that she has always been ashamed of. She rarely smiles. A little half smile rises to her lips but sinks again, never reaching her eyes which are deep blue, almost black. "You don't believe me, you know what he did?"

"What? we better hurry," I help Stephanie pull the meat off the pile of steamed chickens.

"He touched my breasts."

"Have you lost your mind?"

"Hey, it wasn't me, he did it. He didn't ask. He just did it."

"What did you do? Jump away, run, leave the scene of the accident?" Stephanie sighs. She is six months older than me. "You're younger, there's a lot you don't know. I liked it."

"What about how you were going to stay out of trouble no matter what it takes?"

"Don't you ever like anybody?"

"No, I know what men and women do together, and I don't want to have to do it," I say emphatically, biting off my words.

"All right, all right."

"Where are you gonna go when you get kicked out?"

"First of all I'm not going to get kicked out."

"That's what you think."

"Secondly, my dad and stepmom are back together after ten years. George said divorced people could be together, so my Dad went down to see her and my half brothers and half sister, and now they're together again."

"Are they coming here?"

"No. They're staying in Massachusetts; they're selling firewood for George."

"We're going to finish on time. Want to go on one of our Sunday night walks?"

Outside the air is the dark, twilight blue of Stephanie's eyes. The mountains surround the school, a dark ring of shadows, a few stars are out. "Where should we go?" Stephanie says.

"Where do you want to go?"

We walk down the school lane that I walked with Luke. I say, "C'mere, look at these," and Stephanie follows me off the road. By a small stream, in the dying light, we can make out several large pink flowers. "I love them," I say, almost whispering.

"Do you ever pick 'em?"

"No, I know we're not allowed. You know they said we couldn't. Grownups call them 'ladyslippers.'"

"I know, I like that name;" Stephanie touches the pink flower tinged with darker pink around the edges, shaped like an elfin slipper. We are both whispering. "Think of the foot this would fit."

"I know, a little fairy or something. Think of a lady with a slipper." She cups the flower in one hand. "I like them not being picked; the Indians called them 'water moccasins,' and I like that name."

"Like a moccasin for a water creature."

"Sounds earthy." I lie down on the ground, and Stephanie sits beside me.

"It's getting dark."

"I know." Stephanie touches my hair. "I wish I were a water moccasin growing here. Nobody could touch me." She stands up breaking the sound of water rushing over quiet stones.

We turn toward the road. "I just think of all the things we can't do," Stephanie says. "We can't have boyfriends, we can't read. We can't use the front doors, but the counselors can. We can't pick water moccasins."

We climb the hill, and stand for a moment looking at the stars before we go inside. A figure appears silhouetted against the dark, standing on the Faculty Room porch.

"Stephanie, report to the Faculty Room double quick." Stephanie's eyes never meet mine again. She turns and runs. I walk alone toward the barn; I shiver. The twilight-blue air has turned black. The air is stiff and motionless. I hold my fingers up for that slight movement of air that tells rain might come, but there isn't a breath of wind.

In Nathan's and my little room, it is quiet except for the scratching of pens. Yellow-white light comes in during the early morning; in the afternoon, the room is grey and full of shadows.

We are supposed to write a story, something we would like to have happen. We are supposed to sit down and write the first thing that comes into our minds. "I come back to the Farm after many years," I write. "I have been exploring for a place where the Farm can move. I am riding a white horse with a long tail. As I ride around the corner of the school lane, my long blond hair streaming behind me, the sun setting and lighting me so I look like a silhouette against red and orange, the horse rears. I quiet him, and he comes to a stop, stomping his beautiful hooves."

"Luke comes out and looks jealous, but I hardly notice him. George comes out, and I dismount to speak with him. I have found a South Sea Island everyone can move to. I have bought the island, and I am ready to fly everyone there in my own plane. I will be visiting them on the island quite often, but I will not be able to live there since I have other important things to do. I pay off the Farm debt of three quarters of a million dollars, and everyone is very grateful to me. I know, and everyone knows, that I will certainly go to heaven because I am very much in George's good graces. But I do not have to live under him because I will only be visiting the island which is covered with palm trees and coconuts."

I take the paper, rip it in tiny shreds and throw it away. Nathan looks up at me for a second, "George calls me into his office and tells me that God would like me to work in the garden. I go out and start pulling weeds," I write.

In the spring of 1981, Nathan and I are finishing up our senior year. When we are not doing schoolwork, we take care of the goats, so we are together almost constantly.

"I think we're supposed to go together," Nathan says while we're driving to a nearby farm to buy two more goats. He just got his driving license, and he drives slowly and cautiously. I watch him, a little surprised at him for putting the words right out into the air.

"But there's no hurry to anything," I say.

"No," and he keeps looking at the road. "No, I just meant . . ."

"I know, George said when he put us in charge of the goats that we have his blessing."

"Yeah."

"Don't you think we would kind of go together like other people do before they get married? I mean, what do you think?"

"I don't know. I mean they just take walks together on Sabbath Day, and pray together. We're already together a lot. We pray together every morning before school." I watch his hands on the steering wheel, large, white hands like the underbelly of a flounder. I can hardly stand to watch them gesture, but I am fascinated by them as well.

"Oh, I think they do stuff." He lets go of the wheel with one hand and waves it limply. He has long legs and arms like a spider. We drive under tree boughs that cover the road. The leaves are in full bud, and the road is shaded and dim. "Springtime," he says, and sighs.

"It's very dark here," I say, and we don't speak until we arrive at the little farm and load the goats into the car. We ask for a drink, and the old man points to the garden hose. Nathan washes his long piano fingers in the water, and the droplets sparkle in the air as he shakes those white hands. I watch him for a second, pictures of him flashing through my mind: Nathan playing the piano while we all sing, Nathan singing to the sheep in that golden tenor to quiet them. I wonder if the adults who are going together really do kiss. I watch his lips move in the water like a fish's. I think of a kissing fish's mouth spasmodically opening and closing. For a moment I think of what Luke told me about sex, and I see Nathan's long white body moving in some jerky fashion. I push the picture from my mind with a shudder.

"Is something wrong?" he says, smiling like sunshine, looking boyish and harmless.

"No," I say, shrugging away my thoughts.

Because You Never Said Goodbye

You said, why can't you?
Ah, I remember you asking
me questions with your mouth.
Your eyes, even your hair twisted.
Your body writhed; your thin hands
curved around each other like question marks.

Why can't you obey? follow?
You're rebellious. That blocky word.
Rebellious—unwilling to comply
with you or God, or a Christian marriage
arranged so nicely.

But when I thought of white dresses, white flowers,
lying down with a foreign white body,
I wanted to attack.

I'm anti-marriage, I told you.
You've always been anti-God,
anti-Christ.

I shook your hand goodbye
and felt in your palm
a scaly belly.

Chapter 16

One of the insufferably long meetings drones on in the restaurant which is always closed on Saturdays for the Lord's Sabbath. People who come to the restaurant find this closing on Saturday less than amusing, but as a child, I find it surprising that anyone would expect a restaurant to be open on the Sabbath. I am in the kitchen making dinner for everyone in the meeting when Nathan and I discover that the French fry maker is not working. We turn it on and light a match, but nothing happens. We are supposed to be making French fries, meat loaf and peas. Dinner should be ready in forty-five minutes and the French fry maker sits there inert, the cold grease around the edges, the oil unmoving.

"All right," Nathan says, "we have to get this moving or we'll be in trouble."

"I know," I say grimly. "What do we do?"

"I go into the cave; I figure out which line might be providing fuel here."

"All right." The cave is a dug out portion under the kitchen which one can get to from the basement. The walls and floor are dirt, but one can walk in and see the wiring and pipes that lead to the appliances in the kitchen.

"When I think I have the right one, I'll turn it on, and then you light a match under the French fry maker."

"Gottcha."

He disappears and I get my matches in order. I am wearing a crew necked short sleeved shirt, a knee length blue skirt, white knee socks and penny loafers. I am wondering whether I will get my clothes dirty and whether I should get an apron, when I hear Nathan's voice muffled by floor boards and scant insulation, "Now, light it." I flick the match under the French fry maker and for a moment, I lose all sense of time. There is a huge explosion; the building shakes and the kitchen is instantly on fire, I am on fire; I am dimly aware of my hair burning, a horrible singing smell, my clothes, and then Nathan is grinding the fuel line off, I can hear him screaming below me, and then kids are around me, and an adult appears in the doorway. Someone is dashing water on my head. The next thing I remember is a tub of ice water and the smell of my skin bubbling and the horrible burning pain over my limbs, my face. Throughout the night and into the next day, I descend in and out of consciousness. I sometimes talk although I do not want to as I am afraid of betraying myself. I am afraid of thinking aloud.

Finally my days settle into a routine as the pain fades. Peace comes every two hours and dresses the burn wounds with a mixture of vitamin E and vitamin C, and I am given a thousand milligrams of vitamin C every hour with calcium. There is talk of whether I should be taken to a hospital, but it is decided that it is too cold. I am given books to read; I am considered at risk of infection, so only Peace enters the room dressed in white. Everything in the small room is covered with sheets, and I wear a T-shirt and underwear and the room is kept warm. I sleep, read and do school work. I eat very little, and I dream constantly. I sleep more than I have ever slept, and I dream of escape. I am not bored, and I do not want to leave the room which feels like a womb, a nest. The accident occurred, I am told, because a French fry maker had been removed and there was an uncapped gas line which Nathan turned on. Someone comes to apologize for leaving the gas line uncapped. I am draped with a sheet for his arrival, and I say that it is fine. I am very glad to be alone week after week. The room is my safety, so it is with regret that I leave it after four months of slow healing.

The fountain behind the restaurant glows red and green in the darkness. George calls a meeting after dinner, and we sit on the grass in squads. The fountain is huge, copied from the one in Buchart Gardens, Victoria, British Columbia. One tall, forty foot spike of orange water knifes the air. It melts into several shorter spikes splashing orange and blue and then becoming a fifteen foot wall of water alternating blue and green. I watch as the whole wall becomes red and then descends into the dark water. The lights flicker, and an eight track stereo plays Vivaldi's *Four Seasons*. We sit on the grass casually, but no one talks. We see George's hair with its halo in the doorway. He is talking with Don. Mary stands behind him, clipboard in hand.

He walks down the steps, and our bodies stiffen to attention. He stands with his back to the fountain, the red light glowing behind him. There is no sound but water falling. It is spring time. I have just turned eighteen. I think of Nathan for a second and look across rows of heads, I meet his eyes looking back at mine. His face glows green; I hold up my hands in the light. They are blue. Then the fountain turns all colors, and George raises his hand to indicate he is going to speak.

I remember British Columbia, getting up early in the morning to go salmon fishing, pulling a long pink coho salmon into the boat. Most of the time we caught dogfish, little four foot shark, and sometimes we ate the shark anyway, although they weren't nearly as good as salmon. Once Alexa pulled a fat dogfish into the canoe, and it thrashed in the couple inches of water, and then starting giving birth to babies until we all had our bare feet up on the gunwales, and the bottom of the canoe was alive with baby sharks. We got to shore and lit a fire to start cooking the salmon we had caught and Alexa, scooping pail fulls of babies into the ocean, called, "Don't start cooking yet, these babies might smell it."

I think about that salmon cooking, pink in the sunrise. I sit on the grass, waiting for George; I breathe, close my eyes, and smell.

George looks through a sheaf of papers. He never shuffles papers like some underling might, nervously. He flicks through his papers. The only card game I know is a French card game we played to teach us the names of animals, but I watch George with the papers and thinks he handles them like a dealer of cards.

"You are going to have dinner here tonight with the Farm family, but first your plans for the summer." He pauses, and in the silence, behind him, the water shoots up, gloriously orange to the music of summer. "You are going to BC." Silence. In that silence, a hundred in-drawn breaths, a hundred speeded up hearts. "You can clap," he says, "you can cheer," and the clapping and cheering breaks toward the wall of water in blues and greens.

"I will now read the teams you will be living with." He begins to read lists of captains, teams, which bus they will travel in. The names begin to cave in around my ears, one name piling on another. I feel that something is wrong. He is finished. Everyone is on their feet, teammates hugging each other. I look around and see Nathan watching me, "We're not going," he says. I can't think properly. The fountain splashes red, and red shadows snake across the water.

"Dinner will be in a half hour," George shouts.

"Whatever the Lord wants," Nathan says, and I look at him, like I'm looking at him through the wrong end of binoculars. I can hardly see him. I turn to walk up the road that goes behind the fountain; I want to be behind something, away from the light. I don't feel like crying. My chest and belly feel black and heavy. I can't remember if I have ever been happy. I lie down in the grass. "God," I say, "I have never wanted anything so badly, let me go to BC."

For the next few days, I move in a daze, everyone except us is leaving next week, George and Mary have already left. I tell Lucy that I am praying to go, and Lucy promises to talk to George on the phone. The answer comes back "no." Nathan and I are to take care of the school animals, live at the school by ourselves and take care of the grounds, and during the afternoon to walk down and help with the boat crew.

Fiberglass dust burns into our noses. Nathan and I stand side by side, our elbows almost touching. We each hold a heavy sander against the side of a forty foot boat. Glass fibers, millions of them float on the air, the sun shining through them. The sanders quiver in our hands, and when we put them down at break time, our hands continue to shake. "How long do you think it will take to finish just this one boat?" I ask in a tired dry voice.

"Probably a few months. Come on, this is a good stopping point. We're finished sanding this layer Let's step outside for a second, take a breather." Outside the greenhouse, the air moves a little.

"The glass grows into your skin."

"I know, you okay?"

"Yeah, I'm just always thinking about getting in trouble, and I don't want to get in trouble."

"Well, you shouldn't worry if you're not guilty about anything." He touches my arm, and I pull away. "Sorry, I know, feels disgusting to be touched, digs the glass in."

Back on the boat, we paint the whole side with green resin. Then we place the next layer of heavy white fiberglass resin to be sanded down the next day. The sun-heated glass particles and moisture hang heavy in the air.

"We're going to sail around the world in trimarans." George announced at a meeting for adults only, the first adult meeting Nathan and I had ever attended. "The Lord has made it clear how we are to leave the country. We are leaving by boat. Ten trimarans; trimarans do not flip over in high seas. Each main hull has two small hulls attached to either side of it. The mini hulls are used for storage. We will build these boats, and we will escape this country which will be punished by the wrath of God for their disobedience, for forsaking his laws. The people of this country have been blessed by God like no other people, and instead of obeying him, they have turned their backs on him. People no longer pray every day, they no longer fully support Israel, and they care more about issues like the environment than making this a strong country that has God-fearing men leading it, like George Washington and Abraham Lincoln. We must leave the country by the end of 1982. We must prepare to leave. You're on a sinking ship. You are drowning."

We sit still taking notes. "God will not bless you unless you keep his commandments. God has given you business after business to run, and you have failed. The ungodly people of this town protested when God has us clear cut the mountain and sell firewood. You did not make a profit selling firewood. God had you run a bakery, a restaurant, a thousand sheep, a thousand chickens, a thousand rabbits. If you want God to bless you, if you want him to help you, you must repent. As a corporation, you are three quarters of a million dollars in debt. God is saying to you, 'Wake up, work.' He will come upon you like a thief in the night. God is coming at any time. Will he find you ready?"

I have known all my life that the Lord might come at any time. The Rapture. The Lord will suddenly descend from the sky with a trumpet, with all his angels. The dead in Christ will fly up out of their graves and will be transformed from corpses. They will be given new and heavenly bodies. George always ended sermons on the Rapture with these words, "Then, we which are alive will rise and meet the Lord in the air, so will we ever be with the Lord." I heard those words many times. I have come back from walking, and found no one in the building and been terrified that I was being left behind.

For when the Lord comes, those whose names are not written in the Lamb's Book of Life will be left behind. I have woken up at night dreaming that I have been left behind, woken up sweating, frantic to see if the others are still in the room.

"Do you think we'll ever really like each other?" Nathan asks as they're walking down from school. The full wet air hangs around us; the leaves newly rained on drip.

"It's going to rain again."

"I know, what do you think?"

"We could; we're allowed to." I stop and look straight at him and he stops too. A slight rain begins, and the air, pregnant with moisture, moves around us in the wind. I am wearing a brown corduroy skirt, a shapeless thick grey sweater, glasses. My breasts are hidden as my mother taught me, my eyes are covered by my glasses. I never smile and show my teeth.

Nathan smiles rarely. His walk is angular, a boy who grew fast and never learned what to do with his knees and elbows. The straight lines between them seemed simpler. He turns to face me, his body straight.

"What do you want to do?" I ask.

"The right thing," he says, "that's all I ever want to do is the right thing."

We walk quietly, just the rain wetting our hair. "It's a cold summer," I say.

"We could touch each other," he says breaking off a branch and snapping the woody stem. His walk is a half march. His arms swing in rhythm. "At least we could hold hands."

"Why would we want to?" I say, and then look at him. His pale face, transparent as glass turns toward me. His green liquid eyes darken. I say, "I'm sorry, I mean."

"I know what you mean." I stop and hug him. I say, "Nathan, I love you," and he understands the bread crumb coating to the words. He knows I love him like a brother or a good sexless friend.

He says, "I love you too," earnestly, trying to put more into the words than my words, as if his words could drench me. The rain stops. He takes both my hands.

"What do you want to say?"

"What do you want to hear?"

"That you want."

"Yes."

"That you feel."

"Yes."

"I want to marry you. I think they'd let us. I want us to be together. We could be." I step back.

"Come on, what's wrong?"

"Can't we be friends without all that stuff?"

"I want to touch you." I stop and look up; the sun shines on wet leaves. His eyes follow mine. "I wonder if there'll be a rainbow," he says.

"Nothing's ever happened to me," I say.

He snaps a twig. "Can't you see yourself having children?"

"Can you? I can't see myself at all. I can't see myself doing anything." I watch the ground where I walk.

"We're allowed," he says.

"I know," I say. "I know. There isn't going to be a rainbow."

Weeks later, on a Sabbath Day, we've finished up the chores and are standing facing each other. Nathan is moving from one foot to the other. "I need time to be alone."

Nathan gives me a look, his blond brows pulled together. "I need time to pray." He nods.

"Okay," he says slowly, "there's nothing wrong with that. You sure you don't want me to go with you? We could pray together."

"Not this time," I say. "I just need to be alone this time." I look at him pleading to be forgiven and liked anyway. He takes one hand and kisses my forehead lightly. I hug him and say, "I love you, Nathan."

I call my dog Toby, put him on a bailing twine string. Together, we break into a run, and we run all the way down the school lane before we slow to a walk.

I found Toby a year ago, just wandering along a road, and Lucy let me keep him as long as I trained him. He is a mutt with silky long black hair, probably part Labrador. He is the only one who I am sure loves me.

During the six miles to Long Pond, I watch the cars going by. I wish I could walk anywhere, but I'm not sure where I would like to go. It's an unusually dry day, yellow dusty air blows up from the sides of the road, settles on my skin. A car passes with a California license plate. California, so far away, another country practically. The girls in the car are laughing, their heads thrown back. I can't think why they would be laughing.

At the pond, I dive into cold water, swim, and then sit on a rock looking out toward the island out in the middle. It was a big deal to be allowed to swim out to that island, one mile out. First we had to do it with someone paddling near by in a canoe, then we could do it alone. Swimming races, swimming the mile, I was good at that. A lot of kids were good at short races, and I wasn't, but I could swim a mile, two miles, clear, slow steady strokes.

A girl in a two piece swimsuit comes to sit beside me. "Where you from?" the girl asks.

"Six miles up the road." I am doing the forbidden, talking to a stranger. The girl is slender, tan, has a flat belly, and long waves of blond hair down her back. She tosses the hair.

"I'm visiting from California; it's cold here. What's your name?"

"Andie. How old are you?" I can't tell; there's something grown up about the girl, but she has the body of a twelve year old.

"Nineteen, you?"

"Eighteen." The girl looks at me as if searching for a compliment. I'm wearing an ugly one piece blue suit. My hair hangs wet and brown down my back, and I wear glasses.

"Nice day," the girl says, "see my parents, gotta go." She waves, and as she walks away, her long legs glow in the fading sun. Her butt twitches from side to side as if it were beckoning.

I start walking back, while Toby bounds along beside me. "You want to go California?" I ask him. He wags his tail and gives me a dog smile.

He seems more intelligent than most people I know. I take him on walks through the woods, and in a clearing, I would kneel with my arms around him. I love him more than any people I know.

Sometimes, when I walked with him down to Long Pond, I'd wonder what it would be like if just the two of us kept walking away from the Farm, never coming back. I'd stop, bury my face in Toby's neck, and say, "I love you, I love you. I love you."

Isaac and Rebecca

And he said to her, let down, I pray you,
thy pitcher and give me to drink. And Rebecca
said, I will get thee drink and thy camels also.

I see this woman kneel in wet earth,
her pitcher deep in the well, pouring
out water that slides into the man like life,
Sweat on her neck like slime.

The man tells her father, I want this woman,
to be my master Isaac's wife. Her father says, "Go,"
and she says, "Yes." "Yes" as she rides off
in darkness. "Yes," many days later, in a strange city.
A strange man, Isaac, lifts her down, smiles
until his teeth show. She follows him
to his tent, lies down where he tells her.
Says, my God. He gives her the blood of grapes
spilling down breasts and belly, into hard earth.

Chapter 17

I walk from School through the rain. Water falls through grey air, soaking my hair, soaking Toby. We smell like wet animals; we walk slowly. Toby's tail drips; my wet ponytail hangs down my back like a stick.

It is September; orange red leaves beaten by the early rains lie scattered on the road. I pick up a red maple leaf like a jagged heart and walk with it in one hand. The school kids will be back any time. George is back from BC. Hope called the day before to say that she is getting married to the same man she was in love with fifteen years before.

"After all this time, George gets married, and now you can," I said leaning wearily against the refrigerator door.

"I don't like the sound of your voice."

"I'm sorry, I'm happy for you, but wouldn't it have been more fun back when you were young?" I wouldn't say this to anyone else, but Hope is unlikely to tell on me.

"That was not the Lord's time for us, now I want you to repent."

"For what, now?"

"You know." I felt immediately angry with myself for not being kinder to my mother; Hope deserves a better daughter, but that's what Alexa's for.

I feel that I should be more interested in this marriage of my mother, but it seems far removed from me. I haven't seen much of my mother for the past few years, and I feel disconnected from Hope. My own problems seem weighty, and Hope's marriage is something that will happen whether I think about it or not.

At the Farm, I tie Toby outside and go in to comb my hair. I am to report to the office for a meeting with George. Don is the school headmaster again. When he called to tell me to come down Saturday afternoon for a meeting, I knew it wasn't good.

My face is a yellowish grey in the mirror, my hair flat, my eyes say nothing. I feel a dead knot in my belly, and I wonder just how bad it is this time.

I knock on the door of the office and hear George say, "Come in."

I hesitate a moment and open the door. It's bad, really bad, I can see that immediately. George and Mary sit facing me. On my right are Don and his wife, and on my left, Alexa and Hope.

"Close the door," and I feel it clang behind me like the gates of heaven shutting me out forever.

"We have been hearing about you," George says, and pauses. I think of what it could be, but nothing comes to my mind. No one knows about my talking to the girl at Long Pond. Maybe taking walks alone on Sabbath day, idle words, working too slowly on the boat crew; it could be anything.

"Alexa, would you repeat for us, what you told me earlier?" Everyone turns toward her, and I think, "This should be interesting," because I don't know a thing I've done that Alexa would know about, I hardly ever see Alexa.

Alexa's large nose lifts a little, and her jaw looks determined. Her whole square body, and chunky dark hair leans forward. Her elbows rest on the arms of the chair, and her fingertips press together, as if what she is about to say is infinitely wise and important.

"The other day," she begins, and George says,

"Exactly what day was it? It is important that we deal with facts."

"Thursday, day before yesterday. I was going through the hall, and I heard Andie talking on the phone." I keep my face unmoving, but I'm thinking, "talking on the phone," and wondering why nothing flashes through my mind that I said wrong. "She was talking to someone about a goat Nancy purchased for the Farm. She said, 'What a buy, stole the shirt right off his back.'" Alexa looks around triumphantly, for a moment her square face encounters my round one. Everyone looks at me. There is a moment of silence.

I'm thinking, "Okay, all right, so this is it?" I feel lonely. I feel like everyone in the room knows what is going to happen. The light slants in on my head and hands. Everyone else sits partially in shadow. I feel pale, invisible in contrast to Alexa's solidity and dark skin.

I remember Hope telling me that Alexa looks like her ex-husband. "He was Jewish," she said, as if he were already dead. "You take after my side of the family; we're Danes." I shiver. I try to remain still, I try to hold my face so it doesn't move. Across from me, is a round mirror facing the door. I see my grey eyes looking flat with soot pools in the middle.

"Implying that a saint could steal," George says each word slowly and distinctly. He looks at me, speaking each word slowly, letting me quiver on the edge of hellfire. "Andie," he stares me up and down, as though he is thinking of what to say, although I am always sure that it has been decided long ago.

I think of a verse we memorized, "For the children not being yet born, it was said, Jacob have I loved, and Esau have I hated." I remember my mother saying, "There's a black sheep in every family," and Hope looking at my blackness until I wanted to turn away.

"You have rebelled against the Holy Spirit throughout this whole summer. Your attitude stinks; it is from the devil." George looks at Don who throws back his head, a defiant shake.

"Andie has been rebellious. She has not been spending time with Nathan reading the word of God. She has been off by herself, thinking her own thoughts instead of staying with the fold. She has been seen reading books other than the Bible. She has not been open with anyone. She has not been telling anyone everything that she is thinking." His voice keeps going on. I wonder if Toby is okay. I think of walking down the mountain road with him, and what if we had just kept walking? When Don's voice finally stops, everyone looks at George.

"We are asking you to leave." The long silence that follows is broken only by Hope crying. I think suddenly of a story I heard of a man who was allowed to be king as long as he would consent to have a large sword hanging above him all day. I feel sweat break over my body. I move my arms a little, and they still move. The sword I have been waiting for all my life has fallen, and I am still alive. "The axe has fallen," George says in a deep rich voice like God or Satan. I keep standing there. I move one foot, and then the other. I open my mouth, but my lips are dry.

"I, I," everyone looks at me, "I'll go." Another long silence, the adults all look at each other surprised, questioning. Don stands up, stands over me.

"The voice of God is telling you to repent so that you may be accepted into the fold. Even now, you may be forgiven. Repent, on your knees, do not let Satan take over your mind," and I tremble like a sapling in a storm, and stumble to my knees.

"I pray God to cleanse this wicked girl in the blood of Christ for her wickedness for her rebellion against the Holy Spirit for not walking in the light," he says.

"Thank you Jesus," the others say.

"I pray to you, Lord Jesus that you bring this child of the devil out of the darkness in which she sits and make her a child of God."

"Thank you Jesus."

"Cast Satan out of her life. Give her a new heart, a new life, come into her heart that she may be transformed, made new and clean in thy sight."

"Thank you, Jesus."

"Andie, pray, I have prayed on your behalf. You pray."

"Lord Jesus, please forgive me for all my sins, for rebellion, for idle words, please cleanse me in your blood. Please make me clean."

"Thank you for dying on the cross for us," Mary prays.

"Thank you Jesus."

"And thank you for rising again on the third day," George says triumphantly.

"Thank you, Jesus." After what seems like hours of praying, George says, "Amen," and I glance at the wall clock, and see that it has been one hour since I entered the room at noon.

"Well, Andie," George says after a pause. Everyone is sitting in their chairs except for me. I am on my knees in the middle of the circle. "What do you have to say?" I know what to say. I have said it before.

"I have been forgiven, and my sins washed away by the blood of Jesus who died on the cross for me. I ask to be accepted back into the fold. Thank you Shepherd of the sheep for catching me before I strayed too far." But I don't say the words. I don't say any words because so many are spinning through my head.

I want to sleep. I want to be alone. I want to be away. I want to walk with Toby. I want to close my eyes and open them to find everybody gone. I feel sure that the room is getting smaller, stuffier, that the walls are closing in.

"I'll leave," I say, and I hear my own voice as though it were coming from far away, outside my body, through miles of clear flowing water. I listen to the words and wonder if that is how my voice sounds. "I have been asked to leave. I'll leave," and it seems such a relief to say it. The words come so easily; they want to come.

"You don't have to . . ." Don begins, but George cuts him off.

"Go pack your things," and I stand up, feel my body is weightless. I hold onto the doorknob for support. "You are dismissed." As the door closes behind me, I hear Hope crying. I turn in the doorway, looking again at all of them. The corners of Alexa's lips turn up.

While I'm tossing my clothes into a green utility sack, I look up to see Hope in the doorway. Her face is red, her eyes swollen. "I'm sorry I won't be able to see you get married," I say, not sure what I should say, but wanting to say something.

"You'll never make it," Hope says in a whisper. "You'll be broke or lose your virginity in two weeks." Her hand slips over mine, and I look down at that hand, small, the raised blue veins. I hold the two dollars my mother has given me, wonder what the dollars will do for me. It is the first money I have ever had. I wonder if two dollars will get me a place to stay.

"Can I write to you?"

"When you leave here, you are no longer part of the family of God. You are one of those who has fallen by the wayside." She's still whispering, shaking her head, her eyes looking huge and dark in her white face.

Suddenly Hope throws her arms around me, and I take a step back to catch my balance. "I love you," she whispers into my hair, and I can't think of any words. I wanted my mother to love me all my life.

I remember writing to her that one of the counselors had made me stick my head in a garbage pail for fifteen minutes for speaking idle words. I remember writing to her of being beaten. I wanted my mother to champion my cause, to show me love, to do something. But she never did, and I've given up hoping that my mother feels anything for me at all. And now she's hugging me, minutes before I walk out the door.

I won't be allowed back. George will never let me see her again. I can hold this hug, this love, the words in my hair, I can hold them forever, like a desert woman holds her last water for a trek across sand.

Then she's gone, gliding out of the room, afraid, and I'm getting my bailing twine string for Toby's leash, and Alexa comes in. I look at her, standing with her hands on her hips, standing over me, as I kneel on the floor tying my bag shut. I don't say anything until I'm standing up, standing over Alexa by two inches, feeling good because of my height. Then I smile, a real smile, a laughing smile, because there's nothing anyone can do about it, and Alexa frowns.

"Be good to Hope," I say, "you're all she's got. You should have been her only daughter anyway," and Alexa doesn't say anything, like she's been expecting something else.

I say, "Well, this is it sister, shall I write?" I don't know why I say this, but it pops into my head. The sensation of being able to say something just because it popped into my head is too exciting.

"You're not my sister any more," Alexa says lifting her broad nose like that's what she has been waiting to say. Her small eyes narrow.

I think of Pinocchio saying to the fox, "Adios, false friend," but I don't say it. I say, "Here Toby." He lopes over from his place in the corner. I tie on the string and leave the room, pulling Toby, forcing myself to whistle, forcing myself not to look back.

On the hill of the school, as I start down the lane, I turn back. The afternoon sun is setting in front of me and reflecting on the tin roof of the new barn. The front door is open, and inside I see the animals sitting quietly in their small cages waiting to be fed and watered. I wonder about dinner. I shiver; it's going to be an early winter.

As I walk down the slope, I see beside the road, a clump of dying water moccasins. I reach down and pick one.

I Am Not Pretty

I cannot listen to you, sir.
There is one way to walk, you say, left, right.
The children in this place write their names
last name first, Gale, Andie.

Andie, Andie, Andie, I repeat
making the word more than God's name.
You can't even see God, you know that?
You can't even see him.

By the left quick, march.
Company halt.
Stand up straight.
Like men, like soldiers.

You pour my child bones into
your soldier hands
and crunch them
and crunch them.

I admit I was not good.
I wasn't even pretty.

You said I was God's daughter.
God wants us
to be soldiers.
He takes a child
and makes it march, left right.

I cannot listen to you.
But I hear anyway, at night, now.
Left, right, daughter of God.
Scrub that floor, soldier, and I kneel,

and I am not always good,
and I am not pretty.

Chapter 18

September air blows cold around my face as I walk down the lane and out onto the tar road. The sky is empty of clouds; the road curves down into the woods. My green utility sack is slung over one shoulder, and I hold a bailing twine string with Toby trotting at the end. I'm not sure where I'm walking or what I'll do when I get there. I think about sleeping with Toby on the ground, and I feel good. I'm used to sleeping on the ground, and I have a sleeping bag in my green sack.

I walk past a row of tamarack trees and remember myself in Nursery School being allowed to spend a day with my mother. We were walking through the woods, and Hope was teaching me the names of trees. "Oak, maple, elm, beech, birch, tamarack."

"Hatmatack," I said, and then because I liked the sound, "Hatmatack, hatmatack." I remember now that it must have been September then, too. The leaves of the trees were turning, the wind was blowing and the dark green needles of the tamarack trees tossed in a sea of gold. I knelt in a pile of leaves and buried my head, and then crawled under the leaves. We had only been at the Farm about a year, and my mother laughed, one of the last times I ever heard my mother laugh, the laugh ringing through the gold and crimson trees. Hope dived under the leaves, and we were buried together. We lay still under the leaves for a while, and I remember how my mother understood just wanting to lie still not doing anything or saying anything. We watched the clouds flying wherever clouds want to fly.

Today is a colder day than that one was. "Hatmatack," I say out loud, "hatmatack." Toby turns, wagging his tail, "Where do you want to go, Toby?" and the dog follows me, confident that I know where I am going. "All roads lead somewhere," I tell the dog. I remember George saying that only the wicked say that all roads lead to the same place. "Broad is the gate that leads to destruction. Straight is the gate and narrow the way that leads to life and few there be that find it."

The sun sets, and the broad road stretches out in front of me. I leave the road, looking for a tree to sleep under. I feel excited, like someone in a story book. I am alone at night, sleeping under the stars. The dog lies beside my sleeping bag; no one knows where I am. I kiss Toby. As I go to sleep, I think, "I could be a princess, and no one would know it. Who knows who my father is? He could be a king somewhere, and I could be a princess, and no one would ever know."

I dream. I am at the Farm, and we are having a skip and sing. We stand in two circles, one inside the other, and we sing, "It's bubbling, it's bubbling, it's bubbling in my soul. They're singing and shouting since Jesus made me whole."

We had sing-skips before every meal, and every Friday evening for two or three hours. Sometimes we held hands and skipped and sang in pairs. We skipped barefoot, so our shoes wouldn't get worn.

I am skipping barefoot, but my feet hurt, and I am out of beat with the other skippers. I don't want to skip any more, but George stands on his chair and blows his whistle twice, which means reverse. Everyone reverses except me, and everyone barrels past me, the wind of their motion forcing me down, and I lie there on the floor while they all skip by, and no one stops and looks for me. It is as if I'm not there. I wake myself screaming, and Toby jerks awake and licks my face.

It's cold and the sun is rising. There's no point trying to go back to sleep because once you wake up outdoors, the cold and discomfort drag you onto your feet and keep you there. I pull out a worn Bible. Inside the flyleaf, is my name, "Andie Gale," and it says, "4/25/77." It was a gift for my fourteenth birthday from my mother. I turn the page not wanting to think of my mother, and I read Psalms 1-4.

I feel something that keeps distracting me from reading, and although I recognize the feeling, I ignore it. I've been hungry before, when I disobeyed and had to go without meals for a day, or when I was locked in a room, and they gave me one meal a day for a week.

I walk more slowly than yesterday, and Toby seems impatient. We drink from a stream, and I feel even hungrier. I try not to think about food, but I keep feeling sure that since it's Sunday, they're having muffins, applesauce, yoghurt and cottage scramble (scrambled eggs mixed with cottage cheese). I could be back at the school in an hour or two.

And then, across the road, a rabbit runs out from under a bush. Toby takes off, his twenty-four hours with no food eating at his belly, and I watch like I'm watching the hands of a clock, relentlessly, slowly turn toward the hour of execution. I hear the car coming before it is on us, the noise seems unbearable, the car screaming to a stop, my own voice screaming and echoing inside my head as if my head were horribly hollow; Toby's silky dog body in mid-leap flattens with a dog scream. When I reach him, he is not quite dead, he opens his eyes and then closes them. I drag him over to the side of the road, and lean over him, my hair and his mixing in the dirt and sweat and cold autumn sunlight. I feel for a heart beat that isn't there. I kiss his face and his cold wet nose, and the driver leaning over me says something. I can never remember what he says, or what I say. I should have said, "I live around here, I'll take care of this, you can keep going, it was my fault," but I'm not sure if I said anything, or if those words just went around in my head.

I stay there all day. It takes me until late afternoon to dig with a stick and my hands, a hole big enough to bury him so animals won't dig him up. I cover his body with pine branches, with dirt, with rocks. I fall asleep sitting up beside the grave and wake up lying across it.

My whole body is empty, the stomach walls rumble and crash against each other. My heart feels like an empty room; my head feels light and weightless on my shoulders. I think about staying where I am for a long time, just lying on the extra pine boughs; it seems like a good place. I go back to sleep.

I walk more slowly. By afternoon, my stomach pains have subsided to a dull ache. I could go back, I think. I remember my mother whispering to me, "You'll be back, you won't make it." For dinner tonight, they might be having stew, big chunks of potatoes, carrots, onions, beef, and then cornbread to go with it. I feel faint. I can't remember why I wanted to leave in the first place. I see a mobile home off the side of the road, and stop to comb my hair. When I have combed all the tangles out, I straighten my clothes, walk to the door and knock.

"Excuse me," I say to the woman who answers. "Can I have a drink of water?"

"Sure, come in," and I step inside. The woman sticks out her hand, "Beth," she says. I carefully consider the hand, take it in both of mine, hold it, press it, and let it go. Beth looks at me oddly, "Like Seven-Up?"

"Yes, please," I say wondering what I am being offered and hoping it's a kind of food.

Beth is sitting in front of what appears to be a large glass box. I don't want to appear stupid, so I don't ask about it, but I notice that someone is talking from it. I know the box must be a television. I wait to see what the television will do. "Look, sit down, I taped the Royal Wedding, have you seen it, want to see it? Look at Princess Diana's dress, will you? She had to be a virgin for him to marry her. Can you beat that? But Chukkie was no virgin. There's no justice. Sit down. My old man's out of town."

"Your father?"

"No, my husband, wantta beer? Watcha doin anyway?"

"Walking, looking for work."

"Look at them kissin, willya? Willya?"

"I am looking. I see them kissing."

"Goddamn rich people get everything, but I've gotta rich aunt's gonna die sometime, look at 'em holdin hands, wantta sandwich, I'm gettin another beer."

"Yes, please."

"Here's a sub, hope you don't mind ham, I bet she is so happy."

"She looks happy. Thank you for the sandwich."

"Where your folks?"

"My folks, meaning, the people I come from? My parents?"

"Yeah."

"I'm on my own."

"Yeah, I was on my own at sixteen; that's when I met my old man. I'd let you stay here but my old man comes home, finds someone here, he's gonna kill me."

"Kill you?"

"You be careful." Beth is tall, and I get the impression of a tree bending over me, the trunk thick, masses of thick blond hair, everything large; large hands, large nose, a large behind that wobbles when she walks. Beth says, as if sensing my stare, "I look great in clothes, my old man met me, I was decked."

"But you have on clothes now."

"I mean, dressed to kill."

"To kill?"

"Old man's a truck driver, God, look at that dress. I'm rewinding this." She gets another beer. "What's your name?"

"Andie."

"Andie, I'll tell you something. You want to hear something. Princess Diana's probably been screwed by now, and I'll tell you a first screwing is nothing special, nothing special at all. You probably already know that."

I shake my head.

"First time my old man and I did it," she says. I try to make myself think about something else. I'm sure this is the sort of thing I could go to hell for hearing, but my ears seem to be practically bending in Beth's direction. "I'm drunk at a party, I'm drunk off my ass, and I pass out, and I wake up, and there's this face above me, and it's his face, but I can't even tell for sure, and I don't even scream I'm so out of it, and this face is like some horrible mask. It's distorted. He was just in the act of coming, and when a man comes, his face is changed like some goblin. God, it was horrible." Her face closes for a moment, and she shakes herself as she remembers. "I shut my eyes now when we screw."

"Sex." I say the word slowly, hearing my own voice say it for the first time.

"It's nothing terrific. I bet that's what Diana's thinking right now. She's saying to herself. Well, this wasn't all it's cracked up to be."

"Then why do you talk about it?"

"Sex," Beth says, leaning back in a chair, a beer in one hand, her other hand thrust into a bag of potato chips. "Sex, is America's favorite pastime."

"I thought you said it's nothing terrific."

"I know, but it's supposed to be. In movies and television, it's terrific. That's America's second favorite pastime, watching sex on movies and television where it's better than real life." She tosses the beer can into a heap in the corner and gets another. "You better get the hell out of here. My old man's gonna kill me when he gets home. He's gonna kill me for drinking his beer. We always fight, then screw. Nice meeting you."

She opens the door, and a cold wind blows in from outside. I step out into the blue green light of a September evening. I hear the tape playing again, Prince Charles saying, "I do." I wish I could have seen the whole wedding start to finish and maybe found out what happened afterward.

Before Teddy, I had a friend in first grade who came to the school in long pigtails. Grace didn't hesitate. "Turn around Melissa," she said, and we stopped to watch. Grace held up the long red pigtails with pink bows at the end and snipped them off. They thudded to the floor, and Melissa stood dead still. "Now don't cry," Grace said.

"I don't care," Melissa said in a still voice. "But my Daddy isn't going to like it." She turned toward Grace, "He'll get you." Grace raised both hands like a witch ready to throw thunderbolts, and the door opened. Melissa's father said.

"Hello, may I speak with you, Grace?" Grace's claws melted into the open soft hands of a loving mother.

"What can I do for you?" He looked at Melissa's hair but didn't say anything. Grace picked up the pigtails and went to talk with him holding his daughter's hair in her hands.

I heard, bit by bit, the rest of the story of Melissa's father, Tom Mountain. He had heard George preaching in Washington D.C., had moved his restoration of antiques to Vermont, bought a few acres of George's property and built a house. His daughter was allowed to go the school, but he was not allowed to be part of the Farm Family. He had questioned something George had done, and he was never allowed to talk with George face to face again. I heard that it had to do with George's wife, who hadn't been allowed to stay at the Farm. She had loved God, but not in the right way. As soon as she was sent away, young Mary moved in with George, and maybe, it was said, Tom Mountain questioned this.

Tom Mountain's own beautiful wife had just divorced him because she did not want to be a Christian. Long hot hours he had sat in divorce court, watching her tiny waist bend. Her long blond curls that he had thought were soft now looked harsh in the court room's unforgiving glare. She accused him while he thought of how intimate they once were. Her Danish accent that he had thought was so charming, sounded like some cruel caricature of the mean wife.

I heard all this, filtered through many people. "Who knows," I thought, "how much of it is true by the time it reaches me?" But what I remember most clearly, what I will always remember is Melissa going home to her Dad one weekend. Her dad didn't bring her back and from the way the grownups whispered, something was wrong. Maybe she was sick, maybe she had been kicked out; it all seemed rather strange.

There had been intermittent thunderstorms all weekend, and the lights were out to save electricity. Don called us together in the octagon. Eerie, muddy yellow-green light washed in behind him from the picture windows. The lightning crackled down the sky like jagged knives, thunder stamping behind it. Don opened the Bible and read, "And God shall visit the sins of the fathers on the children to the third and fourth generation." He closed the Bible. "God keeps his promises. He punishes the wicked." He punched the table with his fist. "He punishes the children of the wicked. God is a just God, a merciful God, but he punishes sin."

I thought about my father, what sins he had committed, probably was committing right then. I had never really heard what type of sinner he was, but I liked to think of him as one of the worst kind of sinners. I never felt he would be a mediocre halfhearted sinner, but a big sinner. He could be drinking or smoking, he might be saying idle words. He might be taking the name of God in vain, forgetting to keep the Sabbath Day holy. When I thought about my father, sometimes I hoped he was being good and would go to heaven. Other times, I just hoped he was having a good time. I would think, "Well, if I were going to be a sinner, I would really do it wholeheartedly, I would enjoy myself if I were a sinner."

"God has taken our sister, Melissa, to a better place. She was struck by lightning while walking by the lake with her father."
No one speaks. No one moves. I can feel my own breath going in and out. "She is in God's hands. Let us sing, 'Holy, holy, holy, Lord, God Almighty, all thy saints shall praise thy name in earth and sky and sea.'" We all sing, our voices rising and falling like sobs, drowning out the loud silence.

Tom's house is set back on his lot, but the high roof shows above the trees. In an area of white farmhouses and solid brown cabins,

Tom's house stands out. He designed it himself, and I've ridden by it many times on horseback when I was out riding with Teddy. Sometimes Tom came out and said, "Hello." I always wondered what his house looked like up close.

Through the trees, one can see that it is large and full of angles and windows. I approach late in the afternoon and knock on one of the doors. Tom opens it, "Hello, what can I do for you?"

"Do you remember me?"

"Yes, yes, of course, you're Andie."

"Well, I left the Farm, and I'm looking for work."

"Come in."

He moves awkwardly, a man used to being alone. "Can I look at your house? I've always wanted to see it."

"Look around," he says. "Don't mind the mess. Maybe you can help me clean." The house is big, sprawling and unfinished. It has three floors. The first floor is all antique restoration. One whole wall is all sloping windows that look out on a garden. The second floor has bedrooms, a kitchen, a living room that has large windows with window seats. The windows look out on the gardens and fruit trees. Between the first and second story, a large area of floor is thick glass blocks. Between the second and third floor, a corresponding area of floor is plexiglass, and above that is a skylight. So in the middle of the house, light floods down through a tunnel and throws shadows in the dirty corners of the house. Books, dust, papers and tools are everywhere.

"What a wonderful house this would be if you finished it, and cleaned it up," I say.

"I've been living alone a long time. You smell like pine and earth."

"You smell like cheese and English muffins." Both of us half smile. "Can I use the restroom?"

He points at it, and I go in, just to look in the mirror and catch my breath. I feel dazed. I look at my reflection. I look pale. My eyes look huge in my white face, and my long brown hair hangs around my face.

I go out in the living room and sit down across from Tom. I haven't seen him up close for years, and I had forgotten that his eyes are so brown and sad.

"Why did you leave?" he asks, motioning for me to sit down and scooping papers off one end of a couch. I explain briefly, and he doesn't say anything, just presses his hands together, and when I stop talking he fixes me an English muffin with melted cheese. "You know how to type?" he calls from the kitchen.

"Yes, I do."

"Well, good, you can start tomorrow. You can clean up the house and type. I'll pay you four dollars an hour."

"When should I be here?"

"Nine o'clock will be fine."

When I get to the door, he says, "I'll walk you down the driveway. Where are you staying?"

"I'm going to ask Emma's family if I can stay with them. Right now, nowhere, outside I mean."

"I'm sure you understand why I shouldn't have you stay here," he says.

"Yes," I say although I have no idea, "that's okay, thank you for the job. See you tomorrow." I wave to him and feel happiness.

I walk three or four miles to Emma's house, and knock on the door. Emma opens it, wearing a tight sweater. Her breasts curve under it, her hair is long and curly, and she's laughing. "What are you doing?" she says, "Come on in, want dinner?"

Emma's parents moved up from New York City, bought one of the lots and built a house on it. There had been some trouble about her father who had been divorced, but insisted on continuing to live with his second wife by whom he had seven children. She was pregnant with their eighth when George told her father that it was against the law of God for a man to marry again if he had been divorced.

All of his kids except one were expelled from the school for one reason or another. The one who stayed, as soon as she was of age, refused to see or speak with her parents. Emma's dad was round, bald, and told a lot of jokes. Her mom was very pretty, small, laughed at his jokes and cooked good food.

Emma's hair is in curlers and her fingernails and toenails are newly polished. "I'm so glad to see you. How you been?"

"Fine."

"Sit down, want something to eat?"

"Yes, please."

Emma opens a bag of potato chips and throws it on the living room table. "Don't make a mess. Mom'll kill us."

"You call her 'Mom?'"

"Course I do. I'm, not living at the Farm any more."

Over peas, mashed potatoes and roast beef, they ask where I am staying. I say, "Right now it's a question of under what tree, but I have a job, so I'm going to find a place. I just don't know how to do it."

Emma says, "Come on, Mom, Dad, let her stay in my room. I got two beds."

Her father says, "No rough housing at night, fifty dollars a week." Emma and I kick each other joyfully under the table like we used to do at the Farm.

In a week Tom pays me one hundred-sixty in cash, and I leave on Friday night feeling very rich, so much money; making money is so easy. I have cleaned the house spotlessly one room at a time. Tom comes up for lunch from the studio, and I fix us sandwiches or soup. He says I am doing a good job and gives me a hint of a smile. No one has ever told me, "Good job," and I like it.

Emma's room has a big open closet with stacks of Emma's sweaters, skirts and blouses hanging up; pictures of Emma are all over the place, in all of them, Emma is laughing. Emma lies on her bed, legs up, and looks at the ceiling. "So, tell me everything," she says. She begins to pump her legs.

"They asked me to leave,"

"Because?"

"I was getting to that. Because, I said, 'stole the shirt off her back,' talking about somebody who is a saint like they could steal."

"Who ratted?"

"Ratted?"

"Who was the slime ball who told on you? Spilled their guts, did their bit for George?"

"Alexa."

"If you don't mind my saying so, she's one terrific sister. I'll tell you something else, you know our counselor Sue, remember she had the baby at the end?"

"Yeah, he's real cute, he . . ."

"Did ya ever notice that after they had that little rushed wedding, that they had the baby which was no preemie, I can tell you, eight months later?" she asks.

"I don't know what you're saying."

"You are so dense, so pitifully dense. You swallow all their garbage. Listen, they had sex before they got married. They did it." She laughs into my face. I see a brief vision of dogs in the back yard.

"I don't want to hear this, I don't believe it."

"All right, all right, so how dy'a like it so far?" she asks seriously.

"You mean, being out? Okay, I guess. I think I like it."

"Wait till you meet some boys."

"I don't want to meet any boys. I just want to save money, and leave, maybe be a travelling fruit picker. I gotta get away. When I was walking over here, Liza saw me and pretended she didn't. I can't keep walking around here."

Emma lies on her back pumping an imaginary bicycle. "Oh, they all pretend you're a walking corpse, come to think of it, they might be more polite to a corpse. Heard from your mother?"

"No."

"You're dead to her, don't sweat them. Listen, I got an idea, let's walk by the Farm and ignore them." She laughs hysterically at this idea.

"That would help." I say frowning.

Emma laughs and rolls around on the bed. "Just kidding, gosh, you're so serious."

"Nothing's funny."

"Lighten up, wouldya? Lots of things are funny." Emma looks at me for a moment in earnest, her pretty face serious. "I swear," she says, "Life is good," and then she starts laughing again.

Mother Troubles

I have trouble remembering
my mother's name
your own mother? you poor thing
how long has it been? ten years

I have trouble remembering
the raised veins in her hands
how she rubbed away
many headaches

Lying in her lap I could see her face
from below, jaw jutting into a V
I lay on her lap
her fingers on my forehead

I don't remember what she said
last I saw her, not much
she was busy, brushed her hands
through air, said, I have to go
back
to work, put her hands
in her grey hair
said she liked the last picture
I'd sent I looked more natural

I can't make out
what you're saying to me
I didn't love her
I don't think she ever loved me

We were separated early
I remember little of our visits
before I left she pressed my head
between her breasts where secrets kept

whispered, do not forget me
I don't know
what she could mean
by that

I am blank
on the subject of my mother
it is impossible
for me

to write anything
about her
without remembering
her hands

on my forehead
in her hair
with raised veins
protecting her blood.

Chapter 19

Taking off is the hard part. After letters and a couple phone calls, my mother's parents invite me to visit them in Colorado. Now I'm flying for the first time. The plane rumbles down the runway, and I keep thinking about collisions. Then it's off, and I feel air under me. Looking down, I see Logan Airport, fast disappearing, an unimportant detail in a collage of houses, little people, little lives.

I think for a moment, "I can do anything I want, fill in the blank," but the sky around the plane, outside the window, is all grey-white, and I can't see through it, and nothing comes to my mind that I would like to do. The little land of make-believe below me, the dolls' cars disappear in a mask of silky white clouds. And as I sink back in my chair, the flight attendant offers me soda and peanuts.

I open my Bible, close my eyes and lay my finger on one page. At the Farm, this is considered to be a good way of finding out the will of God. I hope to see, "The eternal God is thy refuge, and underneath are the everlasting arms."

I open my eyes and read, "The firstborn said unto the younger, I lay last night with my father, let us make him drink wine tonight, and thou lie with him . . . thus were both the daughters of Lot with child by their father." I close the book, close my eyes, and turn the pages. I read, "And the children not yet being born, Jacob had I loved, and Esau had I hated," and I know I am Esau, and my sister Jacob, and looking out the window, I feel hot tears on my face.

Coming down to Stapleton feels like coming down to a desert. The clouds have disappeared, and as we begin to descend, the brown earth spreads out under me. The wheels hit the runway with a bump, and I grit my teeth and wish I hadn't come. I miss the green of Vermont; I miss the wet air.

When I walk off the plane, my grandmother talks without stopping; the flow of words does not need breath; it washes around my head, and I look at my grandfather's white-haired handsome profile. His doctorate must have been in thinking, my grandmother's in talking, I think. He smiles but doesn't say anything. My grandmother's voice goes on about the history of Fort Collins. She says she is writing a book on the subject. She points out square brick buildings and says they are beautiful, historical.

"We're going to stop at one of our favorite places to eat," she says as we pull in to Furrs Cafeteria. The food looks like food at the Farm, an institutional mass of Jello and pork chops. I take a bowl of red Jello. "Aren't you hungry?" my grandmother says, "Call me Granny."

I look at my grandfather. "Call him Grandpa. Now, we wanted to know what you are planning to do while you're here because we're hoping you'll want to go see your cousin play football. You know you have two cousins; your cousin Jennifer is in high school. Your cousin Charles is graduating this year. You'll want to go to their school."

Granny's voice keeps going; the noise of it swirls around me as I look out the window, stirring my Jello until it begins to liquefy. "Are you going to stay in Colorado?" My grandmother's voice sounds like she's repeating a question. I jerk my head around.

"I don't think I'll stay long. I have to go back," and as I say it, I feel relief that I'll be leaving this brown flat land and whatever expectations these people have for me. When I wrote to them and wanted to come visit, I thought I would feel safe with them. I thought I would feel like I had come home, but I don't feel like I've come home at all. I feel completely outside. They seem to have actual ideas about me, ideas that I will do things I'm not sure if I can do. I want to go back, I want to fail alone where no one expects anything of me.

"Give us a chance," Granny says.

At their house she says, "This is your room. The basement living room will be just for you. There's the television. Here's a radio. I've left make-up in the bathroom for you so you can do your face. We're going to a play tonight. We'll let you relax a couple hours before dinner."

I turn the knob on the radio, but nothing happens. I'm not sure, but I think it should start talking to me like a tape machine. It sits there, a brown silent box, no voices in it.

In the bathroom, I find the make-up. I pour the brown liquid from a bottle into my hand. It looks like tigers milk, a mixture of milk, honey, molasses, brewer's yeast and vanilla that we drank every day at the Farm. I taste it, but the taste is dull and chalky. I smear some on my hands and face, and they look dirty. My face looks streaked with drying mud.

I wash it all off and open a small tube of stuff that looks like colored toothpaste. It says on the bottom, "lipstick," and I have seen women with colored lips. I rub the stuff on my lips and look in the mirror at myself. My lips are orange; my face is white, my eyes a dead unsmiling green. But with my lips colored, I look like someone else, someone older, a woman. I don't want to be a woman, and I wash off the lipstick.

I go to the living room and sit in front of the strange glass box, a television, my grandmother had said. It is like the thing in Beth's house. I wonder if I will see The Royal Wedding if I turn it on. I pull a button and turn it. A green other-world glow lights the screen, and gradually coming into focus is the face of a man. "Welcome," a voice says, "to Fantasy Island."

For dinner, I eat a donut that doesn't taste like a donut. "It's a bagel," my grandmother says and hands me white stuff that looks like white butter. "Cream cheese, smear it on the bagel, haven't you ever had cream cheese? It's good. It's actually kind of a Jewish food, but we love it. How do you like it? What kind of food did you eat on the Farm? Sarah never kept in close touch with us you probably know."

"She's called 'Hope.'"

"Well, we named her Sarah Jr. after me, and I see no reason to start calling her anything different now just because she's decided that she wants to have her name changed. She used to be contrary when she was young. I could tell you some things." Granny's voice pours over the table, rippling down between the plates. "What plays do you like?"

"I've never seen a play."

"Well, this should be a good experience."

The play is "The Mousetrap." We arrive early and sit down. My grandparents chat with friends who come in as the audience settles in around them. I feel alone in a sea of faces all turned expectantly toward the stage. I remember sitting in meetings, everyone turned toward George.

The play begins, people moving on stage creating a story, living a story before our eyes, and the audience watches that life, there in the dark. During the intermission, Granny explains acting, "See, these people take acting lessons, and they learn how to get up there on stage and act out a story. Of course, there are film actors too, they act out stories on screen, you've seen films, and television, no, you probably haven't. Well, we have this strange system in this country. Actors for film and television have that job, and people worship them like royalty."

"Just for acting?"

"Yes, some of them aren't even nice people, some are immoral, but they are worshipped, they're called celebrities. Do you like the play?"

"Yes, I think so, it's hard to say yet."

During the last half of the play, I hardly move. The actors live and breathe on stage. I remember camping trips when we ate by the fire and we'd see, in the darkness, the shining reflection of animal eyes watching us. In the darkness, I feel like an animal crouching outside the circle of light, watching the humans play out their lives but knowing that I will never be human.

I wrap a blanket around me. I sit on a high white bench overlooking the football field. Light rain falls on my shoulders and hair. "Do you want to get under my umbrella?" my aunt says. She looks like I expected; blond, assured, smiling.

"I like the feel of rain," I say.

"Won't you catch cold?"

"No, I don't catch cold from rolling in the snow in my underwear or from sleeping outside in the winter or from swimming in April."

"I see," my aunt says. She has a broad face, long braids and grey eyes. Her manner is business like, polite, her hands move through the air in a gesture that forgives me for my strangeness. "Well, how do you like sitting up in the bleachers watching football in the rain?"

"Bleachers?"

"These benches are called bleachers. See Charles down there, they're putting him in the game now. He's number 34."

From up there it looks ridiculous. I have played soccer, and I think it must be something like soccer, but the ball looks like a squashed banana. While I can see that the players are trying to move the ball from one end of the field to the other, they seem to be breaking all the rules of soccer. This game seems to have no rules. The boys charge recklessly around. They don't have any positions that they stick to. They all dive into heaps on top of the ball, a large pile of boys. They wear the most ridiculous clown outfits, huge shoulder pads, tight pants that show off their butts. "Aren't football pants sexy," my cousin says, watching the field breathlessly.

"If you say so," I say, and Jennifer laughs. A whistle blows and I jump; but the whistle is for the boys. They stop, get up from the heap they have fallen in.

"How long will you be staying?"

"Till next week," I say, and they all turn toward me for a minute.

"Why leaving so soon?" my aunt asks, and I shake my head hoping the tears on my face look like rain. I feel alien, like I am still watching the play. They are all the actors, and I don't know how to get on stage. I've never had any acting lessons. My grandparents and aunt laugh at something, and Jennifer laughs too. I don't laugh; I'm afraid that they're laughing at me.

When my aunt takes me to the airport, we shake hands awkwardly. Her voice sounds so much like Hope's that I keep getting spooked and jumping. On the plane, I relax and eat my peanuts.

As soon as I return, Emma's parents tell me that they need for me to move. I am never sure why this happens. They say that they need more room because one of their other children is moving back. I realize this may not be the real reason. I am learning that sometimes one should not ask the real reason. I go looking for another place to stay.

I'm at the library one evening after working at Tom's house. I spend a lot of time there reading everything I was never supposed to read, and when I get ready to check out a book, the librarian says, "Aren't you from the Farm?"

"How can you tell?"

"You all have the same look."

"I left the Farm. I'm looking for a place to live; the family I'm living with, their kids are moving back. I gotta get out." I say this all in a breath, I've been thinking about it all night. It's October, and below freezing every night. I told Emma's Mom I'd be out by the end of the week, and I have no idea where I'll be going.

The librarian says, "I got a full house, but I've got a friend with an extra room to rent. I'll talk with her. Come back tomorrow night."

I go in the bathroom to look at myself in the mirror; I want to see what the librarian saw, to see how I still look like the Farm. I heard my cousins talking about people being "good looking" or "cute." It is a quality they want in people they date. I have never thought about anyone's looks. I do not know whether anyone I know is good looking or whether I am.

I look to see what the librarian saw. I wear loose clothing, loose hair hanging around my white face that looks like a moon, round and smooth and expressionless. My eyes look wet and pleading. I look forgotten, I think, and then hate that word, "forgotten," and wonder whether my mother still remembers me.

The next night the first light snow falls as the librarian and I knock on Charlie's door. Charlie's husband answers it. He is tall, and has a huge black beard, that makes me think of old prophets, possibly Jeremiah, I'm not sure, Jeremiah, or Elijah. His name turns out to be Rick. He smiles, and his teeth show. Rick introduces his wife Charlie who has a face as round as an apple, an apron on, and flour on one cheek. She shows me a room in the attic with two beds, and tells me to be comfortable.

Left alone, I explore the room. I don't want to go down and see Rick; I hear him talking with his wife, maybe about me. Maybe I have already done or said something offensive. I can't remember anything I said except, "here" when I gave the first week's rent of fifteen dollars. I hope that I said, "Thank you" when Charlie showed me the room, but I realize I probably didn't because at that moment, I'd thought she heard a noise on the stair like Rick coming.

The ceiling slants down over one bed, and the wallpaper above the bed is peeling. I have seen beds before but have never slept in one. When I visited Hope, I slept in a sleeping bag on the floor beside her. At the Farm, we slept in sleeping bags on the floor. I try lying on the bed. It is a funny little raised platform. I lie on the floor, but I'm not sure if maybe I should lie on the bed. What if Rick caught me lying on the floor? I get up on the bed, and look at the ceiling. In the corner of the room are stacks of magazines.

I only take food from the family when it is offered. I usually buy a pound of grapes and a package of Hostess Snowballs to eat for dinner. I buy these at the little corner market, and go to my room in the attic. I climb in bed with the grapes and snowballs and read the magazines.

When Tom Mountain runs out of jobs for me to do, I get a job at the ski resort where Emma works, and I hitchhike back and forth.

I come back to ask Charlie about words I heard at work. "What does 'get out of the fucking way' mean?"

"It just means to get out of the way." Charlie raises all her own vegetables in the summer, cans them in the fall, slaughters a lamb in late fall for freezing and cards her sheep's wool during the winter. She stops carding the wool, and gets up to stir the stew which smells wonderful. It's the smell of a country stew, mushrooms, peppers, lamb, potatoes, carrots, onions, rutabaga, herbs, all sizzling together.

"But what does the word, 'fucking' mean? It must be an adjective of some sort, but it's not in the dictionary."

"To fuck," Charlie says, sitting down again, "means to have sex."

"I see. What does that have to do with getting out of the way?"

"Nothing, it's an expression people use."

"Could I use it? Could I say, I'm pretty fucking hungry?"

"You could, you certainly could, but it would be considered not very ladylike; it's bad language."

"I see."

Upstairs under the sloping roof, I fall asleep reading magazines, and wake up to hear a loud thump. My head hurts, although I'm not sure why. I was dreaming about being beaten by Don. George was smiling, and my mother was clapping and singing, "I may never march in the infantry, ride in the cavalry, shoot the artillery, and I may never fly o'er the enemy, but I'm in the Lord's army," and then I'd tried to get away from Don, and run to my mother. I tried to say, "He's hurting me," but my mouth wouldn't work.

I lie on the floor, my face pressed against the cold boards. Don is far away, George is gone, the snow falls outside. I climb back in bed, and look out at it. It lies in new white drifts as far as I can see. I could climb out the window and down the porch rail. I could climb through and over the huge white mounds. Music is playing in the background, some World War II song, "I can't sit under the apple tree with anyone else but me, for there is no secret lover, that the draft board didn't discover."

I wake up to hear Rick and Charlie's son, "What did she do? We heard a noise last night. We did." Peter is almost four, big brown eyes like his father, beautiful skin, his mother's round face. He loves to march around the house in cowboy boots listening to World War II songs, "This is the army, Mr. Brown, you and your baby went to town, you used to stroll in the park before, but you'll find there's no time on K-P."

I come downstairs to the smell of frying sausage. "I fell off the bed," I say, "I'm not used to beds." I wait for Rick to laugh, but he doesn't. Charlie says, "Sit down, and eat up. Did you know Christmas is coming?"

"Christmas?"

"You know what Christmas is, don't you?" I look up from eating, and they're all looking at me, even Peter; it must be important. Peter screams, "You know, you know, he's coming."

"Christmas carols?" I say, sausage on fork in mid air.

"What else does Christmas mean to you?"

"Nothing, we never had Christmas."

"Why not?"

"Because George said that it isn't really the Lord's birthday."

"Is that what they said? You sure they weren't just too cheap to give you presents?"

"What presents?"

"From Santa Claus, and my grandpa and my grandma, and my other grandpa and grandma, and my dad and mom, and my aunt." Peter begins jumping up and down in his chair.

"We'll go to his grandmother's house for Christmas, you can come too."

When we come home after Christmas dinner, I go out for a walk. I think about Christmas, a day you don't have to work, but you sit around and eat a lot, and then people open presents. "They give these presents because they feel like it," Charlie says. That's all there is to it. And they have a tree inside the house making a bit of a mess what with the needles, and some melted snow, and they hang things off the tree. If the tree were alive, it would feel ridiculous with all that stuff hanging off it, I think.

I come back to find Charlie fixing sandwiches. She waves me into a chair, which means she has something to say. "Andie, have you ever thought of going to college? You know, even like the Voc-Tech school where Rick teaches. You could learn a skill, you could meet young people. You never date, and you're intelligent."

"How long does college take?"

"Two to four years."

"See, I don't have that long. The Lord may come at any time. I want to be ready for his coming, and if I start college, I might never finish because he might come, and then I'd have wasted my time."

"Stop," Charlie says suddenly, and I stop eating the sandwich and look at it in my hand to see if something is wrong with it. "The Lord might come before you finish that sandwich, so there's no point starting it." I throw back my head and laugh, tipping my chair precariously, and Charlie sits watching me, her round apple cheeks smiling but puzzled. I stop laughing and look at her suddenly sober, afraid I've done something wrong.

"What'd I do?"

"Nothing, I've just never seen you laugh."

"Oh, I used to laugh, sometimes, by myself."

"I bet you did." Charlie looks at me, "Are you ever angry at the people at the Farm?"

"I don't know about angry. I wish I could write to my mother, but I called her, and she said she never wanted to hear from me again because the road I am going down leads to hell."

"What road?"

"I'm not living at the Farm."

"So you're going to hell?"

"I'd like to think not, but," I shrug.

"Think about college."

"I will, but see, it's not just the Lord coming. The country might collapse, and then I'd have to leave and go live on some desert island, and I wouldn't be able to shave my legs. That's why I don't shave my legs, because the hair would grow back even longer if I shaved it, so I might be on some island, that's another reason, I'm not sure about college."

"How are you going to get to this desert island?"

"I have a passport, don't you?"

"No, I don't plan to go anywhere."

"Are you just going to stay here if the country collapses?"

Charlie looks around the room, at the blankets made from wool she sheared and carded, at the high shelves with rows of jars she canned, jellies, pickles, vegetables, at the onions hanging from the ceiling, at the wood stove. "Where would I go, the Caribbean?"

In the room, I read the *Penthouse* magazines, look at the pictures, wonder how these girls feel. I read letters that are supposed to be from readers and wonder why all the writing sounds like the same writer, the same style. I read a story of a man watching a woman masturbate. I touch myself, and realize that this action has a name which must mean other people do it too.

I hitchhike to work one day, head down, and a white truck pulls up beside me. I cannot see the driver, the snow blows in my eyes. I get in. He is an Indian with long black hair and shining eyes. "Got pretty hair," he says, "know it?" and he reaches out to touch my long uncombed, snow-covered hair. I shy away from him in the cab of the truck. He begins to smile, showing a mouth of missing teeth. He does not look where he is driving; he looks at me, and the smile goes on, like a long bad story. I wish it would stop; there is something strange about the smile. I think of jumping out, but, we are going too fast.

I say, "This is where I get out," but he keeps driving, past the ski slopes, past the town, his arm sits on the back of the seat. The cab is not big enough. He touches my shoulder.

I remember words from a *Penthouse* letter, "I could not wait any more, I had to have her; I tore off her blouse, and ripped at her cotton panties. I had to get to what was inside." He keeps smiling as he pulls into a deserted dump.

The snow has stopped, and the sun is shining on everything. He turns to me, "I just want to talk," he says, reaching for me with two big arms, the muscles on them knotted like ropes, the smell of his breath falling over me. He is trying to open my door. It is stuck, and as it opens, we both fall out. He is on top of me in the snow. My head is thrown back in the drift, my long skirt pulled up to show my long johned legs. He leans over me, and begins to kiss my face, somehow missing my lips, but kissing my cheeks while his whiskey-cigarette breath blows into my open mouth to sicken me. I start to choke; my legs are moving, but it's hard to stand up, half-buried by him with my body sinking into snow. My mind is a mass of confusion, "I'm going to be late for work. Is this what makes babies? Will he kill me? Scream?" I scream, so he covers my mouth with one hand, and his whole body seems to be crushing my chest.

"You wanted this, bitch, you girls, you hitchhikers," and I can't see his face anymore, but I can hear he's still smiling. I hear my skirt coming off in one long tear, like my life tearing, and I try to flip myself over like we did in wrestling class. But it was easier on a hard surface, and I am floundering in a snowdrift. He takes the hand off my mouth, and with both of his hands tears the long johns down, and my white upper legs and buttocks suddenly feel snow biting into them. He sits on top of me. I see pine trees above my head, heavy with snow like his body feels sitting on me; my breath is coming in great gasps. He is doing something to himself, and I realize that he is unzipping his pants; he is reaching for something.

I remember. I know what it is. I realize suddenly; in the letters when the men said, "my cock," and I remember a horse's cock, and someone telling me that was a cock, and I know what is coming, something, huge, monstrous, filthy, to be shoved up in me, like horses and dogs do, while I scream. I have seen the cock, enormous, swelling purple, shoving into a mare—screaming, screaming, while the stallion pushed.

One fist connects with his face. All my body energy rushes, fear surges through me, I feel my adrenaline singing in my ears, hear some high wild screaming like an animal, and the screaming goes on. I throw him backward; I don't look back for a second at the horrible huge thing he is pulling out in the open; I run toward the woods, run, sure he is after me. This is something I have been trained to do, run through woods in any weather. I run kicking my legs up sideways, like running through water at the beach. I hear him yell something, but my head is buzzing. I can't think of anything but, run, run.

I know, before I run out of breath and feel hot jagged pains in my heart from exertion, that he isn't coming after me. The snow and wind blow up around my legs; I am suddenly cold, I fall down into the snow and cry uncontrollably.

"I want to go south where it's warmer," I tell the man at the ticket window the next day. "How far will this money take me?" I hand him a packet of my money from my green utility sack.

"Richmond, Virginia."

I come away from the window and say to Charlie, "Thanks for the sandwiches. Thanks for everything."

"It doesn't leave for an hour, let's have lunch, the sandwiches are for later." We sit down; I sit slowly. I'm wearing a long skirt that covers my legs, whipped from the branches, a mass of red stripes welting and burning. "Did something happen? Are you okay?"

"Nothing happened," I say, "nothing happened. I just have to go. Bad things happen here." Charlie looks at me as if trying to read something, but I'm holding my face still like I did on our first meeting. I know there is nothing to guess from my face, a mask of secrets behind my glasses.

The Doorway of Secrets

Something follows me, a dog or my shadow.
It haunts me on quiet days
in the thick of woods
like a bear or a mountain lion stalking me.
It leans toward me, fuzzes the edges of thoughts.

It stays there, just out of reach,
a maddening itch my arms are too stiff to touch.
I stare in the mirror hoping to see a trace of it
between my eyes or written on my forehead.
But my forehead is a shelf of closed books.

I close my eyes for a moment.
For a moment I am in the doorway of secrets;
but I do not knock.
I fold my arms across my chest and turn away
because in there, I think,
is a bloated, frenzied squaw,
kneeling, bending, wheedling,
covering old sores.

Chapter 20

The Virginia air gets colder every day. I didn't think it was supposed to get cold so far south, but maybe I haven't come far enough. I wear an old sweatshirt, and sit on top of the bed in my hotel room flipping through the *Richmond News Leader* looking for jobs. I circle domestic help jobs. The hotel room is dark; grey curtains blow in the dry heat from a white metal heater. When I open drawers, huge black bugs crawl out. "What are those bugs?" I ask the man at the desk. He looks me over like he's trying to figure me out.

"Cockroaches." He shrugs. "What y'all doing here?"

"Looking for work." He laughs, a strange coughing laugh.

I sit in the doorway of my room, and watch the other residents, mostly women, taking their trash to the dumpster, talking to each other, looking at me strangely. They never speak to me. The women are thin; in the morning they appear pale with long stringy hair, ripped dresses, a grasping look about their hands, a tightness in their shoulders. I feel their unhappiness but don't understand it.

At night, they are different, the pale faces are painted. They stand in their doorways dressed in tight black and red, silver blouses, leather skirts. Men ride up on motorcycles. I watch from the window. The men wear leather and smoke cigarettes. They smile into the women's faces and take their arms. They go into their rooms and come out again puffing smoke and slapping each other on the back. I sit in my room in wool skirts and heavy sweaters. In the mirror I see that good looks are something I don't have. My long hair hangs straight, my white pale face stares.

The first day after I run out of money, the familiar hungry feeling returns, and I call all day to jobs listed in the paper. They ask me whether I have references. I ask what references are. After several calls, someone says, "How do you expect to get a job when you're as dumb as a stick; you know, references, people who know you who we can call and check you out." I say I have references in Vermont. I just got into town. "So, are you some type of transient?" someone asks.

"Yes, I'm a transient," I say. The person hangs up on me. I wonder if "transient" is a bad word like "shit." I am on the way to the dumpster when one of the motorcycle men comes by. He's wearing blue jeans and an old faded plaid shirt like men at the Farm wore. He smiles at me, "You live here?"

"Yes."

"You're new around here."

"Yes."

"Like to go out with me for a hamburger tonight?"

My stomach rumbles, "Yes." "If you like," I say. He smiles again.

He comes in a truck with high wheels. I wear a polyester black shirt and white skirt. We eat hamburgers and onion rings in the parking lot of Burger King, and he plays the radio loudly. "Bitchin' stereo, don't you think," he yells over "My Angel is a Centerfold." Trash blows by, and the wind is cold, blowing in through windows that don't close. He reaches for me, and I pull away.

"Hey," he says, "I'm not gonna hurt you. Thirsty?" he asks. I don't answer. He hands me a bottle of something clear. It tastes sweet and pepperminty. I take a sip. "Drink all you like."

"Thank you." He smiles again.

"Why don't you smile. You're real pretty." I manage a smile. I like the pepperminty stuff. He turns down the music. "You're real pretty when you smile. Have another drink." The stuff is sweet and good. He pours my coke out the window and fills my glass with the sweet stuff.

"What is this?" He looks at me like he's trying to figure something out, and I get the animal feeling, as I call it. Ever since I left the Farm, and watched Toby die, I've been getting the "animal feeling," a feeling that I myself am Toby, a dumb animal in a strange world, waiting to get hit by a car. The humans can't tell that I am an animal; they think because I wear glasses and clothes that I am an intelligent human being, but I know that I am not. I am a dumb animal. The animal feeling is accompanied by a sinking sensation. I drink some more of the pepperminty stuff.

My head feels light and then heavy. I feel the peppermint sliding down my throat, and I feel a heightened awareness of everything, the cold air, the smell of a truck, newly cleaned, the smell of the onion rings, the man beside me. I begin to sing along with the radio. "I love Pat Benatar," the man says. Pat's husky voice sings, "Hell is for children," and I sing along.

The man slides one hand over my leg, and leans forward to kiss me. His eyes are brown and warm. I let him kiss me. I close my eyes and feel the lips against mine. I kiss him back, slowly at first, like I'm tasting something for the first time, then I feel hungry for something, I don't know what. He says, "Come on, I'll show you where I live."

At his apartment, the living room is dark; he doesn't turn on the light. "Come on," we stumble through a hallway; "this is my bedroom. I want you to see my stereo." He points to a black metallic hunk in the corner; he turns buttons, lights flash, music I don't understand, but we start dancing. The dancing seems natural to me, slow rhythmic movements to the sounds from the stereo, his arms around me, his hands on my butt. His hands crawl up to my breasts, both hands on my breasts.

"I can't let you do this," I slur. "I can't." I feel like I am going to black out; he pushes me back on the bed. "I can not do this; I can not, I'm a virgin; I can not."

"You can do *this*," and my mouth hanging open is suddenly force fed something large and hard. "Suck this," he says, "suck it until I come." I feel I will choke, gag, die, and the feeling goes on for a long time. I close my eyes and feel a ringing in my ears. My jaw aches. The man's hands hold my head. I feel my head letting go of my shoulders. I taste water and salt, and tears. He falls back; I scramble to the bathroom. "Come back, lie down."

I lift the toilet seat and retch, wash my mouth and look at my face, a pasty mass. He's asleep when I come back. I walk back to my hotel room, my head heavy and falling from side to side like a bowling ball.

Snow falls lightly on my shoulders, the flakes floating past each other, being tossed back up as if they were dancing or joking about whether they really intended to come to earth. I ring the doorbell again and lay my head against it. I hear footsteps, but no lights come on in the darkened house. A man had said this was the address, and I hitchhiked and walked all day. The house is seventeen miles out of Richmond, he said. I hope this is the right address. The snow blankets my shoulders, and I carry my stuff in the same green utility sack I had when I left the Farm. I have three dollars in my pocket, and I have no more nights paid for at the Cockroach Motel.

The door opens and a man with a glass in his hand motions me inside. He is short, red faced, and smiling, the house is completely dark. I hesitate. "Come in," he commands, and I step inside as he closes and locks the door. A fire is burning, but no lights are on.

"The electricity's out," he says, "I guess it's the storm. Care for a drink?"

"Water's fine," I say. I don't want anything pepperminty.

"Ah come on, I'll get you a rum and coke, you look like you could use some warming up. You must be Andie. I'm Bill." He holds out a hand, and breathes alcohol in my face. I remember the smell and step back. "You look like I'm going to bite you. My wife'll be right out. So what do you want to know about the job?"

"Well, I would like the job. What would you like me to do?"

"My mother lives in the adjoining house," he says. "She broke her hip, but her mind is sound. She's eighty-two. My wife runs a business, so she's often busy. We need someone to look after my mother. You'd have your own bedroom. We want someone to be nice to my mother, sit and chat with her, keep her company. She bathes herself, feeds herself. How are you with taking care of people?"

He looks at me closely, and I get the "animal feeling." He is trying to figure me out. I can tell. I put my hand to my throat in some childish gesture of self defense. I sit on the floor, my arms around my knees.

"I will do a good job. I can take care of your mother. I'm used to cooking. I grew up in a boarding school. I know how to cook and clean. I will do a good job."

"We'll give you a week's trial," he says. "Ah, here's my wife, Iris. Iris, Andie." Iris puts out her hand, and I stand up.

"Oh, don't get up," she says, setting down the candle in her hand. "I can't believe the electricity would go out like this, what a storm." She sits down, and she and her husband talk; the conversation flows around me. They look at me once in a while as if to allow me to speak, but I have no words, and feel that I might be being tested to see if I am the sort who would interrupt an adult conversation. I want to show that I have been well-brought up. Children will be seen and not heard.

Bill is like most of the men I have seen since I left the Farm. His voice is loud and gets louder as he walks back and forth filling his glass with brown liquid from a thick glass bottle. His face is red and getting redder. Much of what he says has to do with money and stocks and sports and technology, all empty words. Iris' talk goes in a different direction, and most of the time, they don't seem concerned with what the other is saying. Iris looks unlike anyone at the Farm. Her hair is red and full around her face, her eyes a piercing blue, and her face smiles constantly. She laughs at things she herself says. She turns toward me,

"So where did you say you're from?"

"Vermont."

"I wondered about the accent. Come on, let me show you where your room is, I'm tired." She stands up, and Bill watches her. I can see that look in his eyes that I am beginning to recognize. Iris' waist is small beneath a full bosom that seems barely held in by her white sweater. She stretches and turns toward him, "I'll be back, sweetheart," she says.

We dash through the carport to the adjoining house, and Iris shows me my room. "Grandma's already asleep. I hope you like it here."

"I'm sure I will, you're very good and very beautiful."

Iris stops, and looks at me. "Thank you, for a fifty year old Grandma I guess I'm okay." She laughs again.

Left alone, I wash up and get into the bed. It is a wooden four poster bed with a white comforter. The dresser beside the bed has a white doily on it. "You can put your clothes in there," Iris said.

"I'm going to like it here," I whisper to myself. I fall asleep clutching my pillow.

I get up in the morning, go out to feed the birds so that they will be eating on the porch when Grandma comes out to eat her breakfast of eggs and toast. I fix Grandma's breakfast and watch her eat. I clean the house and then take an hour walk while Grandma rests.

Bill and Iris let me take driving lessons in their car. I get my driver's license so that some days I can take Grandma to the hair dresser or to the doctor. Grandma talks very little. She smiles and eats slowly watching the birds.

"Do you know how far a bird travels in a lifetime?" she asks.

"No."

Grandma smiles. "No one has counted, but they end up where they started."

"Really, do they?"

Grandma stares at the birds in silence. Iris comes over every day, and has lately discovered what she calls, "your talent for sewing."

"It isn't a talent," I say. "I have no talents. It's just something I was taught to do."

"I want you to make a bunch of those place mats and pillows and rugs, and I'm going to have all my nail customers over and you are going to make some money so you can go to college."

"College?"

"Yes, you are going to college."

"Yes, M'am."

"That's what I like about you. You do as you're told."

"Yes, M'am."

The women walk around the room choosing what they want to buy, chatting with each other and Iris, eating the refreshments I laid out. I give yes and no answers to their questions. When they are gone, I have made five hundred dollars.

"Why can't you be more friendly?"

"I'm sorry."

"Talk to people." Iris walks around the room, shaking her head in exasperation.

"What do you wish me to say?"

"Something, anything, you sit there like a damned robot." I feel my eyes fill with tears. "Listen, honey, I'm sorry," Iris is apologetic. She pulls my head against her chest. "Honey, I'm sorry. Y'all just have to be more friendly. You sit there like some damned statue." She puts her arms around me. "Y'all are getting thinner."

Bill appears at the top of the steps, staggering a little, holding on to the rail. Iris' sculptured nail business is in the basement which is all flowers and pillows and teacups and the light smell of chemicals overwhelmed by candle fragrances; vanilla and apricot. "So the girls are gone?" Bill says.

"Yes," Iris stands up, and suddenly looks defiant. She and Bill have been married for eight years. Her first marriage lasted twenty-five years ended when her husband died. "Bill and I are on thin ice," she says to me. "When I married him, he was married to one of those Michigan French girls who are so sexy, but then she started drinking, Lordy, Lordy. My first husband, God rest his soul, beat me to death. He was Italian, that was his problem. After him, I swore off men forever, and then Bill came along. He was so romantic and what a lifestyle. We got married at Caesar's Palace, and we've jetted everywhere."

"I can see that it would be nice."

"What?"

"To marry someone and then have enough to eat and a place to stay."

"Well, William has started drinking." She always calls him "William" when she is upset at him.

Bill descends the stairs to find us huddled on the couch talking. "Whispering again, talking about me," he says.

"People who don't like being talked about are usually guilty," Iris says. "I have nothing to say to you."

"You still mad about having to pick me up at the police station?" Iris looks embarrassed for a second, and then defiant again.

"Third time this month," she says. "Now get out of here and let me talk with her," she points to me. I am still crouching on the sofa.

"Her," he waves his hands in my direction, "Her?" his voice is mockery. "She's never going to do shit with her life. Look at her. They ruined her at that cult. Look at her, she's a fucking abortion. She's an accident." I hold my face steady. I make sure my face never changes expression.

"Get out of here. You're drunk." Iris rises like a river goddess from beneath the surface of water. She stretches out her hands with their long nails like she will scratch out his eyes. "Get away from her, get away from me. Go," her voice rises, and he blows back up the stairs like unimportant matter.

A World Without God

He told me, never say it's impossible,
rubbing the back of my neck,
nothing's impossible,
kissing the back of my hand,
leather close enough for me to smell
putting down his keys.
I've promised God, I say.
He doesn't stop breathing.
He moves behind me, reaching
for the buttons
of my green dress.
I get up, say goodbye, the word
hanging between us, an icicle
from eaves.
His eyes, my eyes,
stay linked. We move
together. I walk
backward, my hands behind me;
he walks forward
both arms outstretched. I trip;
we fall forward together
into some other world
where there is no God.

Chapter 21

I lie on a single bed in a small bedroom. I lie on my stomach and look around the room which I am proud to have decorated myself. It is the first time I have had my own space to do what I want to with. At a World Bazaar in the mall, I bought two slatted scrolls with Japanese drawings on them for two dollars each. Since there are gold colors in the drawing, I followed that up by buying a piece of gold fabric that is simulated fur and putting that over the bed for a comforter. I hung gold curtains which I found at a thrift shop, and for a final touch I placed a philodendron on the window sill. I lie on the bed, delighted with the matching gold colors. The shag carpet is flattened to non-existence, and there is a full length mirror hanging on the back of the door.

I have been living in this house for two months, ever since Bill's mother died. I visit Iris every week when Bill is at work. It is with Iris' recommendation that I got my present job taking care of another elderly lady.

I turn on the radio slowly. I twist the knob looking for a familiar song, and when I find one, I turn up the volume. I check the curtains, lock the door, and slide across the floor to the mirror. I have been watching MTV, so I have a vague idea of dancing, and I like it. I stand tapping my feet, closing my eyes, letting the beat of the music seep into me. "Gloria, I think I got your number." I begin to dance, a slow rhythmic swaying, "I think I got the alias that you've been living under." I undress, one piece of clothing at a time, "but you really don't remember was it something that they said," the dancing becomes frenzied. I move my hips back and forth like a jazz dancer, "or the voices in your head, calling Gloria." I rub my hands down over my sweating hips. "Feel your innocence slipping away," I touch my thighs, "don't believe it's coming back soon." I dance faster and faster.

The dance starts small; I believe that everything starts small. I begin, still, arms down; the feet tap, first one foot then both, the movement creeps up my legs, the hips, the waist, the arms begin moving like a statue coming to life, a tree whose branches begin blowing in the wind, a tree goddess who begins moving about, and finally my whole body, like a crazy thing, moves, the beat of the music drumming inside me, all my limbs moving outward, my whole body opening and opening.

That summer in Richmond is very hot. When Grandma sleeps, the eight-year old boy of the family and I walk to the park and build dams in the small stream. We go to movies, sitting together in the darkened theater eating popcorn.

I save up money to buy a seven hundred-fifty dollar Ford LTD. The week after I get my license, I drive to Nags Head, North Carolina, and spend my weekend off lying on the beach, swimming, walking in and out of beach shops that sell shell covered jewelry cases made in Taiwan. I lie in the sand, bury myself, to the neck, and then dig back out again. Nags Head is lonely and the beaches are white and clean. I have seen pictures of Virginia Beach, the crowded board walks, the girls parading with threads in their crotches and elastic across their breasts. I wear one piece bathing suits and walk alone on the dunes.

"You must go to college in the fall," Iris says. "But before you do that, you have to get in touch with that father of yours."

"I only know he lives in the Philadelphia area."

"That's enough, find out how many men with his name live in Philly and call them all. Go on, use my phone, I want to know how this turns out."

The third time, I ask, "Hello, Sean Gale, do you have a daughter named Andie?"

There is a silence, and a male voice tentatively says, "Yes, I did."

"Well, I'm her," I say quickly, "I mean I am she. I left the Farm. I'm eighteen."

"I know how old you are. Where are you now?"

"Richmond, I'm just living here and working."

"Tell him you want to meet him," Iris says.

"I don't know if I want to meet him," I say covering the phone.

"Who are you staying with?"

"A family who I'm working for taking care of the grandmother, but right now I'm visiting a friend for the evening."

"Of course you want to meet him," Iris says.

"I don't even know him," I say covering the phone again.

"Well, what can I do for you?"

I pause, cover the phone. "He wants to know what he can do for me."

"You want to meet him," Iris says.

"I'd like to meet you," I say.

"Well, certainly. I'll tell you what, I'm going to be in DC in a couple weeks on business. I can drive down." I hardly hear the rest of the conversation. I write down the time he will arrive and give him my address. I write down the date and circle it again and again.

When the rental car pulls up, I am sitting on the front steps wearing a royal blue polyester dress that I made myself. I have on white knee socks, penny loafers. My straight hair hangs down my back in a single loose ponytail. I know I look scared, but I can't help it. The car door opens, and he steps out. For a long moment, neither of us speaks.

He wears a dark blue suit and white shirt. His eyes twinkle when he smiles, and I get the feeling that this good looking man is laughing at me. He puts out a hand, and I take it, glance at him, stare at the ground and at his blue pant legs and large shoes. "Hello, sir," I say softly, "are you my father?"

"Yes," he says, and when I glance up, he is still looking at me.

"If you don't like me, it's partly your fault too."

"I like you very much," he says and opens the car door for me. "Would you like to get something to eat?"

"Sure, yes please." I lay awake in bed thinking of what I will say, smart things. I'll tell him I'm thinking of being a travelling fruit picker, and I'll tell him how I bought a car and how I got my license. He'll smile. He'll say, "Sure, daughter." He'll put his arm around me. He'll love me. He'll be the first person in my life to love me, and I'll love him.

I went to see "Annie," and I change the words of the songs, and sing to myself, "And maybe, he'll remember, how nice he was to me, and how I was almost his baby, maybe."

Maybe he's rich, maybe he's poor, don't really care as long as he's mine."

At Friendlys, he opens the door for me, and we sit down in a red booth. There are cloth napkins, and I play with mine. A plant hangs over our booth, and I stand up on the seat of the booth, to see why the leaves are falling off. "Philodendrons need more water than this," I say. I water the plant with my water glass, and he watches me but doesn't say anything.

"Can I take your order?" the waiter asks.

"Can I order for you?" he says, and I nod.

The next day I try to tell Iris what happened, and find that I can't remember parts of the evening.

"I was scared during the first half of the night, and during the second half, I was still scared, but not as much."

"Well, what happened?"

"He ordered French fries and a hot dog for me which I had never had, and I ate the French fries one at a time with ketchup although I don't know if that's the way to eat them. I ate the hot dog with a fork."

"What did he say?"

"He wanted to see a picture of my sister, and I showed him one, and then I said he could keep it."

"Do you think he liked you?"

"I guess not. I liked him, but I guess he did not like me."

"Why do you say that? He's your father, of course he liked you."

"Not, of course, he doesn't know me, and he doesn't have to like me. He looked at me funny, and he has two kids by his second wife, and I think they're his real family now. I think he wishes I hadn't turned up."

"Now why do you say that?"

"I'm telling you, he looked at me funny. I don't think he loves me."

"He doesn't even know you, how could he love you?"

"I wanted him to love me," I throw myself on the couch and then sit up abruptly. "Nothing is turning out like I expected. I expected to be free and loved and live in this world where I could do anything, and it would be beautiful, and my father would love me and be proud of me. I'm not going to cry, I just have to get him to love me." I got up and looked at myself in the mirror and picked up my long skirt. "Look at my legs, do you think they're fat? Do you think I could stand to lose a bit?"

"Well, you could, but what does this have to do with your father? Tell me what else happened? What does he do?"

"He's a professor at the University of Pennsylvania. His wife's a runner. She's probably in good shape, and she has a Ph.D., and is an executive at some company. I bet she's thin." I pull the skirt up around my hips and grab a handful of flesh. "That's what I'll do, I'll lose weight."

That year goes by quickly. I sign up for college at J. Sergeant Reynolds Community College, but the week before classes are to start, the lady I am taking care of dies. One night, just after dinner, she stops breathing and falls back in my arms with her eyes closed. When they bury her, she looks better than she has looked in a long while, peaceful and intelligent, as if she has been lucid for months.

Her son says I can continue to stay at the house for one hundred dollars a month and some baby-sitting. I begin tutoring for a living and start college.

The lady who I took care of has a daughter in Arizona who arrives for the funeral. "Thank you for caring for my mother," the daughter, Dinah says kissing me on the forehead. We sit on the screened porch, and Dinah shells peas and husks corn for dinner. "I grew up in the Virginia mountains with Mama, and she always took care of me. I wish I could have cared for her at the end, but she didn't like it in Arizona. I had her with me for a year, and she kept running away. She said she was going back to Virginia." Dinah looks over at me. I am polishing silver, my head down, my hair hanging over my face.

"So, tell me, what do you want to do with yourself?"

"Well, I'm going to college this year. I have one friend, Iris, she said for me to go to college, and I think I'd like to be a travelling fruit picker. I'd like to travel around, maybe go to California. I'd like to be warm."

"I see."

"I'm starting some baby-sitting and tutoring jobs now, because I need to make money to put myself through college."

"And what is your major going to be?"

"I don't know. Iris said to go to college."

"Where are your parents?"

"My mother, I don't see any more. She lives in a commune, a closed Christian commune in Vermont. I only met my dad once. I don't really know him. I don't think he thought much of me. He's never contacted me since that one time he saw me."

"You're okay, you'll do fine," Dinah says, snapping the peas open. "I hope you'll come and see me in Arizona some time."

"Thank you, Ma'am."

"My name's Dinah, and here's my address, write to me."

I get A's in my classes, babysit, visit Iris, and write to Dinah. I diet, first tentatively skipping one meal a day, then eating less and less as my body is accustomed to living on little. Dinah writes that I can come to Arizona for the summer, and I apply to Arizona State University in case I want to stay there.

In June, my Ford dies and I buy a Pontiac Sunbird and pack all my belongings into it. My fingers trace the route on the map while I drive on an empty stomach through the southern United States, across Texas to Arizona.

When Dinah opens the door of her house in Mesa, in June, she tells me later, she does not know who this girl is, standing on the doorstep. She pauses for a moment, there is something familiar about the eyes. My hair is cut short and bleached blond. My eyes, she says, looked huge and hungry in a white face of sharp angles. I am a large framework of bones with no flesh. My shorts cling uneasily on bony hips. Above my purple tank top, my collar bone protrudes like something abnormal. My feet look enormous on the ends of my skinny legs. To Dinah, the whole thing looks like some strange stick figure. The stick figure speaks, "Dinah, it's good to see you."

"Well, it's good to see you, Andie," she says quickly masking her face. "You've changed, you're thinner."

"Yeah, I wanted to get thinner to see. I wanted to lose some weight. I felt like I was a bit heavy."

"Well, come in, tell us about your trip, sit down have a sandwich."

"I can't eat; I'll do anything you want, but I can't eat. I have to stay thin, now, so I can't eat."

My Father and Food

My father and I
do not need each other.
I have a husband,
he has a wife.
I carry a baby
who will never say grandpa.

I met him twice,
the first it was snowing.
I was anxious and dripped
ketchup from my French fries.
He studied me like
leftovers.

Two years later
when I called
he said he had no time
to read my letters,
said I'd seemed fat
when he met me.
I said, "Ah."

The second time was hot,
Philadelphia steamed.
I was California
blond, tanned and
had a plane to catch.
Over chicken salad
I crumbled out my life
for him; he gave me only
select slices of his.

Chapter 22

"What are you doing with your food?" Dinah asks, stopping between the kitchen and the table with a plate of fresh sliced tomatoes. "What are you doing?" she asks again when there isn't an answer. I just sit there like the moon in the sky, white and unmoving. Then my head moves slowly to one side, cocked in a peculiar motion as if I am trying hard, and unsuccessfully to figure out what is being said.

"I want to do whatever you want," I say slowly as if talking is an effort. I push the green beans around the plate with my fork, "Just don't make me eat. It's so hard to lose weight, I can't eat now."

"Girl, you're trying to starve yourself, that's what your trying to do. She's sick that's was she is, look at her, arms no bigger than bird's legs. She's not eaten but two bites." Dinah's husband's belly shoves against the table, and he takes bites of pork chops, gravy and muffins. He pours himself another scotch.

I watch him, my head still cocked like it's stuck or he's hypnotized me. To me, he looks like some goblin feasting. I am better than that. I am not gluttonous; I do not stuff food in my mouth.

"It makes me sick having her at the table, if you want to know the truth," he says. I watch the brown liquid pour into his mouth, fascinated. His mouth looks like some garbage dump for him to shove refuse into.

Dinah bites her lip. "She's okay, leave her alone."

"I'll say whatever I want to in my house."

"I'll eat," I say, picking up my fork and taking a bite of green beans. "I'll eat, see, I'm eating."

"You better keep eating," he says. The house smells wonderfully warm and food-like. I want to just sit there and smell it; I figure I could just live off the smells.

I am alone in the house, walking around smelling the air. Dinah and her husband are gone for two weeks, and the house is all mine. I will not eat anything. No one is there to force me, to make food smells sing through the house, to ask why I am playing with my food.

Dinah and her husband call. "How are you doing? How is work? Are you eating?" I think about Dinah's husband looking at me with troubled eyes. "We feel responsible for you," he'd said.

"We love you," Dinah said. But I couldn't think about anything but my weight.

The dream is always the same. I go to sleep in my bed alone in a room. I have been sleeping alone ever since I left the Farm, but I have never quite gotten use to the absence of fifteen other girls breathing in and out. The warmth of other bodies, the feeling of being part of a litter of puppies. I shiver now, my bones crunching against each other. I dream.

I am at the Farm again, and they are making me stay. They won't let me leave. Sometimes in the dream I am getting six-of-the best. Sometimes I am in a room alone, sometimes I am shovelling manure. I am always trapped. I always wake up sweating and terrified. I always wake up with the rat-in-a-cage feeling. I will be fed, I will be watered, but I will never get out. "Never get out, never get out," I hear myself crying, and I wake up pulling the blankets around myself.

I lie still in my bed, pulling my arms around me, remembering where I am. I close my eyes and see the water moccasins. I see myself kneeling in brown earth by clear water picking the soft pink flowers.

I think of the ugly duckling, and move my thin arms; I wonder if I will ever be a swan.

Weeks after I left the Farm, when I was staying with Charlie, Hope came to visit me. "I'm coming to invite you back to the Farm," she'd said. "On behalf of George and the Farm family, we'd like to invite you back. The Lord is calling you to come back into the fold."

I stared out the window. Snow fell slowly and lazily onto the roof outside. In the room where I slept there was barely room to stand. The roof sloped down over the bed. Stacked boxes had been moved aside to make room for a bed. Wall paper peeled. The place smelled like the wood stove burning below, and faintly of mildew.

"God is calling you."

"Let me pray about it."

Alexa visited the next day. I showed her some poems I had been working on. "What are you writing poetry for?"

"I want to publish poetry."

"God is not going to let you go. He wants you back."

"I'm praying about it."

"God has his hand on you." When Alexa was gone, I pulled out a book of poetry I had bought. It was by Emily Dickinson, and I did not understand it, but the book tingled in my hands. It felt alive, the pages turned in the draft from the stove below my room. "I'm going to be a poet," I whispered to myself.

The dreams are worse now. I am afraid to go to sleep. I seem to be on the verge of hallucinations almost as soon as I lie down. God, a huge white man with a beard, stands with his hands on me, wrenching me from my life, and putting me into a cage where I run in circles all day. I daydream of going back to the Farm, letting everyone out. I dream at night of being in the cage. I dream in the day of inheriting a million dollars, going back to the Farm, buying it, and telling everyone they can leave. In my daydreams, they are grateful to me, they know God is with me. In my night dreams, God angrily takes away my car and gives it to George. God descends from heaven and becomes George. God is George.

"You have sinned against the Almighty. You knew and still you would not listen. You will be punished worse than if you had never heard the Word of God because you knew, and you turned your back on God. Hell is waiting for you if you do not repent and come back." I wake up screaming.

I am being fired from my fifth job. I can tell when it is coming now. The boss stops looking at my little thin body and notices what I'm not doing. "Didn't I tell you? Don't you listen?" I'll shake my head, because if I listen, I don't hear. The words that people say seem so pointless. I don't know why people are always talking to me. Their voices seem too loud.

The manager calls me to his office. He's eating a piece of pizza, and the tomato drips on his chin, like he's some big baby. His fingers holding the pizza are fat and hairy. He says, "It looks like you're not making it here." I try to look surprised although I'm not. He says,

"There's something you could do for me if you want to keep your job."

His eyes travel me, and I think I remember what that hungry look means. Nothing comes to my mind to say. I take a step backward toward the door.

He takes a step forward, one arm goes around my waist, and with his other hand he unbuttons the top button of my white blouse. He smiles down at me, and I smell pizza and feel sick and hungry. His fat hand slips under my bra to cup one breast. I struggle a little, but I haven't eaten for a couple days, and I suddenly feel dizzy. He sinks into a chair, and pulls me onto his lap.

I'm feeling sick and looking down at my black pant leg across his lap I think, "This is bad," but my mind feels sluggish, like something important is about to happen, but I can't think what it is.

"Let me go," I say dully, but without conviction.

"You're such a baby." He smiles, and the smile looks hungry. I try halfheartedly to get up, and his hand moves on my breast. I feel an unfamiliar shudder run through me, as if some electric current between my breast and the rest of my body has been charged. His fingers start moving in a circle. I try again to get up; this time more feebly. He nuzzles my neck, and I don't notice his breath so much. "You're very pretty," he says.

His free hand reaches for the button that fastens my pants shut, and my mind turns over like a cold engine on a winter morning, and I remember what is happening.

As I'm running away, he calls after me, "Get back here, bitch." On the way home, I get lost twice.

Back at the house my heart is still pounding when I open the refrigerator. My head feels huge. I feel my blood pounding and singing between my ears. When I realize what I am doing, I am sitting on the kitchen floor with a half gallon of Rocky Road icecream between my legs. My mouth hangs open, and my hand moves mechanically stuffing bite after bite. I can't taste or think, and breathing seems difficult. One spoonful drops on the floor, and I immediately slop it up with one hand and eat it.

When I wake up, my head against the refrigerator, I dig my nails into my arm. I cover my face, and then slowly crawl to my knees and begin praying, begging God's forgiveness for ever eating, for being a glutton, for being so filthy and disgusting.

At the grocery store, I buy a replacement half gallon of icecream, and I buy a package of laxatives. At least I can get rid of what I've done to myself. I take eight on the way home.

By the time I move out by myself, I'm afraid of any place where there might be food. I keep my curtains closed and walk around naked so I can weigh myself any time. On one wall, I keep pictures of Christie Brinkley, Daryl Hannah, Brooke Shields. I make myself a poster that says, "Discipline, Discipline, Discipline," and I paste pictures of models around it. The only foods I buy to bring home are citrus fruit, carrots, laxatives and diet sodas. On good days, these are all I eat. On bad days, I will go from the 7-11 where I'll buy Ding Dongs to the grocery store for yoghurt covered pretzels and to McDonald on the way home for a sundae. Then I'll take fifty or a hundred laxatives. Sometimes, I don't count; I just stand by the kitchen sink, taking handfuls of them. Now that my weight is up to 115 lbs, I am more desperate. I weigh myself after every meal, trying to get back to 108.

The first course I sign up for at Arizona State University is abnormal psychology, since I consider myself abnormal, possibly mad, and the second week I learn about eating disorders. When the professor has us give oral reports on a particular psychological abnormality, I decide on bulimia. I turn the word over in my mouth on the way home to eat a carrot and weigh myself. "Bulimia," actually a name for what she does; the starving and binging, and taking laxatives.

I pray every day that God will help me recover, and vow every morning not to overeat, not to take laxatives. Some mornings, I wake up with a peculiar buzzing in my ears. I know I will overeat that day as I know the sun will rise.

In the counseling office at Arizona State University, the therapist says, "I am working here because I myself am a recovering bulimic."

I look at her, and I'm not sure I want to recover. Flesh hangs on this woman, she must weigh at least 130 lbs. She seems unnecessarily large.

"What have you eaten today?" I ask.

"A bagel," the woman says, "And it's three o'clock."

"You're having a good day." I sit on the floor, my bony knees wrapped in my arms. "When was your last bad day?"

"I'm asking the questions. Why do you think you are doing this to yourself?"

"It's the one thing I can control."

"What would you like to control?"

"Make my parents love me."

"Is this making them love you?"

"I sent them both an eight-by-ten picture of myself thin. They never answered."

"So, it didn't work, but you're still starving yourself."

"I'm into it now, and I can't break out."

"Do you want to get better?"

"Yes," I say slowly.

"Which do you want more, to be thin or to get better?"

"Both."

"Suppose you can't have both. Which do you want more?"

"To get better."

"Then I think I can help you."

"Good. What do I do?"

"That's also good. You are aware that you have to do something. You have to stop taking laxatives. Knowing you can take laxatives is encouraging you to binge. If you couldn't, you wouldn't binge so often. How often do you binge now?"

"Two to three times a week."

"That's not bad, I know people who binge two or three times a day."

"It's bad for me."

"I know. All right, no more laxatives."

"But I'll gain weight."

"Let that be okay. This is the only way you are going to get better."

"I don't want to be fat."

"Do you exercise?"

"No."

"Well, start."

I begin to swim in the university pool one mile a day. I stop taking laxatives by fits and starts. I quit, but take them again once in a while for a few months. I pray every day, and visit the therapist who becomes the highlight of my week.

I take modelling classes and get a few low paying jobs. I send my father a head shot. My eyes are big and sad, my hair perfectly curled, my face made up like a porcelain doll. I try for a cool Mona Lisa half smile, but the smile looks like it's hanging precariously on my face and may fall off. On the back of the picture I write, "Andie Gale, sophomore, Arizona State University, 115 lbs."

Modelling classes are early Saturday mornings. We learn how to put on make-up, how to sit, how to walk. Most of the girls in the class are teenagers; one woman in the class is older than me, but just as thin. She always looks tired, and when I ask her if she works late at night, she replies, "Saturday morning is a stupid time for a class. Who isn't hungover? What's your name? I'm Tanya." Tanya wears long tight pants and sweaters that show her large breasts. Except for the breasts, she is skeletal, and her face looks even tinier, surrounded by bushes of blond hair.

Tanya turns out to be the only friend I make in my first two years in Arizona. "What I want to know," Tanya says, late one night when we're both lying around in her Jacuzzi, "do you think men are nutritious as well as delicious?"

"You can't eat men."

"You can too eat men. I eat men." She leans back, her eyes closed in luxurious contemplation. "Munch 'em, chew 'em up, swallow 'em, suck them, squeeze them." She takes another sip of her margarita. "I adore men, except for my louse of an ex-husband. He isn't too bad. He just better keep on paying the bills."

"I don't know anything about men."

"Are you a *virgin*? How the hell old are you?"

"Twenty-two."

"Twenty-fucking-two! Do you know how old I was the first time I fucked somebody?"

"How old?"

"Thirteen, thirteen sweet years old. It was great, it was great."

"I thought sex hurt women."

"Who have you been talking to, some pervert? Sex is the best thing that ever happened to women. Sex is like, it's like, God, I can't even describe it. You gotta do it. I tell you what, want to go with me to hear this band tomorrow night?"

After my second rum and coke, I am gyrating beside my bar stool. A boy who I've never seen, comes up behind me, and puts his arms around me, and we move together. I feel something hard pressing against my backside, and it feels good. I want to grind into him. He's whispering in my ear; most of it I can't understand. I get the word, "Baby," the rest is lost in the noise of the band. Tanya must be somewhere, but it doesn't matter. The hands travel up under my sweater, and I moan, lean into him, and put my head back on his shoulder. He kisses my neck, and I wonder vaguely why I waited so long to do this. Nothing is more important. He grinds his hips into my backside, and his tongue goes into my ear. He smells good, like smooth drinks and warmth.

Later we're sitting on barstools, and the band's taking a break, and we're having a conversation that seems very important. His dark hair falls in his face. He says, "I want you, baby. You are the most beautiful girl in this room. Hell, you're the most beautiful girl I've ever seen."

I say, "I've always wanted someone to want me."

"Hell, girl," he says. "A man can want anybody. I'm talking anybody. A man can want a wet stone if it's shaped right. A man is a wanting machine, that's what he is. I bet half the men in this room would fall over themselves to fuck you, and the other half would fall over each other." I look around the room. There are a lot of men. "You're special though, baby, I'm telling you, you are special."

"So lots of men have probably wanted me?"

"You bet, baby, fathers, stepfathers, uncles, poets, clerks, fancy preachers, probably most of the men you've met have thought to themselves, 'Hell, I could fuck her.'" He takes a long drink, "Hell," he says, "You're special baby, I want you to know that, I love you."

In the restroom, I look at my smeared eye shadow and my smudged lipstick, and Tanya's dress that I'm wearing. It slips off one shoulder, and I look bony underneath. My hair, which was poufed out at the beginning of the evening is mostly flat, and my eyes look yellow and glassy.

"What the hell are you doing with that Mediterranean looking guy?" Tanya asks.

"What's the matter with him? He's good looking."

"I like six foot muscular blondes myself, but whatever. He's dancing with someone else now. Come on, we're going backstage to meet the band."

"The band?"

"I'm gonna take that cute drummer home with me. He's a doll."

"Home?"

"Would you quit repeating me. Come on, you look great."

At Tanya's house the band members mill in and out of bedrooms. "What are they all doing here?"

"Coke, possibly acid, what do you think? They're all so cute." Tanya's eyes roll around like marbles. She says, "You are going to get fucked tonight."

"By whom?" I am beginning to feel things, like my head hurting, and my dress slipping off. The white chimney looks like a Corinthian column swaying, and then like a statue.

"Drink some more." A guitar player comes up behind me and kisses the back of my neck. The lights go dimmer. I am sitting on the guitar player's lap, and his hand is between my legs. He asks if I want to try anything. It is getting very dark in the room. I say that he seems to be the one doing all the trying. We both laugh as if this is very witty. I kiss him on both cheeks. I feel this is a very cool thing to do.

The light outside goes on, and I see a man walk by naked and step into the Jacuzzi. Tanya is on the couch, and the drummer has his face between her legs; possibly he is kissing her thighs, I'm not sure.

"Your guitar picking hands are getting very insistent," I say, very seriously. We both laugh; everything is funny and the light coming in from outside seems grey and hangs softly in the room. From the couch come moans. Outside, naked bodies walk back and forth. I stand up. The guitar player follows me outside and asks if I want to see his car.

In his car he says, "What do you want? I'll get it for you."

"A job," I say. The window is rolled down, and the cold air rushing around my head makes me feel wide awake, makes me think about going home, pushing open the door of my dark apartment, feeling safe and warm in the alone darkness.

He says, "I never marry, I have many girlfriends, but I never marry." I am holding a copy of the band's record in one hand. "Let me see that." He writes, "You can sit on my face any time."

He says, "Suck me off, and I'll get you a job," and we both laugh. A white line of light shines down through the car window, and the cool dark air wakes me up. The moon is hanging huge and yellow, like God's eye watching me. "Gotta go," I say.

At home, the shadows on the walls look the same as every night. Nothing has changed.

About Peaches

He wears blue jeans, a plaid shirt,
smells of grease and after-shave.
She picks the hard dry peaches
that fall out of season.
The wind is cold. She wears her resistance
lightly like her worn cotton shorts and shirt.

She wants college in the fall.
He wants babies in the springtime.
She saves money at the bank
and goes across the street to the thrift store.
She kisses him in his car on Saturdays.
He takes her to Burger joints and parties
where his friends drink beer.
She hugs her knees and looks at the stars.

It is a warm summer.
She smells ripe peaches on the wind;
She has decided to be a doctor.
Their kisses become wetter.

He takes her hand and says,
here's a lesson in anatomy.
His laugh grinds over her,
stops the flow of wanting
that edged her toward him on the seat.

He starts again under a full moon,
patient, hungry, his breath in her ears.
He dips his face in the V of her legs
and comes up smiling and wet
like a dog from a stream,
and she has lost her mind now.

She can't remember how it all happens:
it's okay, only she wishes
they could have talked first.
her brain feels left out,
her body and his conspired alone.
The ripe peaches she'd brought
squish beneath them and
juice runs down the seat.

Chapter 23

Arizona State University feels like a jungle of buildings. The first night of poetry class, I sit in the front row. "I am going to read you the 'Love Song of J. Alfred Prufrock,'" the professor says. He turns to write the title on the board, and I watch his butt. I can hear Tanya's voice in my head, "The thing I adore about men is their torsos, the whole way they move like their hips are alive and hungry. I like the curve of their jeans on their asses. That movement like music, just lying there watching a man sometimes can drive me wild. I'll wonder how long it's been since he's had it. Making a man happy is no big fucking deal. Actually, just a little fucking will cut it most of the time."

He reads in a melodic tenor, swaying slightly. I wonder if he sleeps with his students. He asks whether anyone has brought poems to the first night of class. I watch his large hands move. Tanya tells me that a man with small hands has a small penis. I wonder why Tanya thinks a large penis is better. Wouldn't it hurt worse? He cups the huge hands explaining something about energy. I watch his legs move. He calls on someone to read.

The girl reads a poem in which she is sucking a man's penis while Chaka Khan plays in the next room. In the poem she says that the rhythm gives her mouth something to move to, "the wet salt on my lips, sweetness" She asks the class whether the word "sweetness" is out of place since semen is actually salty. The professor says the poem works fine. He sits down and stays seated for a while.

I stop at Tanya's house. "He was sitting down because he had a hardon," Tanya says.

"A hardon?"

"I'm gonna slap you if you don't quit the hell repeating everything I say. You know what a hardon is."

"I think so, isn't it like, when their thing gets hard?"

"Oh, my God, I totally despair of you. Get me a drink, and let me know when you've done it."

During astronomy class, I strain to see the stars through light pollution. I glance up from the telescope into blue eyes. "You have beautiful eyes," I say, and he smiles.

He is painfully thin, with thick dark hair and long fingers. He reaches up and touches my cheek with one long finger. It is the most romantic thing anyone has ever done to me. His name is Chad, he says, as we pile change into the soda machine. "Do you like this class?"

"It's okay, what I really want to do is go to San Diego tomorrow and go to the zoo. You want to come?"

"You're going to ditch school to go to the zoo?" he asks.

"The tortoises are mating," I reply, seductively I hope. He smiles like a child.

We talk for eight hours about everything as we drive. We eat ice cream, fudge and cotton candy. We watch the tortoise shells clack; sailors wink at each other. Chad holds my hands. He takes pictures of me wearing a big shirt and a short skirt.

The next night he leaves poems and flowers on my car. I go by his dorm room to thank him. The place is tiny, my first glimpse of dorm life, beer cans manfully crushed in the sink, huge naked posters of girls on the walls, a strange odor; the mixture of male sweat and different colognes.

I sit on his small bed and look through his books. "I made the bed and ironed the sheets in case you ever came up here," he says shyly. I wear a short pink dress and enough makeup to cover a clown. He holds my hand as we leave and his roommates whistle.

"I've never met anyone like you," I say. "The flowers are so nice."

"I got them from my grandpa's mortuary," he says.

"Does he have a lot of flowers?"

"Yes, I'll show you someday. Have you ever been to a football game?"

"Not a college one."

"My roommates said this would be a good date."

"When does the game start?"

"Not for a while, we can walk and eat. I have to do something," he says, and as I turn toward him, his arms go around me, as young and tender as my own arms, and he kisses me as if I were a child. There is nothing needy in the kiss, nothing pressing or pushing, just the wet kiss of giving lips sliding into warmth. I close my eyes, open my mouth into the kiss and fall in love.

Several weeks later, he comes to see me at my new job as an assistant apartment manager. I have closed the office and I am locking up the vacant apartments. He walks with me along the balcony; we stop and lean over the pool surrounded by tall palms, the water shimmering in the heat, the sun setting into yellow and brown mountains. He kisses me as we enter the apartment. The lights are out, but the sunlight filters in over the clean bed. I stand by the window and undress as naturally and easily as if I were preparing to bathe. As I unfasten my bra, he catches his breath, and I feel I could live forever on the balanced air of that caught breath. He moves close to me slowly, barely breathing, both hands coming up under my breasts. I lean back into him, my face looking up into his and laugh.

I am unprepared for his undressing. It is strange to see his white thin torso, his lean wiry muscled arms very pale in the dark room. His long legs covered with dark hair, seem alien, straight, a body with no curves. When he slowly pulls down his underwear to reveal something hard, long, much bigger than I expected, I am undone with curiosity. I forget what we are about to do.

"Check this thing out," I say. "I gotta see this. What does it just spontaneously stand up on its own?"

"Well, yeah, I mean, if you're thinking about something sexy. Like if I'm thinking about you." He tries to put his arms around me, but I push him away.

"No, wait a minute, I need to get this, this is so fascinating. Okay, so you're in a locker room and you're talking with this other guy, and suddenly you just think, I mean, it just flashes through your mind, someone you were naked with last night, and then you get one of these."

"A hardon," he says.

"Yeah, okay, so you get one, is he going to think it's strange, is he?"

"Well, he might, I mean."

"Or, what about if you're talking with your teacher, and she's like, fifty years old and ugly as sin, and then you think about some cute girl and you get one, and she notices and thinks it's for her, I mean, wouldn't you be embarrassed? I can't believe you have this huge thing that can just spring up at any time."

"Let me show you what I can do with it," he says laughing.

I run around the bed; he hops over it, grabs me; together we land on the bed. We cuddle like children, rolling from side to side, laughing puddles of relief.

I have been taking a Human Sexuality class, I have visited the health clinic for birth control. I am sure that I know everything when it comes to sex, so when the lovemaking is over before I can say the word, I know that we are not right for each other or it would be fireworks. When it is right, fireworks go off over the bed like in movies, when it is wrong, the guy comes as soon as he is inside. "We're not right for each other," I say.

"You don't understand," he says while we both dress. His blue eyes look huge. On the way back to the dorm, he says, "Let's stop at the airport and watch the planes."

At Sky Harbor Airport, I follow his directions and drive the car out to the end of a runway. The darkening desert sky is tinged yellow and pink. I lean back across the car, and he is on his knees with his face between my legs. The car feels warm under me, an American Airlines 747 takes off above my face, and rises into the gold air as I feel a sensation I have never imagined. I emit the tiniest, "Oh," as I sink down onto the runway, and we make love with the car crouching over us and the roar of take off above us.

Two years later I sit on Tanya's couch while Tanya mixes drinks. "What is this?"

"A Golden Cadillac, just drink it, you're going to love it. So what's happening?"

"What's going on with you, first?"

Tanya stretches out on the opposite couch. "Do you ever use the fireplace?" I ask.

"When a man is here to light it for me."

"You count on men for everything."

"Of course. My Grandma always told me you can have anything you want. Any fool can have a job and work nine to five. I like being taken care of."

"How long have you been divorced?"

"Three years now," Tanya looks suddenly sober, and I wonder for the first time, how old she is. I have always assumed Tanya to be five or ten years older than me. Tanya is always smiling and laughing, her strawberry blond hair fluffed out around her petite face, her body thinner than a mannequin, her lips bright pink.

"How's your eating thing?"

"You act like it's baggage I'm carrying or something. I'm much better. I've been seeing the therapist every other week for the last year, and she thinks I'm over it. She says since I had the eating disorder for about a year, I should have gotten it over it in about a year."

"Do you think you're over it?"

"I guess, I mean, I think I'll be obsessed with my weight all my life."

"I remember when you used to come over here, and you'd be fasting one night, and the next night you'd eat everything in the house," Tanya sips her drink and plays with the rim of the glass.

"It's a wonder you're still my friend. So how's the love life?" I asked hoping to deflect this conversation away from dissecting me.

"Well, we've been together for two years, and his business is going under. I've got the house sold, and I am moving to California." Tanya frowns as if she doesn't like her own answer.

"Is this for real now? I mean you've been saying you were just in it as long as the good times last, but I mean, are you seriously ditching him?"

"We had great times together. He took me to Hawaii, Tahoe, San Diego, but he is going to be broke. He doesn't need me around, he needs some time to get on his feet."

What I thought was, "Well, if you sell this house, you'll have some money, you've been living off him, why can't he live off you until you get back on your feet?"

But what I said was, "Well, you have to do what works for you."

"Andie, if there is one thing that drives me crazy about you it is your utter stupidity about relationships."

"Clue me in, what am I missing here?"

"Here's what you're missing. I want a man to take care of me. I don't want a gigolo."

"Tanya, we're talking about two human beings here, you two care about each other."

"I've already decided to move to Los Angeles and live with my son."

"Your son?"

"He's taking a college course at UCLA. So, tell me what's going on with you and Chad."

"I don't know, I mean you know our basic story. We met and fell in love when in our sophomore year, got engaged; we've been living together for two years now, you realize that? and he's been living on my money and my student loans most of the time."

"I don't know why you put up with this shit."

"I love him, I get so lonely when he goes for the night to see his parents. I want to feel like someone cares about me. I want to feel, I don't know."

"That's exactly your problem, you don't know."

"Well, what do you think?"

"I think you're stuck in a lousy relationship. I think you ought to get the hell out and move to California with me."

"Where would I live?"

"My son's got a house. I'll get him to rent you a room too."

"Well, I don't know what to do about Chad."

"Do you still love him?"

"I'm fond of him. I guess I'm tired of supporting him."

"See, it does come back to money. Check this out, whenever anyone is having a problem, it always comes back to money or sex."

"I feel like I want to leave before we start hating each other. I don't have the heart to kick him out of the apartment, and if I move to a different apartment, he'll come along."

"This guy must be the greatest fuck in the universe if you're putting up with this shit."

"Actually, he was a great lover, but I think the stress of knowing that I am upset with him for not making enough money gets to him. We haven't made love in months."

Tanya's voice comes out in a scream. "You don't even fuck? Oh, I give up all hope for you, how can you stay with a man who doesn't even, does he eat you?"

"No, not for a long time."

Tanya gets up, "I might as well go to bed. Obviously all my lessons are useless, you don't listen to anything I say. Men who don't pay their way and eat you, are a dime a fucking dozen. They're losers, you don't need them. Are you going to spend the night?"

"No, I have to get back to Chad."

Tanya refills her drink and sits down. "What the hell do you see in this guy?"

"I'll tell you a story."

"I'm all ears." We watch our shadows flicker on the wall opposite us.

"When I was a kid at the boarding school, we would make dinners for the counselors once in a while, we'd get to make the whole thing ourselves."

"Sounds like fun so far."

"We'd have a whole day to prepare the food, decorate the room, everything. We used to lay sheets on the picnic tables and make huge plates of cornbread and beef stew and for dessert we'd make cakes and decorate them. Well, one year we decided to make an obstacle course." I pause to drink. "It took all day to haul enough pine boughs into one wing; that's what we called the dorm rooms. We completely filled the room with tops of trees and boughs, so when you opened the door it looked like a forest; and we let rabbits go in the forest room. There was a certain path through it, and at one place you had to crawl through a tunnel of pine boughs, and between the two wings, we lashed a log, so they had to walk across it."

"Sounds like a whole lot of fun, so what was the point of this?"

"Well, they opened the door expecting dinner, and the smell of pine was overwhelming, they were plunged into a forest, and they had to walk and crawl and climb over things, and then go across that log, and then, there they were in a candlelit room with dinner served. I think of this now, because I feel like I am in an obstacle course, and I keep waiting for dinner. I'm hungry all the time, plus I remember the smell of pine, and I keep feeling like I'm missing something."

"It must have been a bitch to clean up."

"It wasn't too bad, life is much messier. I just wish I could get back to some place where I knew what I was going to eat and, I don't know, I had animals to play with."

"You're weird, and you need a man to take care of you, and anyway, life is an obstacle course, there's no free dinner."

"You don't think I'll ever be relaxed?"

"Have another drink, that'll relax you."

I drink and lie back on the couch watching our shadows on the ceiling. I talk in a low voice as if I am talking to myself. "I fell in love with him because he didn't want anything from me."

"Except your money."

"No, you're wrong, he never wanted anything from me or took anything from me. I asked him to move in with me, and he just never made enough money to pay his part of the rent, and he felt badly about it, but he wanted to be with me."

"But not fuck you."

"We made love in the beginning, and then less because I wanted him to make more money, and he couldn't so we fought. But he always accepted me, he never bitched at me about anything. He made model airplanes in the evenings while I made rugs. We went to dollar movies, and we went to Mexico and drank cheap tequila while we studied for finals. We stayed in this one cheap hotel with white cool flagstones, and we'd walk out in the morning and look down at the water, and our mouths would be all fuzzy, and we'd have to brush our teeth in tequila because of the water."

"It all just sounds like too much fun for one person. Face it, we are talking about a loser here, I hate to tell you this, but this guy is not all that good looking."

"You and I have different tastes in good looking. I think Daniel Day Lewis is the epitome of male handsomeness, and you think, who, Arnold?"

"Yeah, or Robert Redford. What I'm saying is, you should seriously consider going to California. I'm serious. You can find some rich guy to take care of you."

"I never wanted anyone to provide for me."

"You'll never have a house with this guy, and kids and a life."

"I've never had a life."

"Oh, God, I'm going to bed, you work this shit out, let me know if you can break up with Mr. Chad; we'd have a hell of a time in California."

Sand and Hair

The first time I pressed myself against a man's chest,
my bare breasts ached and pushed against all that hair,
ready and warm, a wet god at the center of me.
The wet energy of the universe pulsing open and open.
I bloomed against the chest of the man I covered.
We coveted each other. We moved against each other.
I tasted him, and the rare soft flower
I had dreamed of bloomed in my fingers.
I tasted salt. By the ocean,
sand came between him and me,
the gritty sand of our lives.

Chapter 24

"Oh, my God," I think as I pull up to the little house in Los Angeles, California. It is three o'clock in the morning, but the city is not silent. It moves around me like an animal, the blackness reflecting nothing. I don't want to get out of the car that holds everything I own. My body feels stuck into it. I cannot move.

The little guest house is in back he'd said, the old servant's quarters. The house looks small in the darkness, and the guest house looks like an addition to the garage. The guest house door is open. I switch on a light; cheap panelling, a bed in one corner, a bar for hanging clothes, a bare light bulb, a sink in one corner. "I guess I'll go inside to shower," I think. The carpet is stained, but the place is clean. It is one of the best places I've ever stayed. I turn out the light, throw myself down on the bed fully clothed and I am asleep almost instantly.

In the morning, I wake and begin to unpack. I am hanging a David Hockney print on the wall when a male voice says, "May I come in?" and I say, "Yes," and wish for a moment that I look the way girls do in movies when they are unpacking. They always have on fetching shorts, crop tops and their hair in bandannas. My hair is long straight and blond and hangs down my back. I wear a big sweater and shorts that show off my legs which don't look so great in my opinion. I want long thin legs; like models, mine have shaped calves.

"Glad to meet you. You must be my new tenant," he says, and smiles. "I'm sure Tanya told you all about me."

I am sure he is well over six feet; he bends down to come into the little house. "I hope this little house is okay."

"It's fine." He has thick dark hair and a boyish lopsided smile. "Was this really for a servant?"

"Yes, a lot of houses in the Valley have these. They're fifty, sixty year old houses, but these people had servants. Come on in, see the house, such as it is."

The paint on the house is peeling. He shows me the bathroom I can use. Boxes are stacked everywhere. "How long have you been here?"

"Two years, I just never got around to unpacking."

"When is Tanya coming?"

"In a couple of weeks, she's on one last vacation with her soon to be ex."

"I know."

"Well, I have errands to run. I'll be back around five, want to go to for a drive?"

"Okay." He waves as he gets into an old Ford and drives off. The main house is incredibly filthy. If I am to live here even to go in and out, Tanya and I will have to do a complete overhaul. I shudder, opening drawers, expecting to find bugs or cockroaches. The refrigerator smells like bad meat, and I quickly close it. It will be enough the first day to get myself unpacked and settled into the little house.

"So what are you going to do in California, you didn't say," he asks over dinner. We have driven out to Malibu, walked along the beach and are sitting at a window of the Sea Lion looking out at moonlit waters. I think about romance and why it doesn't occur automatically in places like this. I order vodka.

"I've been accepted to graduate school at California State University Northridge in English."

"I know, but what are you going to do for a living?"

"Tutor probably, then I'll teach at community colleges. I want to write. And what do you do?"

"I'm a gaffer."

"A what?."

"I do lighting for film and television. I set up the lights for the DP."

"What's the DP?"

"The camera man. So where do your folks live?"

I finish the vodka and order another. "You want to hear a story?"

"Sure."

"When I was a little girl, we used to go swimming every summer in this pond called Dodge Pond. Right beside it was this big hill and the whole hill was a graveyard. We used to wander around in there after our swim looking for names, and they'd say things like 'Died in Peace,' or 'May she rest in Peace,' and we used to think it was really creepy, because that pond was so black with bracken that we wondered if the dead bodies had seeped into the pond."

He knits his brows but doesn't say anything. "Anyway, I'm sorry I said that about the bodies when we're getting ready to eat, but here's the point; I never thought about that pond for years, and then I went to college and I tried to make friends. People would always ask me where my family was from. The truth is that I'm twenty-five and neither of my parents has spoken to me in years."

"I don't know how to lie well, and I got tired of explaining. At first I said they were dead, but I could never keep that story straight, and I began to think maybe it would be easier if at least my mother were dead. I've found a lot of people understand if your parents were divorced and you didn't see much of your dad, but my mother, I can never explain it in a few short sentences, and then people look at me like I'm some criminal. My own mother doesn't want me so what does that say?"

"What happened?"

"She's living in a closed Christian commune, and she doesn't want to have anything to do with me because I'm not living there."

"That didn't take long."

"But then people would want more details, and I remember growing up at the Farm, sometimes wanting to be dead, and then after I left sometimes wishing she were, and I wondered if maybe the pond water did seep into me." I can feel that I'm talking way too much. The vodka lying on my empty stomach is working me over, but the thing that bothers me that I can't explain is that I really wish I could be a normal person. I am getting the "animal feeling" very strongly. I want to be a normal girl who could just say something chic like, "the folks," here I would wave a hand dismissively, "live in New Haven," and one would picture my family, serene, out walking through the snow. They would wear plaid mufflers and have a golden retriever.

He smiles, "Here comes our waiter. Let's eat." We crunch into their salads and bread and he raises his glass, "To your success in

Los Angeles," he says, and I clink his glass which I'm fairly sure is the right thing to do. I've seen them to do it movies.

"I'm sorry I went on like that, I'm sorry I run at the mouth sometimes. It's one of my worst traits. I know I talk too much."

"You're fine," he says.

"What I want to know is, how old are you?"

"How old do you think?" I put down my fork and look at him. He has large brown eyes, a big nose, a charming wholesomeness about his demeanor. I think briefly about Chad who never tanned and was white and black haired, "Like something that would only come out at night" I had always thought. This Mark looks like an advertisement for America. "Not at all my type," I think.

"Twenty-five," I guess.

"I'm thirty-four."

"Thirty-four? That means that Tanya's got to be in her fifties."

"Indeed she is, how old did you think she was?"

"Thirty-four."

He laughs. "She fools a lot of people. Those facelifts."

"So did you grow up with her as your mother? It's hard for me to picture her being anyone's mother."

"No, actually, I was raised by my grandmother, who was Mom to me. Tanya's always been more of a sister."

"Where did you grow up?"

"Illinois."

"And what's your dream here in L.A."

"Well, I came out here because I was going to direct, produce, but it didn't turn out that way. I got into lighting, and now I'm just doing that. I'm not very ambitious. I have a house, and I want to marry a woman who already has children because I like children, and I want to spend most of my time at home. I like to be in jeans. I like the middle class life. I like barbecues."

"Well, that's good. We can be comfortable together."

"Why?" he says biting an oyster.

"Because we aren't made for each other. I want adventure. You want to stay home. I want to dress up. You want to dress down. I like parties. You like barbecues. I want to travel the world. You want to stay in your own back yard. I want to achieve great success as a writer and lift myself way above the poverty in which I find myself to be on a wonderful piece of land with a horse where I don't have to

223

worry about money. You want the status quo. So, we can just be friends." He laughs.

"You have everything figured out. Here's to friendship," he says, and we raise our water glasses. I set mine down on the bread basket and water pours into our laps.

I work temp jobs, go to graduate school, start working out. I know he's watching me. He tells me that I'm immature. I smile. I wear jeans and cut them off when it gets hot so my butt shows.

Tanya moves into the master bedroom, decorates it with long lace peach curtains. The bed looks like a love nest. The room smells of soap, perfume and candles. She and I play "I Can't Get No Satisfaction," and "It's Raining Men" loudly while we scrub the house from top to bottom.

Mark's friends come and go; Tanya watches them and invites them in her room to fix her television or VCR. They think she is Mark's sister. Tanya closes the door, while Mark and I raise eyebrows to muffled sounds. Tanya makes money for clothes by babysitting on week nights, and she goes to Spago's on Friday night. "I saw Jack Lemmon," she sighs. "I wonder who I'll see next week."

She goes to hot dance clubs requiring sequins and bare bellies. I watch her as she strains into the darkness in lines outside of bars for men who will look at her as they all did when she was seventeen. I go with her on these excursions at first. I wear tight black pants, and try to look seductive. I watch men crowd around Tanya, their breath coming hard and fast and I wonder what they smell. "Be friendly," Tanya advises. "You're cute enough." But the lines turn me off.

"You're the most beautiful babe I've seen tonight. I could dance with you all night." The smell of smoke irritates me, and it all seems so tiring, the dance of the sexes for the thing they both want, but will not admit to wanting. The men strain to cover their intentions. The lights sparkle overhead, the silver balls twirling faster, and I come back to the little house, and wish I hadn't gone. Tanya finds new friends to go the beach and the bars with. I cook soups in the kitchen and write poems. Mark comes back and finds me alone.

We sit in the living room and talk. "Do you like kids?" he asks.

"Yes, I'm wild about kids."

"If you were married, would you want kids right away?"

"I don't know. What do you think about the present

administration?"

"Sucks. Reagan is building up the military and increasing the national debt. People have no idea, they just buy into it."

"We've got to end the welfare system, replace it with jobs."

"You got that right. Would you work if you were married?"

"Definitely. I believe every human being has the right and the privilege to support themselves. I don't believe in living off anyone. Do you think Bush will win?"

"He may, but I hope not. Would you expect your husband to help with housework?"

"Or let me hire a housekeeper. The environment cannot take another four years of Republicans. Do you go to church?"

"No, I'm not religious. It's hard for me to buy the idea that God is just waiting to send most of mankind to hell. So, you're going to be a teacher?"

"Yes, and a writer, I don't understand why the Republican Party ignores every issue that has to do with the future, like education and the environment. Are you pro choice?"

"You bet. You know we could just date and date other people too. We're living in the same house, and we keep meeting at night and having these discussions. It's natural for us to date, but since we know we're not right for each other, we should see other people too."

"Good idea, I have a date tomorrow night."

"Who with? I wanted to take you out tomorrow night."

"Your brother, he was by yesterday. He's taking me to some concert."

"Oh, really?

"Well, I better call it a night, I'm a temp at some law firm in Beverly Hills tomorrow. Good night."

A few minutes later the phone rings by my bedside. "Yes?"

"This is Mark, I hope you won't mind, but your date with my brother is off. So, let's go to the Cineplex."

I pause for a second, and say, "Okay."

"See you tomorrow. Good night." I lie down and as I fall asleep, I try to figure out if I'm mad at him. I don't think so, but I'm worried that his brother's feelings may have been hurt.

In the summer we drive to San Francisco and visit some of his friends. The drive is the longest time to talk we've ever had. We find things we agree on; children, money, vacations.

I watch his hands on the steering wheel, the secure way they turn the wheel. He tells me stories of growing up with his Pappy, riding on his grandfather's shoulders, the two of them riding in a train to Chicago to watch the Chicago Cubs at Wrigley Field. I see him, a little boy, eager, laughing. He says, "I can see us together, I really can. We both like children."

"I'll grow up eventually," I say, "and I won't seem so immature."

"You're fine," he says, "You're a beautiful girl."

"I am? me?"

"Yes, you," he says, and takes my hand and kisses it.

We pull over as the sun sets across the Pacific. It sinks slowly, and he wraps his arms around me, bends down and kisses me. The sky flowing out from the sun is pink, the highest clouds are shades of violet. "I love you," he says, and I smile.

"I love you," I whisper, and feel danger, like the car is too close to the cliff and may slide off.

Mark's friends in San Francisco offer their forty foot boat as sleeping quarters. "Where are you going to sleep?" I ask, when we've said good night, and are exploring the two bedrooms at either end of the little boat. "It's like a little home for elves or something. Everything is so cute. But, would you want to own a boat like this?"

"Not as long as I can borrow someone else's. This thing probably cost a fortune, and they said they've only been out on it twice this year. Plus, she said it cost $500 a month just to dock it here."

"Oh, I agree, but it's nice, isn't it?" He climbs up on the deck, and helps me up. We watch the other boats bobbing in the harbor.

"Imagine a storm," I say. "I bet in a storm, these boats are dancing up and down."

"It's hard to imagine a storm. It's so peaceful." The ocean looks like a lake, the last of the sun's reflection flickering across it. He puts his arm around me. "In storms, these boats just have to be prepared to weather them. See those two, real close to each other, not even covered up properly, I bet they bang each other up pretty bad in a storm."

"What if there's a storm tonight?" I grip his arm.

"Oh, I don't think so, let's sleep in the same bed though, it's kind of cold, and it would be cozier."

"Yeah, I agree; it's kind of lonely by yourself."

He lies down beside me, his face very close to mine, kisses me, pulls his face away, looking at me, studying me like a map. "I wonder if he wants to," I think. He touches my forehead. "He's decided not to," I think, but then he begins kissing me. It's funny because what I think about is that in movies people always spring at each other, clawing off each other's clothing, and I wonder if anyone does that in real life. We proceed slowly. I smile in the dark, I feel victorious. I wonder for a moment if I've forgotten how to do this. What if he thinks I'm bad in bed?

He pauses for a moment and points out the window. The stars are showing faintly on the horizon, and a boat is going by, lit up, looking black and twinkly against the deep blue of an almost-night sky. I've never heard of anyone stopping in the middle of everything. I think of sex as a silent procession toward an inevitable end. He whispers in a witch's voice, "I'll get you, my pretty," and I laugh. The blue night air outside the window and the lights in the distance look like fairyland.

Hours later, he opens the door to the deck and cool air flows in around us. He climbs up on deck naked, and I climb up wrapped in a sheet, and we wrap it around both of us and sit quietly for a while. "Want some juice," he says handing me a glass.

"If this were a movie, we'd be smoking cigarettes now."

"Or watching television."

"Or asleep." The moonlight pools on the white sheets. We move our feet and watch the moon pools change shape. We sit quietly for a long time, and then he says, almost as a statement,

"Can you imagine us having children together," in an offhand way like it doesn't matter, and I say, "I guess I can, do you want to?" and he says,

"Maybe, sugarplum."

Sex and Rainbows

I expected to be raised
to some point where drugs
take you, my soul swimming
higher like a salmon leaping
upstream, flashing in sunlight,
pink water diamonds around me, unaware
of the conscious world, my body an instinct.

In a dark room, I shed my clothes one by one
like a prisoner for inspection. He
shed his clothes like a boxer
in the ring. My head down
waiting for approval,
his head up, waiting for everything.

When I started melting, it wasn't a dream;
it was a deliberate male act; as I
dropped to my knees and slipped
down, his hands roaming
my body like the Gauls plundered Europe, I could
still speak, my world, my world, my beautiful
world, as the shining rainbow of a salmon
twisting upward blackened, and I
opened my eyes. I never
expected anything
this big.

Chapter 25

A year later, I sit at my computer, pecking away at a short story when the phone rings. "Hello," I say cradling the phone and continuing to slowly tap away at the keys.

"Hi, this is Stephanie."

"Stephanie, Stephanie," I think, "How many Stephanies do I know?"

"Stephanie, you mean, Stephanie from the Farm? It's been so long. I haven't heard from you in well, how long has it been eight, nine years? What have you been up to?"

"College in New Hampshire, and now I'm living in Boston, but I'm going to be in Los Angeles next week, and I wondered if I could come by. I heard from Ann that you were out there, she gave me your number, I hope it's okay, so I decided to call. If you're busy, and this isn't a good time, that's fine."

"No, I'm glad to hear all's well with you. Yeah, come on out, we have a lot of catching up to do."

I wait for Stephanie at the bus station and jump when someone walks up behind me and touches my shoulder. Stephanie still has unbelievably blue eyes, the same uneasy look on her face. She is much thinner than she was at the Farm, her thick brown hair is partially braided, partly loose, but there is something severe about her bearing as if she has been marching a long time. We talk on the way back in the car, about college, Stephanie graduated with honors from the University of New Hampshire, about the Farm, we have both strayed far from keeping the rules. But I keep trying to figure out what it is about Stephanie that bothers me.

"So what happened to your brothers and sisters?"

"Well, after my Dad was allowed to be reconciled with my stepmother, he left the Farm, as you know. They live in Connecticut now; two sisters married, one brother engaged, one in college, one at the Farm, one in Alaska."

"All happy?"

"Happy? I don't know about happy. Are you happy?"

"I think so."

"Liar, tell me about this husband of yours. How did he propose? Was it romantic?"

"No, it was not."

"Come on, give me the play by play."

"I dated him for about a year, then one night he's watching a Bears game."

"Football?"

"Yeah, so he says, 'Why don't we get married.' I said, 'If you're serious stop watching the game for a minute and come over here on one knee and ask me.'"

"You didn't do that archaic knee shit."

"Ah, you swear too."

"I fucking well do, not being able to swear for all those years, and now I say, 'fuck' all the time."

"Well, lay off it around me, will you, it's annoying."

"Okay, whatever, so what happens?"

"Well, he says, 'Just a minute, this is a really good play, and then I'll stop,' and he watches until someone fumbles the ball, and then turns the sound down and comes over and asks me, but I bet he was still watching the game out of the corner of his eye. So, we got married in Vegas on New Year's Eve, and then gambled. When we got back, his mom was a bit upset, she was living with us at the time, and she had to move out, so we could have privacy. We went skiing for our honeymoon, and I got pregnant."

"This guy sounds like a prince. So, where'd you meet him? Ann just told me you were married and pregnant, by the way congratulations."

"He was my landlord, and he's really a sweetheart, you'll like him."

"What does he do?"

"He's a gaffer, so you haven't told me what you do or where you live. Speaking of where people live, here's where I live. He's not home, so let's go out in the backyard."

We settle down with ice teas in the hammock, as if it has been no time since we saw each other. I feel strangely comfortable with

Stephanie as if all my years of pretending to be normal are unnecessary; Stephanie and I know we are not. "I manage a theater in Boston, and I live with my boyfriend. I lived with my dad and stepmother for years after I left the Farm, and it was a nightmare. My dad runs his house like a military establishment. He used to scream at my brother, make us meet for daily family Bible readings that were excruciating. He dictated our every move. He criticized everything we did."

"How about your stepmother, was she the wicked witch of the East?"

"No, she was pretty much indifferent to me. The boys are important to her; I am not. If you go into the fridge in the house, she's always saving whatever is good in there for the boys when they come by, so you can't eat it. She can be very smooth though."

"I met her a few times, I always thought she was kind of aloof and genteel."

"I don't know, I never understood getting kicked out of the Farm, and I never found happiness as such."

"Not even with your boyfriend?"

"He's okay. So, are you faking it, or are you really happy with this Mark?"

"I love him, I knock him sometimes, but I feel like I'm home when I'm with him. Anyway, my life is better than it's ever been, I'm writing, I'm teaching, I'm pregnant, I feel like I'm not stagnant. I do feel like I have some loose ends to tie up."

"Like what?"

"Well, I've been trying to figure that out. I've been corresponding with Teddy for years; she's a missionary in Central America."

"Oh really?"

"Married, has a kid. I correspond with Emma and Ann and I talk on the phone, I feel like I'm trying to figure something out, or say good bye or discover my father. I don't know."

"Maybe you have unexpressed anger."

"You took too many psychology classes." I laugh. "You could be right, against God you mean?"

"Well, or George, or Don."

"Maybe Don, it might be Don, it might be my dad."

"You got together with him once, right, I think Ann said something about you seeing your dad once."

"Yeah, I did, and then I called him once and talked with him, and I wrote letters to him which he didn't answer, and I gave up."

"Okay close your eyes."

"What?"

"Just do this. Close your eyes, and see your dad."

"Okay."

"What do you feel?"

"Nothing."

"Okay again, close your eyes, see George, what do you feel?"

"Fear." My shoulders hunch.

"Okay Don. What?"

"Anger, I suppose." I don't want to admit that I might be angry. I feel guilty.

"I thought so. Don is the one you need to confront, maybe George too."

"Really?"

"Yes, so what are you going to say to them?"

"I'll say, you used to beat me, shut me in rooms, you told me I was wicked, wicked, wicked, that I was going to hell, that God did not have his hand on me, that I was a child of the devil, and you were wrong. I throw everything you said to me back in your face. I will not accept it."

"Sounds good."

"I've been thinking of taking a trip back East because after the baby comes, I won't be travelling for a while."

"So who are you going to see?"

"Probably my dad, Ann, Emma, Don, George, if I have the guts, maybe I'll see my mother."

"You should go. I'm telling you."

"So, do you feel like things will get better, happier for you?"

"I don't know, I just feel my life going on and on, but happiness seems pretty far fetched, like something you see in movies." When I say good bye to her, she is wearing sunglasses. I cannot see her eyes or anything else about her clearly.

"Good luck," I say.

"Luck?" she says, and shakes her head. She steps on the bus and disappears.

I stop to see Dinah in Arizona. She hugs me in the airport. "Glad to see you're staying filled out," she says, and I feel loved. At her home she pours me a rum and diet coke and cooks trout with lemon and onion. When I've told her everything, she says, "So, explain to me again why you're going back to see your parents. What are you hoping to gain?"

"Their love, forgiveness maybe."

"Forgiveness for what? What have you done wrong?"

"Oh leaving the Farm, having sex before I got married."

"Oh, honey," she says hugging me again. "You've got to stop doing penance. Go see them if you want, but if they don't want you, believe me it has nothing to do with you."

"You know what my favorite story was growing up? It was the story of the "Ugly Duckling." I always think of myself like that, I'm this little ugly duckling that nobody wants. I'm always doing and saying the wrong things, and I don't belong, and everyone can see that. I keep hoping that I'm going to become a swan. I keep waiting for that to happen, and I keep looking down into the water and I see the ugly duckling."

"Well, I see you as a swan, and everybody else sees you as a swan, but maybe you need to go back to the nest to see that you've flown away."

A few days later, my father returns from lunch to find me sitting on his desk. I can tell right away he doesn't recognize me. I'm slimmer now with long blond hair and no glasses. I guess I don't look much like the big ungainly girl with shaggy brown hair, ugly thick skirts, shapeless sweater and glasses who ate French fries with him years before. He looks unchanged to me; broad shoulders, twinkly eyes, unfairly handsome, "Where did these looks go when I was being conceived?" I think.

"I'm your daughter," I say, and we shake hands for the second time in our lives.

This time we talk over chicken salad. I swallow aspirin between bites, and nervously touch my neck in an old childish gesture. He watches me steadily, looking unbothered as a tree on a windless day.

When we've talked about college and whether or not I will get a Ph.D., I say, "I wish we could keep in closer contact."

"You can call me any time."

"My grandparents are angry that we haven't kept in closer touch. They thought you would help me with college or something."

"Are you angry?"

"Anger isn't something I feel that often. I feel sometimes sad, sometimes downtrodden, sometimes rejected. I guess I mostly don't care about the past, but I'd like to try harder to keep in touch with you."

"Well, I'm not one for letters," he says softly, "but you can call me any time. Let me give you a couple new phone numbers." He hands me a card, and his hand touches mine. I feel tears coming, but I don't let them. I watch people walking by the window, walking through the city, and I think that any one of these people walking by could be someone who sees my father every day, has lunch with him. There could be a thousand people in the world who know him better than I do.

"I'll call you," he says.

"I'll call you too, I'm better with letters, but I'll call." there are a lot of questions I haven't asked yet, whether he ever thought of me, why he never got in touch. I wonder if I ever will. He takes my hand.

"I'm proud of you," he says. I feel confused by this, unsure what he is proud of, but I like him saying it, and I smile.

He walks me to the train station. I feel comfortable walking beside him. I wish someone I know would walk up, and I could say, for the first time in my life, "I'd like you to meet my father." I want to take his photograph, but I don't know how to ask. I am almost afraid that even if I do, he won't appear on film, that maybe he isn't really there at all. "Can I take your picture?" I say, and he stops, turns toward me, takes off his sunglasses. Later, when I see the picture, his face reaches toward me in a half smile holding as many questions as answers.

On the flight to Vermont, I make a list of the people I want to see: Charlie and Rick who gave me a place to stay when I had no place, Ann, who left the Farm to take care of her parents. Ann is still living with her parents in a trailer and working in a nursing home. Emma, who was kicked out for kissing, has written once a year. She has just gotten married. I wonder if she is still beautiful.

Charlie and Rick greet me with hugs and kisses. Charlie's cheeks are round apples, her smile spreads calmly like it has never left her face since I left. Charlie gets up early in the morning to pick five gallons of strawberries. By breakfast, she has made fresh strawberry shortcake, whipped up fresh cream, and we eat outside under the pine trees. The garden is coming up wet and green, and the air smells like pine.

I try to explain why I decided to make this trip.

"So is that what you're doing, trying to connect?"

"I don't know, really, but I wanted to come back and see you and everyone. I don't know what I'm doing. What I want to do is confront Don and George. I want to tell them that they really messed up my life, and that it's taken me years to recover. It's wrong the way they treated me. I thought of each of them like this evil father, and it made me afraid of men. I feel like I can't move on with my life until I figure this thing out. Then I have to go home."

"Well, I'm glad you came to see us," Charlie says.

The next morning she comes out to say goodbye. "Well, maybe I'll be back before another five years," I say.

"You're gonna make it kid," she says, and we laugh.

"Yeah, I guess so. I guess I'm a survivor. Thanks for everything. Remember when I was eating that sandwich, and you told me to stop in the middle because the Lord might come, so I wouldn't get to finish it?"

Charlie laughs, "Yeah, you were a case."

"I think that's when my life started moving. Thanks a lot for everything."

"It was nothing."

"Oh, I know, what nothing is, it was something."

She hugs me, and as I turn the corner, I see the sun rising behind her.

Emma's house is a mile from the Farm, a modular home set in a circle of trees. Inside we sit down, and Emma offers donuts and coffee. I look in her face trying to find some trace of the Emma I used to know, the laughing flirting eyes, the curly hair. Emma's hair is cut short and permed, and it sits unmoving on her head. Her face is round. She still smiles readily, but her quick movements, the way she used to jump up to mimic someone, have been replaced by slower quieter movements. She reminds me of the way Vermont feels to me now that I have lived in California, like time is standing still here. She says, "Do I look bigger than the last time you saw me?"

"I don't remember exactly how you looked; it's been so long," I say although she has lost the slim wild coltish look. "So what are you doing?"

"Getting the baby room ready."

"What are your goals?"

"I don't know, what do you mean, goals?"

"You can't know a person until you know their dreams," I say with a forced laugh wishing I hadn't asked the question.

"I want to be a good wife and mother. I don't know. I might take home courses to be a legal secretary. The Farm didn't prepare us for much, you know? But I'm happy. I'm doing what I want to do. I gotta go check the casserole. You like tuna casserole? That's what I'm making. It's one of John's favorites."

I feel vaguely happy for her, she seems to be in a good place, like she's chosen a life that suits her. I think for a moment about how unhappy I'd be in this life, and then I realize that doesn't matter. "I'm making curtains for the baby's room. Want to see them?" I follow her into the baby's room, and then look around the house while Emma picks up things off the floor. "He's such a slob, my husband. I'm always picking up after him. It keeps me busy."

"What's he do? What's he like?"

"Well, we both believe in God, that's the important thing, and we go to church where he went growing up. He's a janitor, and we're hoping he'll get a raise soon to eleven dollars an hour."

"That would be great."

"He may go into industrial cleaning eventually."

"That would be nice."

"But you haven't told me about yourself."

"What is there to say? Teaching college, just a bunch of courses, writing, being pregnant, nothing much." She laughs and throws her arms around me. I feel good and bad. I find myself glad she is happy and angry at myself for wishing a different life for her, a life more like my life.

"I wish you could visit us more often," she says. "I think about you all the time."

"I think of you too," I say softly, and I think for a moment how deep down in the blood, in the marrow, Emma, Stephanie, Teddy,

Ann and I are connected. Most of our lives were spent in the same place, hearing the same words. I think for a second that if our souls could take shape and be laid side by side, we would all look alike. "We survived," I say.

"I love you," Emma says, and we look into each other as we say goodbye.

Going to visit Ann the next day, I drive past a waterfall, through green woods. Ann has called me every two weeks since I left the Farm; she has kept in closer touch than anyone else. Her parents' trailer is tucked away in the woods, down a dirt road, and then down a muddy path. Ann still works at the same nursing home where she's been working since she left. She doesn't date, and her mother is still dying.

The trailer is dark. When my eyes have adjusted, I see Ann's mother slumped in a wheelchair in the corner. The air is warm and smells of cat litter that needs changing and of hospital antiseptics. Ann offers me a tuna sandwich and iced tea. I accept, although I'm not hungry. Ann looks very much the same as she did at the Farm. She is wearing a big skirt and a big sweater, but she seems relaxed, happy.

"Did I tell you I saw Jake and Joyce?"

"No, Jake and Joyce who used to be our counselors?"

"Yeah, well, you know they left the Farm after you did, and moved to Pennsylvania. When we were down there, we went to their church. We talked with them, and they got five kids now."

"Five?"

"And Jake works three shifts to support the kids. Joyce stays at home. She is completely white-haired now."

"Oh yeah, what does he do?"

"Works at a toilet paper factory. Charmin, I think. He boxes toilet paper." I laugh. "What's funny?"

"Nothing, I just always thought he was so mean, and I can't believe that he ended up in a toilet paper factory. So are you still glad you left?"

"It was the right thing for me to do. The Lord didn't want me there any more. He wanted me here to help my mother."

"Do you like working in the nursing home?"

"Yeah, I do, and I really love gardening on weekends."

I think of my own life in California, the visits to the beach, the classes I teach, having a housekeeper, writing, going on set to visit Mark, a relatively exciting life, a life made possible by education and work. I wonder about the superiority of an educated life.

"I like to collect leaves in fall and press them," Ann says. She is content in her mushroom life in one place where it is safe as I am in my life as a fern unfolding in the sunlight.

When we leave the trailer, the outside smells wide open and alive compared to the stuffy trailer. "Do you like living here? Would you ever move, maybe come to visit me?"

"I don't think I could leave my parents. They need me to take care of them. They depend on me. Maybe some time. So, do you still believe in the Lord?"

"Well, let's just say this. At the Farm, we were taught that God is this white man in the sky who sends most people to hell for idle words and such sins. I don't believe that. But I still talk to God, I pray that this baby will be healthy. I am going back to the Farm to confront Don, though, maybe George too."

"Well, Andie, there's just one thing . . ."

"This is what I'm going to tell Don. I've been practicing it on the plane, and on the train up here from Philadelphia, and all day. I'm going to see him this afternoon."

"This afternoon?"

"Yes, okay, listen, tell me how you think this sounds. Don, I believed you were a man of God. I looked up to you as a father. You were George's right hand man, and therefore I believed you were a servant of God. But you beat me, you called me a child of the devil, you told me I was going to hell, and I do not accept your words. Here is everything you ever said to me, every time you convinced me I would have been better off born dead. I give it back. You will have to stand before God for what you have said."

"Andie, he already has."

"Has what?"

"Stood before God."

"What do you mean?"

"I mean that I got a call from the Farm two weeks ago, and they said that in the middle of a skip and sing, he dropped dead with a heart attack."

"You're kidding."

"No, he's dead."

"Oh, wow." I lean into a tree. I'm stunned.

"Well, it was very shocking. I believe he is in heaven now. Are you still going to the Farm?"

"Well, I guess I'll still see my mother."

"Are you okay?"

"Yeah, I just feel unfinished. What about George. Maybe I should confront him."

"He's not living at the Farm any more. He had a series of heart attacks, and he moved away. He and Mary are living someplace else. I don't know where, some other town. The last time I saw him he was walking with a cane. He's an old man, Andie."

"How does the place keep going without him?"

"His son-in-law runs the place now."

"I didn't think it would outlive him."

Ann hugs me for a long time. We kiss, and I get into the car still shaking my head. Now I cannot be sure what I have come all this way for.

I feel butterflies in my stomach as I get nearer to the Farm, and then a dull sick feeling. I feel this whenever anyone calls me into their office, someone who is in charge of me. My stomach feels like lead. I drive around for a while, up the mountain road to the school lane. The mountain road curves and then levels out. The tar is chipped, full of potholes; green trees cover and shade it. When I drive out into the sunshine at the top of the mountain, it feels like I've come such a short way, like the mountain I thought was so big is actually small and old. No one knows or cares about the Mountain Road that has been so big in my mind all these years. I drive to Long Pond where I used to sneak away and swim. It is smaller too, the island we were finally allowed to swim to looks close, the big rock I remember diving from is a small piece of granite jutting out over cold dark waters.

When I pull into the parking lot of the office, I'm shaking a bit, but I'm telling myself it doesn't matter. No one can hurt me, no one can touch me, no one can get me or catch or keep me. My legs keep shaking anyway, but I force them to walk right into the doorway.

To my left, I see my mother behind glass working at a desk. My mother gets up, she's got a bit of a belly she never had, but she's still pretty thin. Her white hair makes her face look paler, and her eyes larger. Her mouth shapes a polite, stretched-across-the-face-just-for-you smile, and the scar across her face looks red against the whiteness. She says, "Hello, can I help you?" in the voice she uses for talking to customers, outsiders.

"Yes," I say, and wait to see the face change, but it doesn't. My mother smoothes her skirt, stands a little straighter, as though this person staring at her is a little disconcerting.

"What can I do for you?"

"Well, I just happened to be in the neighborhood. Of course it took me two planes and a rented car to get in the neighborhood," I say, and the polite mask drops. My mother's face changes like a street light that's out of order. She's happy, she's loving, she's afraid, she's blank. The blank face, rearranged to nothingness says, "How are you?"

"I'm fine."

"I didn't recognize you."

"I recognized you. Are you happy?"

"Yes, I'm happy, a lot has changed since you left. I am happy to be married. The Lord has blessed us, and you, are you still walking with the Lord? I heard you went out west somewhere."

"Arizona, then California," I replied. "I'd like to talk with you."

"I have to get back to work."

"Can I write to you?"

"There wouldn't be any point. You're no longer following the Lord the way you were trained to here at the Farm. You're outside. I can't accept letters from you." The mask turns to pity, maybe regret, back to nothingness. "Nothing has changed."

"No, everything seems the same." I want to leave, I feel a churning of fear; I have come so far, to get something, to let go of something.

My mother says, "goodbye," softly. I watch my mother's face and back out the door to see if it will change. I wait to hear, "Come back." Hope does not return to her work while my eyes follow her. She stares back and then down to the floor, the mask of nothingness securely in place.

I drive away, sick, feeling the awful distance away from Mark who does love me. He insists I call every night. He held my face in

240

his two hands as he said goodbye. Maybe he will be father and mother, maybe my own father will come to love me. Maybe the baby will love me. I cradle my belly.

There is something, an idea too faint for me to grasp. I came back here for something. I drive back up to the top of the Mountain Road. I drive fast, chasing something.

I park by the road near the school. The sun is setting. I get out of the car and walk across a field into the school orchard.

We planted it while I was in school, little dwarf golden delicious and red delicious apple trees. The trunks were the size of a thumb with tiny, uncertain twig branches.

Now, the trees spread out thick, heavy branches covered with snowy apple blossoms. The orchard hums with honeybees departing for their hives. I feel the hum of hive life around me. I touch branches; the sun seems to hover on the horizon, a huge orange ball. I remember digging holes for these trees, years of mulching. The sun sets as I walk from tree to tree. The air changes color, becomes twilight blue and heavy with the scent of the blooms. I hold my belly in two hands.

I close my eyes. I had wanted to finish this part of my life, then throw it away, like a ball you throw far into the woods and then walk away, let it rot, unseen. I was to end up in the lake of fire if I left here. Now I want to leave it all, finally, take flight.

Around me I feel the breeze rushing, petals falling in the soft wind. The orchard darkens around me in the swiftly thickening twilight. I put my hands on my belly and feel a kick, the first real kick, another kick, three kicks. I hear singing, and I listen until the singing dies away. The last bits of my old life linger on the purple air until they disappear, then even the echo is gone. I walk back to my car through the orchard full of growing trees. I think of leaving, flying west and south. It's all a matter of direction, of knowing which way is north, which is south, which is east, which is west. Pick a direction, find a place, I tell myself spreading out my arms for wings. I think of getting on that plane tomorrow. I can almost feel it rising.

Cactus Dreams

I do not know what makes cacti
rise in the desert,
their insides wet, like my dreams
coming from nowhere.

I rise from the floor of oceans
damp, curved as the neck of a sea horse.
Irises fall from my hair.
My skirt splits to the waist.

I am not a cactus,
not a sweet nothing on your pillow.
I am light curtains blowing
across your face tonight.